Broken Things

Devon Taggart Suspense #1

SUSAN ANN WALL

Pamela —

I hope you enjoy your birthday, & hope it isn't one over!

[signature]

♪ ♪ ♪

Broken Strings

Heart of Jupiter Publishing

Copyright © Susan Ann Wall 2016

All Rights Reserved

This is a work of fiction. Names, characters, places, and incidents are a creation from the author's imagination or are used fictitiously.

ISBN: 978-1-941852-08-8

Edited by Mary Ann Jock

Cover Images:
© Kelliem | Dreamstime.com,
© Curaphotography | Dreamstime.com,
© Alhovik | dreamstime.com,
© kmiragaya | depositphotos.com,
© Tadeni | depositphotos.com,
© dnaumoid | depositphotos.com
© Adamsi | depositphotos.com
© stokkete | depositphotos.com

Cover Design: Heart of Jupiter Publishing

♪ ♪ ♪

Acknowledgements

It takes a village to write a story and that is especially true of a romantic suspense that requires accuracy in police procedures and emergency response protocols. I'd like to thank Chief Pinson and Sergeant McKinley for answering all my questions about police procedure, Sabie-baby for answering my questions about other legal matters, including grand jury, subpoenas, warrants, etc. I'd also like to thank Sabie and John Z for sharing their vast knowledge on EMT responses and protocols. Any errors in the story are mine.

I'd also like to thank my NHRWA sisters who helped me plot this book prior to NaNoWriMo 2014. Their expertise and insight helped the story come together with great pace!!

And last, but not least, to my editor who not only meets my ridiculous deadlines, but challenges me to be a better writer with every book! You are the best!

♪ ♪ ♪

Praise

National Bestselling Author

"I could not put the book down. I found myself lost in the story and characters. I cannot wait for more!"

~ 5 Star Amazon Review
A Flame Burns Inside
Fighting Back for Love series

"I absolutely enjoyed everything about this book! The part I enjoyed the most however is how Susan Ann Wall sheds light on the fact that you don't need to be a perfect size two for you to be loved."

~ 5 Star Amazon Review
For the Love of Chocolate
Superstitious Brides series

"Susan has done it again! Great story line with twists and turns! ...Highly recommend the entire series..."

~ 5 Star Amazon Review
The Sound of Circumstance
Puget Sound ~ Alive With Love series

♪ ♪ ♪

Dedication

For 2K, my favorite radio show host.
Thanks for the inspiration and a great show to get my day started!

♪ ♪ ♪

♪ Chapter 1 ♪

COLLEEN COOPER was under siege by men she couldn't have. One was blowing up the phone strangled in her shaking hand. The other scowled while gripping the pistol he'd taken from her.

Colleen returned his scowl, a scant attempt to ward off the onslaught of emotions terrorizing her.

Looking across the street to the casino, she searched the shadows beneath the second floor deck for the *dragon* she was sure she'd seen before pulling her gun. Tourists strolled along, but there was no sign of the monster.

"You have to stop pointing your gun at people," Detective Devon Taggart demanded, drawing her attention away from the ghosts of her past.

The pink Ruger .380 felt pretty badass when she fired it at an unwitting paper target at the range, but it looked meager in Devon's capable hands.

Awareness pushed aside the panic. Colleen forced a long exhale, hoping to expel the heat coursing through her. There was a time when that deep voice and the way he cocked his head to the right made her whole body quiver, but those days were long over. Lucky for Devon he was holding the gun now, otherwise she might be tempted to point it at him.

His slow perusal of her body made the late summer sun even hotter. Colleen wished she wore something other than spandex shorts and a form fitting tank top on her afternoon run. When his gaze stopped at her chest, reading the bright yellow letters that stated *The More Men I Meet The More I Like My Dog,* the condescending expression shifted to amusement before transforming into one of lust-filled approval. "You look good."

"How's your wife?" she snarled, reminding him of the reason his bawdy opinion wasn't welcome.

She released the stranglehold on the cell phone and tucked it into her pack, reminding herself the man who kept texting was also off limits, but not because he was married.

"Coll—"

Her hand shot up, stopping Devon's plea. "Don't *Coll* me, Devon. Am I under arrest or what?"

Devon spun the gun around before offering it to her grip first. Colleen snagged the small weapon from his large hand and shoved it into the holster clipped inside her shorts.

"Let me give you a ride home before you wreak more havoc on the boardwalk."

Colleen sucked in a resolute breath and turned away. "I ran here, I can run home."

"Don't argue with me. You terrified that couple when you pulled your gun and you're lucky they aren't pressing charges."

"I'm lucky?" Colleen argued, swinging around. "That woman ought to be thanking me for coming along when I did. Who knows what her boyfriend might have done to her if I hadn't."

"Couples argue. It doesn't mean it will escalate to assault."

She knew that, but her past made her a little ... paranoid? Skittish? *Defensive.*

Yeah, that was a good descriptor and made her seem less crazy. After what she saw in the shadows across the street, she needed reassurance she wasn't crazy.

She stepped off, focused on keeping a moderate pace, only to realize she was heading in the opposite direction from her house.

"Get in the damn car, Colleen." The commanding tone of Devon's voice was all cop, as though she were a criminal being detained. The couple she'd pulled the gun on stared at her from the other side of the parking lot where a patrolman still talked to them. Fear tightened the woman's expression, annoyance the man's.

Colleen wondered if she would have pulled the gun had she not seen something lurking in the shadows just moments before she came upon the arguing couple. She didn't have a murderous bone in her body. Carrying the gun was a tool for self-preservation. *Tania*, as she'd named it, was loaded, but the first round wasn't chambered. She doubted she could shoot an actual person if the situation called for such a thing.

Turning away from the couple, Colleen surrendered to Devon's command and stomped toward him. He held the door and gave her space as she climbed into his badass black SUV. Everything about the man screamed cop, from the pimped out Tahoe to the stick up his ass posture beneath the department store suit.

As he put the cop-mobile in gear, the adrenaline plummeted and Colleen's worst fears claimed her. She'd held it all at bay until now knowing the panic attack was inevitable. Having it in Devon's presence was beyond humiliating.

"Just breathe through it," he said, the commanding voice gone, replaced with something so much worse. The cop was easy to hate. The empathetic guy she'd once cared about, not so much.

"I don't ... need ... your help," she managed between gasps.

It wasn't the first time Devon had witnessed her struggle through a full-blown panic attack. To escalate the vulnerability she despised as much as men who preyed on women, he'd also seen her naked.

Damn him for being married. Damn him straight to hell for not telling her.

Colleen didn't succumb to panic attacks often, but it was often enough that she knew she was at the point of no return. Rather than fight it, which was futile at this point, she let go, sobs replacing the gasps as memories of her college years and all the horrible things that had happened since raced through her mind. She had thought carrying a gun would help her leave the demons behind, but every time she pulled the damn thing in defense, the demons possessed her once again.

A hand landed on her shoulder, startling her. "Don't touch me," she growled, but Devon didn't let up, his strong hand kneading some of the tension from her body. She stared out the window, watching the waves crash on the beach as Devon drove north.

They were beyond the boardwalk now, into the more residential and less touristy part of Granite Beach, the historic New Hampshire town she'd called home for the last two years. Colleen rented a small bungalow on the bluffs at the northern tip of the beach. The house teetered outside her budget, but the view and sound of waves crashing thirty feet below the patio was worth what she sacrificed to afford it.

That was what she needed now. The sea air and hot sun and crashing waves didn't care about her ridiculous panic attack, didn't care that she'd once again pulled her gun when she didn't need to, didn't care that deep inside, the frightened twenty-one year old who had beaten off her attacker eight years ago still cowered at the site of a man threatening a woman.

Her chest ached, the tight knot of fear and humiliation making it difficult to breathe. She tugged the elastic band from around her tight ponytail, hoping to ease some of the tension in her scalp but mostly wanting to hide behind the unruly waves. Yes, Devon had seen her cry. That didn't mean she wanted him to see it again.

Colleen slid the elastic around her wrist and snapped it one, two, three times.

Breathe, she reminded herself as she helped herself to a tissue in the glove compartment, unwilling to further the humiliation by wiping the snot away with her bare arm. Devon continued with the firm massage despite her demand that he not touch her.

Stupid, stubborn alpha cop.

"Do you want me to keep driving or take you home?" he asked as they approached the bluffs.

"Home," she mumbled, snapping the hair band on her wrist another three times. While she didn't like to be alone during a panic attack — something he knew all too well — she couldn't continue to accept comfort from Devon. She wanted to believe he had taken advantage of her that first time, but the truth was a married man should not have done what he did when a panic-stricken, lonely woman threw herself at him.

A shiver pillaged her body as the sobs petered out. Colleen Cooper was famous for making bad choices when it came to men. She'd already made one bad decision when it came to this one. She'd righted the situation as best she could. As much as the terrified woman inside her wanted to lean on him now, the strong-willed woman she worked hard to be wouldn't allow it.

Plus, she had a dog now. Nola was all the comfort she'd ever need and would never lie to or betray Colleen.

She pinched the elastic between her fingers once more. *Snap. Breathe. Snap. Breathe. Snap. Breathe.*

The road up the bluffs was narrow and windy, small bungalows crowded together on either side. Halfway up, the road forked to create a circle with a small park inside. Even though it was quicker to get to her house by going left, Devon went right as he always had. It was a strategy that offered him an immediate exit if called away.

"You have company?" he asked as they approached her house.

Colleen looked up to find a small sedan with a New York license plate parked in her short driveway.

"No, I ..." her voice trailed off, the panic seizing her chest again. "Maybe they parked in the wrong driveway," she tried to reassure herself, but as Devon's hand vacated her shoulder, she could sense his tension as he returned to full cop mode.

Parking at the end of the driveway, he blocked the car. "Stay here. Lock the doors." He left the keys in the ignition and got out, hitting the lock button before he closed the door.

Colleen didn't play the damsel in distress well. More than succumbing to panic attacks, she abhorred helpless women. She snapped the elastic again, hard enough to inspire her to push the panic aside and embrace the adrenaline rush.

After grabbing the keys from the ignition, she slid out of the SUV and put the keys in the small pack strapped around her waist. Then she pulled *Tania* from the holster and fell in step behind Devon.

"I don't know if you're stubborn or if you just live to be a pain in my ass," he said over his shoulder.

"Yes," she replied.

The adrenaline kicked back in, pushing aside the panic and replacing it with anxious terror. If someone was in her house, it'd throw her off of the deep end, but she couldn't just sit in the SUV and wait for the horror to play out.

After climbing the steps, Devon tested the door handle. "You lock up when you leave, right?"

"Always." She lived alone, and had escaped an attack as a college student and another over a year ago. She followed her laundry list of safety protocols religiously.

"I suppose telling you to go back to the car is pointless."

"I want to know who's in my house," she said, forcing a brave facade.

"Then stay behind me, and for God's sake, put that thing away."

Colleen wouldn't fire the gun, but gripping it in her hands made her feel a hell of a lot more invincible than if she wasn't holding it.

Devon rolled his eyes as she stood her ground. He pushed the door open and stepped inside.

As Colleen stepped in behind him, the bathroom door creaked, giving the intruder away. She held her breath as Devon lifted his gun and pointed it down the hall. Standing behind him and slightly to his left, she pointed her gun as well.

"Jake," she sighed when her best friend stepped out of the bathroom.

He stopped whistling as he turned down the hall and saw two guns pointing at him.

"Whoa, I surrender," Jake said, throwing his arms in the air.

"You know this guy?" Devon asked over his shoulder.

Colleen released the white-knuckled grip, holding *Tania* firmly in her right hand as she rested her left hand on Devon's arm.

"He's a friend. Jake, what are you doing here?" Now she was surrounded by the two men she couldn't have.

"You didn't get my text?"

Shit. He'd texted, multiple times. With all drama on the boardwalk, and the distraction that was the detective standing next to her, she'd forgotten about the texts.

Colleen pushed by Devon and almost tackled Jake. His arms came down from his surrendered position, pulling her in for a tight hug.

She hadn't seen Jake since the opening show of his latest tour six months ago. JD Donovan was one of the hottest acts in country and his *Country Bad Boy* tour kept him on the road.

"It's good to see you, too," he said against her ear before planting a long kiss at her temple.

Without warning, the panic bubbled up again. Before she could swallow the sob, it claimed her.

Jake released her from the circle of his arms and gripped hers. "Coll, why are you crying?" His gaze drifted down to her hand. "And why do you have a gun?"

"I'm just, just so happy to see you," she stammered through the sobs. "I wish I'd seen your text."

"Who's this guy?" he asked, nodding over her shoulder.

"Detective Taggart," Devon answered with emphasis on the Detective.

Colleen turned from Jake's hold to find Devon returning his gun to the holster over his ribcage.

"Detective? Coll, what's going on?" Jake rested an arm across her shoulder in that casual, best friend way he had for years. At Devon's glare, Jake's hand seemed to tighten around her muscles, sending a forbidden thrill straight to her nipples.

"I was running and there was this couple fighting," she explained, leaving out the part about what lurked in the shadows since she wasn't even sure of what she'd seen. "And well, Devon's an old friend, so after the incident was cleared up, he brought me home." That was about as much information as Colleen was willing to offer. Jake might be her best friend, but there were some things she didn't want him to know.

"Are you hurt?" Jake asked, spinning her around and giving her the once over in a brotherly way that made Colleen flinch.

"I'm fine. Stop fussing. Where's Nola?" she asked, realizing her loyal dog hadn't greeted her with that affectionate loyalty Colleen adored.

"She's out back," Jake said, his hands still running up and down her arms.

"Let her in. I'll see Devon out."

Colleen stepped away from Jake but neither man made a move, locked in some stupid alpha man stare down. When she reached the front door, she pulled Devon's keys from her pack and jingled them as though he was Pavlov's dog and might respond to the subtle hint for him to leave.

She couldn't be that lucky. "Detective Taggart, don't let us keep you. I'm sure you have a case load requiring your attention." She jingled the keys again for effect.

Devon turned, his brow furrowed. Jake's face mirrored the expression.

Stopping in front of her, Devon's expression softened. "Get a whistle for when you run. Sports stores have the kind you wear on your fingers. You don't need a gun on the boardwalk."

"Good-bye, Detective," she said, ignoring his logical advice. She was used to the gun. Even though she knew she didn't need it and wouldn't fire it at a person, she still felt safer having it near.

Devon glared at Jake one more time before stepping out.

Before Colleen could breathe a sigh of relief, she turned to find Jake's disapproving glare.

"You're sleeping with him." The curt accusation seethed with disapproval.

"I'm not sleeping with him."

"Slept with, then."

"So? You sleep with everyone." She didn't tend throw his reputation in his face, but where the hell did he get off judging her?

"I don't like him."

"You saw him for all of two minutes. Anyway, it's history. Ancient history."

Jake shook his head. "He doesn't look at you like it's history."

Colleen laughed. "Jacob Daniel Donovan, if I didn't know better, I'd think you're jealous."

Disappointment crashed through her as he shook his head. "You're my best friend. I don't like you hooking up with shady men."

She'd meant her accusation as a joke, but the best friend card was a bitter pill to swallow. "He's a detective. He's not shady."

"Being a cop doesn't exempt him from being shady. I don't like him."

While she knew that was true and Devon was far from being an upstanding man, Jake's angst surprised her. She brushed by him, heading straight down the hall to the back door where Nola wiggled outside the screen. Colleen stepped onto the stone patio and crouched to accept a kiss from her sweetest girl.

"Hi, baby. Did you miss me today?"

Nola tucked her head beneath Colleen's chin, rubbing against her neck in an affectionate hug. Colleen rubbed her girl's back.

"There was a time when she loved me that much," Jake said as he crouched next to Colleen and gave Nola a loving stroke. Nola flopped onto the stone pavers and offered up her belly.

"She still loves you. You rescued her, after all."

"And you gave her a home."

Colleen scratched Nola's belly, her hand bumping Jake's. The dog was nearly in a coma. Colleen would be too if Jake touched her with that kind of affection, but he hadn't since college and given his playboy reputation, doubted he ever would again.

"She gave me a home," Colleen confessed. She and Nola had been together for almost two years now, after Jake found her scavenging through the remains of a tipped over trash can at a rest area in Tennessee. He'd nursed her back to health as he traveled from arena to arena on that tour du jour until admitting the concert circuit was no place for a dog. That's when he called Colleen. She'd been reluctant to take the dog, but when she met up with Jake and Nola in Massachusetts for his Gillette Stadium concert, she'd fallen in love with Nola immediately.

"So what's going on? You're supposed to be on tour. Don't you have a show in Chicago on Thursday?"

"I thought you'd be happy to see me." His hand brushed her palm before his fingers tangled with hers. A familiar longing fluttered in her belly.

"Of course I'm happy to see you, but you never show up unannounced, especially in the middle of a tour."

"I texted."

"Texted today," she reminded him. She released the strap from her arm and pulled the phone from the pouch to read Jake's messages. "*Got a surprise for you.*"

She looked up at him, raising a brow.

"Surprise," he laughed.

She read the next message.

"*Don't you want to know what the surprise is?*"

Jake shrugged. "You usually respond right away."

Usually, but more pressing matters demanded her attention. "*It's me. I'm the surprise,*" she read with a laugh. "*I'm in town. See you in 5. I'm here. Where are you?*"

"You know I'm not very patient," he sighed.

Since the messages spanned about ten minutes, it was clear he didn't have any patience.

There was one other unread message from a number she didn't recognize. Colleen clicked on it to find one word, her least favorite word in the whole world. As the shadow she'd seen earlier flashed through her mind, the panic threatened once more. She sucked in a deep breath and hit delete. As a radio station host, she sometimes got hate messages. That's what this was. It had nothing to do with the day's events.

After tucking the phone into the strap of her sports bra, Colleen turned her hand into his, sliding her fingers between his. "Jake, what's going on?"

He never showed up without notice, especially not while on tour. Jake lived by his calendar, if for no other reason than his personal assistant demanded it.

"Let's go inside. I could use a drink." Jake pushed off the stone with his free hand, pulling Colleen up with him and awakening Nola from her pleasure-induced coma.

♪ Chapter 2 ♪

DREAD SWARMED Jake's chest as Colleen stuffed the small gun into the backpack of a monkey he had won for her at the Eastern States Exposition — the Big E — back in college. She couldn't know about the threats against him, so why the hell was she carrying a gun?

Following her into the kitchen, Jake tried to work up the courage to tell her about his current mess. She'd be disappointed — well, more likely she'd be pissed — but the disappointment would be there and that wrecked him. Colleen and Gramps were the only two people he never wanted to disappoint, but they seemed to be the ones he let down the most.

Nola was at her side, Colleen's hand stroking the dog's chestnut-colored fur. It warmed his heart to see the bond the two had formed. He loved Nola as much as he loved Colleen and they seemed to love each other that much too.

Jake decided to table the gun conversation for later. Right now, he wanted to make sure the detective wasn't going to be a problem. It boiled Jake's blood to see the way the guy had looked at her.

Colleen pulled a bottle of wine from the rack over the sink. He took a seat at one of the bar stools at the small island.

"I don't drink much. Wine is all I have."

He'd kill for a Jack and Coke — okay, maybe kill was a bad metaphor since drinking too much had gotten him into his current mess. He'd settle for wine just for something wet.

She uncorked the bottle and collected the only two glasses from the same rack over the sink. Colleen didn't drink alone. Jake wondered if she kept a few bottles around for when she entertained that detective.

"Tell me about Joe Friday."

"Joe Friday?" She raised a brow, which also lifted one corner of her mouth.

"Detective Loaded Gun," he clarified.

Colleen shrugged. "There's nothing to tell."

"Is he the reason you carry a gun when you're out and stuff it in the monkey when you come home?"

"I carry a gun because I'm a single woman who lives alone in a busy town full of sketchy tourists and vagrants."

Jake didn't buy it, but he needed other facts right now. "How long were you sleeping with him?"

She slammed the bottle down on the counter, her complacent demeanor transformed into anger. "You make me sound like a slut. Maybe it was a meaningful relationship."

Jake wasn't about to back down, not after the way that detective had looked at Colleen and not with his plans for them. "If it was meaningful you would have told me about him."

"Three months." She held up three fingers, as if he didn't understand the number. "That's how long I have to be with a guy before I tell you or my mother about him. I was with Devon for two and to me they were meaningful."

To her. Was she saying they weren't meaningful to the cop? "What went wrong?" If the guy had hurt Colleen in any way, it didn't matter how skilled he was with that gun, Jake would make him pay.

"It was over months ago," she said, the complacency back in her voice. "I'd rather not rehash the boring details."

"You're avoiding the topic," he pointed out.

"You're one to talk. We came in here to talk about why you showed up without warning at my house."

She pushed a wine glass across the small island and held up her glass. "To old friends," she offered.

"To best friends," Jake emphasized, tapping her glass. The searing gaze she afforded him over the rim as she took a long sip of the Merlot inspired a swirl of heat in his chest and stomach that dove right to his groin.

"Speak," she commanded, breaking eye contact and setting her glass down.

"I'm not a dog."

"No, dogs are much better behaved than you," she laughed, leaning over to give Nola a quick pat.

She was right, after all, if he hadn't earned his reputation, he might not be in a world of trouble.

"We rescheduled the next five shows to the end of the tour. I have a couple weeks off. I needed someplace to lie low."

"You're always welcome here. You know that."

He did know that, but it wasn't the only reason he'd come. "How's work?"

"I love the morning show." Colleen's smile brightened the room and sent Jake's heart into a twelve-eighths tempo. "I'm two years in and I love every day of it. I know a small town radio station doesn't sound like much, but this is what I've always wanted."

It wasn't small town radio. The station broadcast to every corner of New England and featured some of the biggest names in country music. Colleen and her co-host had even been nominated as *Personality of the Year* last year at the Country Music Awards. Of course, Jake hoped she was miserable because that'd make his proposition all the more appealing.

"You're a great DJ, Coll. You make small town radio big."

"Thanks, but your opinion's a little biased." She said it with a smile, but it made him crazy how she was unwilling to accept a simple compliment. "So why reschedule the shows? Are you all right?"

He couldn't dance around the topic all night. He'd barged into her life without warning, she deserved to know what was going on.

"I'm fine, but Margot isn't. I have a stalker and she went after Margot."

Colleen stared at him over the glass again. She abandoned the drink, setting the glass on the counter. "Is she okay?"

"She will be."

"Jake," she urged.

"She was stabbed. The knife missed all her vital organs, but she still needed surgery and she's going to be off the road for the rest of the tour. We're looking for a new opening act."

Margot Potter was a rising country star who got her start writing music. Jake had recorded several of her songs and was happy to invite her on tour when she cut her own album.

"Are you still sleeping with her?" Colleen asked. The sting of that question lanced all the way to his heart.

"No," he said while she raised a brow. Colleen was born a skeptic but Jake had earned the reaction. He held up his hands. "I swear. I haven't slept with her since *Set It On Fire*." Margot had written or collaborated on half the songs on that album two years ago. They'd spent a lot of time in the studio together — it was no surprise she ended up in his bed.

"Any leads on the stalker?"

"Islynn Gray. She's been following me around for years. I thought she was harmless, but who knows."

"A woman? Women don't normally use knives. It requires too close of contact and unless she's built like a brick house, she'd be lucky to stab someone and get away."

"A lesson from the detective?"

"His pillow talk was a relationship killer," she smirked, but Jake detected the hurt behind the sarcasm.

"Yeah, well, Islynn has an alibi."

"Don't tell me you were in bed with her." Colleen lifted her glass and took a long drink.

Jake laughed without any humor. "No, not me. Marky."

"Your drummer is screwing your stalker?"

"Apparently. The cops on the case said the same thing you just said, that women don't use knives."

"So do they have a suspect?"

Jake chuckled. "Yeah, yeah they do." He took a long drink of the wine. It wasn't a brand he recognized, but had a nice balance of earthy flavors and tannins. No surprise. Colleen always had good taste.

"You going to keep me in suspense all night?" she asked.

"It's me. I'm the prime person of interest."

~ ♪ ~

Devon strolled into Captain McKinley's office ready for an ass chewing. Rescuing Colleen was below his pay grade and the captain didn't like his detectives handling uniform issues. Devon couldn't ignore the call, though. As soon as he'd seen the dispatch, he knew it had to be Colleen. Not many female runners in Granite Beach would pull a gun on an arguing couple. Since a panic attack was guaranteed to follow, he wasn't inclined to let it pass.

At the scene, Officer Kendall seemed happy to let Devon take the manic Colleen off his hands. That woman needed a whistle. Devon made a mental note to hit the sporting goods store on his way home. It'd be a good excuse to stop by her place.

"Devon, good to see you." To Devon's relief, the captain was cheerful. Maybe he wasn't getting his ass handed to him after all.

"You too, Sir. What's going on?"

Captain McKinley laughed. "Always right to the point. I've always liked that about you. We got a courtesy call from Deputy Carmen French this morning from the Jefferson County Sheriff's Department just south of Denver."

"Denver?"

"Yep. Seems there was a stabbing there a few nights back involving a popular country musician." The chief flipped through his notebook.

"Margot Potter. She's the opening act for JD Donovan. Any of this ring a bell?"

"I don't listen to country, Captain. I'm more of an AC/DC and Metallica kind of guy."

"Right, well, JD Donovan is one of the biggest selling acts in country music. My wife is a huge fan."

Devon nodded, wondering what this had to do with him.

"JD Donovan is a person of interest in the case. He doesn't have an alibi, but there's also no evidence against him. They couldn't keep him in Denver, but according to Deputy French, he is cooperating. He rescheduled his upcoming shows while this is being sorted out and he's laying low here in Granite Beach."

"With all due respect, sir, babysitting a person of interest in an out of state case is a little below my pay grade."

"I agree and you wouldn't have been on my radar at all except you showed up to handle the rogue runner on the boardwalk this afternoon. Officer Kendall got the impression Colleen Cooper is a friend of yours."

Devon resisted the urge to chuckle. He'd like Colleen to be a friend. Hell, now that he was legally separated from Sarah, he'd like Colleen to be more than a friend, but he knew her well enough to know she wouldn't make that easy. He'd hurt her, lied to her. She had every right to hate him. The captain didn't need to know all that. Sarah didn't even know about his affair with Colleen. No one did. "She's more of an acquaintance than a friend, but what does she have to do with this?"

"JD Donovan told the Deputy French he'd be staying with her for the foreseeable future."

"Does the J happen to stand for Jake?" Devon asked.

The captain consulted his notes again. "Sure does. Jacob Daniel Donovan. His home of record is South Royalton, Vermont, but according to Deputy French, he mostly lives out of a big, fancy RV." The chief gazed at him over the frame of his reading glasses. "You've had contact?"

"I brought Colleen home after the incident this afternoon. A car with

New York plates was parked in her driveway and she wasn't expecting anyone, so I entered the property. Mr. Donovan was on the premises."

"You think Ms. Cooper is his lover?"

Dammit, he hoped not, but it was hard to tell with Colleen. She was affectionate but guarded. The guy could have just as easily been a brother or cousin for all Devon knew. Donovan was protective of her, that much he'd garnered during their silent appraisal of each other.

"I don't know. You want me to check him out?"

"Do that. Check with Marie," the captain said, directing Devon to the department's lead research analyst. "Deputy French was going to send the case file. Donovan has a stalker fan, but she has a solid alibi. It seems our country rock star doesn't have an alibi and has a history with the singer who got stabbed. French said she'd appreciate any help we can offer while he's in residence."

Devon was happy to help. Something hadn't felt right about the guy being inside Colleen's house, but Devon wasn't beyond thinking his suspicion was due to his own jealousy. When it came to Colleen, the lines between professionalism and everything else were easily blurred. Now, though, Devon had to give his instincts a little credit. The guy was mixed up in something bad. Devon just hoped he didn't plan to drag Colleen into it.

~ ♪ ~

Jake's hand shook as he waited for Colleen's response. She poured herself another glass of wine and topped off Jake's.

"Why are you a suspect?" she asked, obviously bewildered.

"No alibi." It was funny considering a year ago he wouldn't have been alone after a show, but his new plan only had room for one woman, so he was now spending all of his nights alone.

"How can you not have an alibi?"

"I just don't," Jake shrugged. "I know it's hard to believe, but I'm not that guy who sleeps with a different girl after every show anymore."

He expected her to laugh, but instead she raised her brow again.

Jake made an X over his heart. "I swear to you, Coll. I've turned over a new leaf."

She took another drink, tapping her pretty nails on the counter and staring at him like he had three heads. For the better part of a decade, he'd been the country playboy, ever since Colleen told him they could only ever be friends. She'd broken his heart and he still didn't understand why.

Jake coped by drowning his sorrows in the lifestyle and throwing himself into songwriting. Unfortunately, the stipulations of his contract only allowed him to record a couple of his own songs on each album. None of them were hits, so he had to keep playing the game. While he loved performing on stage, it just never felt quite right. He needed to play his own music, perform by his own rules, and he needed Colleen by his side. She was the only person besides Gramps who ever believed in him.

"Why the sudden change?" she asked.

It wasn't sudden. His new life was a year in the making, but the light at the end of the tunnel grew brighter every day. "I didn't sign a new contract with Southern Rebel Records. I'm recording one more album with them and then I'm breaking out on my own."

Colleen squealed and bounced around the island, nearly jumping into his lap. Some of the tension crippling him for the past couple weeks faded as he slid from the stool and held her close. She was warm and soft and smelled like an ocean breeze and all Jake could think about was kissing her.

And more, so much more.

"I am so proud of you, Jake," she sang, squeezing him before planting a chaste kiss on his cheek. "Tell me everything."

A surge of energy shot through him, excitement replacing the leashed desire. He had so many plans. Some things were already in place and he hoped Colleen didn't get mad for not telling her sooner. Most of all, he hoped she would say yes to his proposition.

"I'm starving. Let me take you to dinner."

Colleen stepped back and glanced down at her clothes. She looked incredible in the workout gear, inspiring Jake's over-active imagination to run wild, his fingers twitching to trace ever curve. He could picture her long, lean legs wrapped around his waist, her soft and curvy breasts pressed against his chest. "I need to grab a shower and change. You can keep yourself entertained for a few?"

Entertained? He wouldn't mind entertaining her in the shower, but he was trying to take baby steps, not leap head first off the cliff.

"I'll steal some loving from Nola. That is if she doesn't hop in the shower with you."

Colleen laughed, the sweet sound music to his ears as she gave Nola an affectionate scratch. "No. She prefers to have the shower to herself."

♪ Chapter 3 ♪

From Viper:

Settled in. Tide is high.

To Viper:

B thr 2moro.

♪ Chapter 4 ♪

ALL JAKE wanted to do was strip down and climb in the shower with Colleen, to touch every inch of her silky skin, taste her, make her scream his name.

Instead, he sat on the sofa, rubbing Nola's ears as the dog snored, and silently rehearsing his proposition. Colleen deserved better than the man his reputation painted him as. He had to prove he was worthy of her love first. Confessing his love now would also be a stupid move. She'd turned him down once, using his music career as an excuse for them to stay just friends. He'd bought it, but all these years, something scratched beneath the surface, something that told him there was more to the story.

He was breaking free of his bad boy reputation now. He hadn't been with a woman in over a year and had only indulged in one or two drinks after a show. He'd stepped back from the after-show parties, using that time to meditate and rest so he had the focus to develop his business plan.

When this tour ended in three months, he'd announce he owned Old Red Barn Records, the label that launched Margot's singing career and had signed three other up and coming artists. By then, the barn at his grandparent's farm would be converted into a fully functional recording studio, equipped to record raw, traditional sounds in one sound room while a second room housed state of the art recording equipment to accommodate those artists who preferred the technological evolution in their music.

The loft was reserved for Colleen — he hoped. That's where JD Donovan's Rock and Soul Internet radio station would broadcast from. The business plan was fully developed, all it needed was Colleen's seal of approval and commitment to manage the station and be the online personality.

His phone beeped and Jake dragged himself away from Nola and the comfortable couch to pull it from his leather jacket hanging on the hook just inside the front door. He loved Colleen's bungalow but was glad it was only a rental. He knew how much she loved the ocean, but she was a mountain girl at heart, part of the reason for his decision to convert the old barn into a studio and radio station. Plus, she loved the big old farmhouse as much as he did. How could she say no?

Jake opened the text message, not at all surprised to see what it was. *SHE is next.*

"Right on schedule," he murmured, the disgust tightening his gut. The three-word message was just like the others. He never knew who the 'she' was in the messages, although in hindsight he now knew the last one was Margot. He wondered how many other crimes would be tied back to the obscure messages. He hoped to hell none, but he couldn't be sure.

He studied the words, trying to piece together who the *SHE* was. There were too many women in his life besides Margot. Kasey Ferris was the fiddler in his road band, there were half a dozen women in the road crew, Rebekah, his personal assistant, not to mention everyone who worked at Southern Rebel Records. *SHE* could be anyone.

His phone vibrated before the song *Mean Woman Blues* played. Jake cringed, knowing he was about to face Rebekah's wrath, but he couldn't avoid it forever.

"Hello, Chuck," he said.

"You son of a bitch," Rebekah yelled. Fortunately, he'd been smart enough to hold the phone away from his ear. "How dare you not tell me you were leaving Denver."

"It was a last-minute decision," he lied.

"Bull shit. Deputy Stick Up Her Ass French told me when she came by to question me yet again. I can't make your life smell like freshly cut roses if you don't keep me in the loop, JD."

"You know I don't like the smell of roses, Chuck."

"And you know I hate being called that. Seriously, JD, when were you going to tell me you left town?"

"I was going to call you once I got settled, I swear." It was another lie. His goal in coming here, aside from enticing Colleen to say yes to his proposition, was to get away from JD Donovan and everything that went along with the persona. That included his moody assistant.

"Are you sleeping with her? Is that why you went there? You promised I wouldn't have to clean up any more of these messes and look at where we are."

So the deputy hadn't just told Rebekah he'd left, he told her where he'd gone. Shit. "I haven't done anything wrong, so there's nothing to clean up."

"Then why are you hiding out with your little girlfriend?"

Colleen wasn't his girlfriend yet, but that was also part of Jake's plan. "She's my best friend and I'm not hiding out. We postponed the next five shows and the detective advised that I keep a low profile."

"It doesn't get much lower than CC."

"Watch yourself, Rebekah," he warned. The two women had been roommates in college. For reasons Jake didn't understand, Rebekah didn't like Colleen — and Colleen didn't have a lot of affection for Rebekah, either. "Colleen is family to me."

"And I'm just the lowly assistant who cleans up all the shit you leave in your wake. I don't get paid enough to do this job."

"I pay you very well and you know it."

"And I hate this job and you know it."

She made no secret of that, yet, she refused to quit. Jake thought she'd be happier now that he wasn't screwing up at every turn, but it seemed the further he got from the life he'd been living, the more miserable Rebekah got. She wouldn't admit it, but it seemed that cleaning up after him made her happy.

"This situation sucks, but we have to make the most of it. Did the fine deputy have any new leads when you spoke to her?"

"She questioned me like I'm a suspect, even though I have a rock solid alibi ... unlike some superstars I know. Alone in your RV, JD? Really? You couldn't come up with something better than that?"

"It was the truth."

"Right, in bed before midnight so you could be up early for church in the morning." Her sarcasm was thick, making Jake weary of this conversation.

He hadn't screwed up in over a year, yet that didn't seem to ease Rebekah's attitude. It seemed the longer he went without getting into trouble, the more bitchy she became.

"Is there anything else you need, Chuck?" he asked.

"My name is Rebekah," she emphasized and Jake bit back a chuckle. She was so easy to rile up. "Next time, tell me where you're going before you go. I don't like being blindsided."

She probably deserved the courtesy of that information, but Jake hadn't told her because he knew what her reaction would be and she'd have made it difficult for him to leave.

"Okay, then. Bye-bye now," he said, aware of how condescending he sounded, but unable to scrape up an ounce of give a shit. Rebekah had been what he needed for the past six years. She'd kept him out of jail, kept most of his exploits out of the press, and kept his life in order so he could move full speed ahead with his career. He didn't know how she did it all and he wasn't sure he wanted to know, but now that he was settling down and taking a new direction with his life, he was eager to let her move on too. She would do great with a new musician, one who didn't know how to balance the excitement of being a rising star with the demands it required.

Jake wanted to turn the phone off, but he'd made a promise to Deputy French to be available should she have any additional questions. He wanted to cooperate, to find whomever had stabbed Margot and put it behind him so he could focus on the future.

"I take it Rebekah isn't happy you're here," Colleen said from behind him.

~ ♪ ~

"You don't eat like a girl," Jake said, tilting his head and offering a smirk that sent sparks straight to all of Colleen's girl parts.

"I run five days a week so I don't have to eat like a girl," Colleen admitted, digging into the fully loaded garlic mashed potatoes. It was carb overload and might send her into a food coma, but potatoes were a comfort food and with the events of the day and Jake's wicked smile, she needed some comfort.

They'd opted to hit a small bar and grill at the north end of the boardwalk. They had walked, enjoying the late summer sun and cool sea breeze. Being at the northern end of the boardwalk, the restaurant catered to locals more than tourists, and on a Tuesday evening was relatively quiet. The table in the back corner gave them some privacy and Jake sat with his back to the rest of the place to avoid being recognized.

Since Jake was a Jack and Coke guy, Colleen was surprised when he ordered a bottle of wine. He claimed giving up the hard stuff was part of the whole turning over a new leaf thing.

She liked it. He seemed more like the young man she'd known in college than the big country star he'd become.

"Do you remember that night in the Campus Center?" Jake asked.

Colleen's fork dangled in front of her mouth, the steak tip just inches away from lodging in her throat and requiring the Heimlich. "The night we watched *Enemy at the Gates*?"

She'd never forget that night, for good reasons and bad.

"The night I kissed you," he elaborated.

Colleen returned the fork to the plate, the steak uneaten. "Yeah, well, you were just channeling your affection for Rachel Weisz," she joked, hoping to keep the conversation light. She could tell from Jake's expression that there was nothing light about it.

"You smiled after. Let out one of those happy sighs as if you'd been waiting a long time for me to kiss you."

Two long years she had waited. Colleen had never been assertive when it came to men — or boys — and especially not when it came to sex. Devon was the one exception to that rule, but even then, she was way out of her element.

At twenty-two, she didn't have a lot of experience and had always been the type of girl that guys liked to be friends with, not the kind they wanted to date. Even now at thirty, she still didn't have much experience with men. What experience she did have was mostly based on bad decisions.

When she and Jake had both applied to DJ at the campus radio station, and they'd been offered the opportunity to host a show together, she'd fallen head over heels in love with him almost immediately. Back then, she was smart enough to know not to mix business and pleasure. Being a DJ was her dream. She did not intend to blow it it by going out with her co-host.

For two years, they worked together and formed an unbreakable bond. She was grateful for his friendship and knew that was more special than anything else they might have shared. They'd been so young, she feared if they ended up going out, it would end, but a friendship, that could last forever.

Then he kissed her and all logic washed away like footprints in wet sand when a new wave kisses the shore.

"It was a nice kiss," she admitted, trying to downplay the impact it had on her.

"I thought it was more than nice. But then you didn't show up for my show and the later said you just wanted to be friends."

"We got caught up in the movie," she shrugged.

"Maybe the movie pushed us over the edge, but we'd been building up to that kiss for a long time."

They had been. It all started when Jake's grandma died. He was different somehow, more serious, more driven. Even though Colleen had fallen for the quick-witted boy who always wore a smile, she'd started fantasizing about the focused and determined man he was becoming.

And the kiss, it had been better than she'd ever imagined.

She took a bite of her steak, unsure what to say. The truth was too terrifying. She tried not to think about that night, not the horror she had escaped, nor the events leading up to it.

"Something happened, Coll. You denied it then and I know you'll deny it now, but you never would have missed a show. Something happened to scare you off and I think I deserve the truth."

"You were offered the opportunity of a lifetime, that's what happened," she countered. A guy was there that night who offered to help Jake record a demo CD. Once he got major radio time, it didn't take long to become a country sensation.

"That was the best performance of my life, and it was all because of you. You believed in me."

"I still do. Now tell me about your plans. I know you've got something brewing if you're leaving Southern Rebel."

"Subtle," he mumbled in response to her change of subject, but his smile soon brightened his face, his eyes wide with excitement.

"You know Old Red Barn Records?"

"The label Margot recorded with?"

"Yeah, and Owen Foster, Greg Felton, and Lacey Graham."

All new musicians, all rising fast with their unique sounds. Foster's country sound was more traditional blue grass, but he was getting as much radio play as the mainstream country artists. Same with Greg Felton, who had a strong blues influence to his music, while Lacey was a lot like Margot with a stronger beat and edgy lyrics. "It's a new label, but it's making some pretty big waves in the industry. Country has never been more diverse."

He smiled, the pride so obvious that the reality hit before he even uttered the words. "It's mine. I partnered with Toby Tibbs."

Colleen's eyes widened. "Wha— I mean, how, uh, why didn't tell me? Why the secret?"

Jake rolled his eyes. "Southern Rebel has been pressuring me to sign again. Specifically, Paul Curran."

Colleen couldn't fight the shiver that raced up her spine at the mention of her former boss.

Jake's hand brushed hers, giving it a small squeeze. "I don't know how you survived working with that guy. He's one sleazy bastard."

Colleen nodded in agreement, unable to offer any words. Paul Curran wasn't a man she liked to think about. He certainly wasn't a man she could talk about.

"He's probably the reason you carry a gun," Jake laughed. It wasn't funny, and it wasn't too far from the truth, but Colleen laughed along with him to try and keep the demons at bay.

"Anyway," Jake continued, releasing her hand and pushing his sirloin around the plate. "Toby and I agreed it was best to keep my name out of it until I'm free and clear of my contract. I formed a holding company with Gramps and it is that company that partnered with Toby to form Old Red Barn. Nobody's looked at it too closely yet, so we've been able to keep my name out of it. It wouldn't take a lot of digging, though, to know who owns sixty percent of the label."

Jake's talent made it easy to forget what an intelligent businessman he could be. He'd majored in business in college even though music was his passion. He always knew he'd pursue a music career, but his grandparents encouraged him to purse a practical education in case the music career never took off.

His success was fast and furious. Jake's first single shot straight to number one. His good looks, charming personality, and unique voice, as well as his talent on the guitar all worked in his favor. Then he took to the road and before long he'd abandoned the county fairs and focused on the larger arenas and stadiums. When he wasn't on the road, he was in the studio.

But most of the time, he wasn't recording his songs and Colleen knew how much that frustrated him. The execs at Southern Rebel kept telling him when one of his songs hit number one, they'd let him record more of them, but until then, he'd record the songs they told him to.

"Paul doesn't think I understand the trends and marketing, but every time I try to convince him otherwise, he tells me to go back to my guitar and let him handle the business. I'm tired of it. They are sabotaging my songs, not releasing them as singles or letting me shoot videos. I've had enough, Coll. I'm tired of playing their games."

Colleen smiled, happy to know he hadn't sold his soul. "You want to come on the show while you're in town? I'll get your songs some air time."

Jake smiled but shook his head. "Paul pitches a fit every time you do that. As much as I'd love to get his knickers twisted, I don't want anyone to know I'm here. It's only a matter of time before what happened to Margot goes viral and when it does, I'll be bleeding in shark-infested waters."

♪ Chapter 5 ♪

COLLEEN IGNORED the badass black Tahoe parked outside The North Beach Tavern. Though Devon wasn't the only cop in town who drove one, she recognized the government-issued license plate as his and had no doubt he lurked behind the tinted glass.

Jake's arm slid across her shoulder as they hit the boardwalk and headed south, away from her house. The sun was due to set in thirty minutes so the walk back would be dark, but she felt safe with Tania clipped to her jeans and Jake at her side.

His embrace was casual, but Colleen's body still tingled with anticipation. She'd long ago stomped out the hope they could be more than friends, but the conversation he'd tried to pursue tonight reawakened every dormant feeling she'd ever had for him. Colleen didn't regret her decision to just be friends, because seeing him achieve his dreams was worth the sacrifice. She'd learned to ignore the tabloids that fed off his playboy reputation, but sometimes it was like staring at a burning building, fascinating and horrifying in equal measure.

Sometimes he told her about the women, looking for advice on how to let them down easy because he really was a nice guy. Colleen did the best she could, but she truly hated knowing about his exploits. Every time, it broke her heart just a little bit more, but she always reminded herself it was her choice to let Jake go.

Self-preservation was such a bitch.

Even when she'd been with Devon, the only other man she'd ever opened her heart to, she still couldn't bear to see Jake on the cover of a magazine with the flavor of the month. He claimed to be turning over a new leaf and now that Colleen thought about it, she hadn't seen him grace the cover of a tabloid or magazine with another woman in a long time.

"You've grown up," she said, letting her arm move across his back. She held on to his waist with a loose grip, aware of the hard muscles beneath her fingers.

"About time, right?" he chuffed.

"I didn't say that." She wouldn't judge. She'd made her own share of mistakes, done things she wasn't proud of, things that bordered on shame. All that was in the past, though, just as it was for Jake. "I'm excited about this new path you're on."

"Me too. The record label isn't the only thing, though."

"There's more?" she asked, though she shouldn't be surprised. When he set his mind to something, he was always one hundred percent committed.

"I'm going to be recording my own music, so I'll be taking a swift turn away from mainstream country."

"I figured as much," Colleen admitted. Country was an easy in when Jake got his start, but it wasn't the beat in his heart.

"To help segue from mainstream country to blues rock with a country lilt, I'm starting my own Internet radio station. JD Donovan's Rock and Soul."

Colleen squealed, loving this idea. Of course, she was a little biased about radio, but she knew other musicians who had found a ton of success with their own Internet radio projects. "I love it. If you need advice on equipment or marketing or anything, I'd love to help."

"I was hoping you'd say that. I have a business plan all written and Dewy Fox gave great advice and input, but I don't want to move forward until it has your blessing."

"Dewy Fox provided input?" He was one of the few country stars bigger than Jake and he had the most popular Internet radio station in the industry. "I'm not sure I can top that, but I'd love to have a look. Do you have it with you?"

"Back at your house, yes."

"Then let's go." She grabbed his hand and dragged him onto the boardwalk.

Her cell phone vibrated as they approached Devon's cop-mobile. She was tempted to ignore it, but she'd been doing that all night and knew there were at least three text messages waiting.

Grabbing the phone out of her pocket, she swept her finger across the screen and opened the messages. Three more from a number she didn't recognize but could be the same number as the message she'd deleted. When she opened the first message, and then the next two, she was sure they were from the same number as earlier. They were all one-word messages, all the same word.

"Slut?" Jake asked, his voice growling in anger across her ear. "Who the hell is sending you messages calling you a slut?"

Colleen shrugged it off. "I'm sure it's wrong number."

Jake grabbed the phone and looked at the message. Based on the movements of his finger and the growing scowl, he was reading the others as well.

"Shit," he muttered. "We need to call the police."

"It's just a stupid message." She tried to grab the phone, but Jake pulled it away. He gripped her shoulder, locking his elbow to keep her an arm's length away as he studied the message. "People text me all the time and it is the wrong number."

"Margot got this same message for weeks before she was stabbed." He lowered the phone and looked at her, anger morphing into desperation. "Colleen, please. We need to call the police."

She peered over her shoulder, looking into the windshield of Devon's SUV. He wasn't there, but movement from the corner of her eye caught her attention and she saw him come out of the shadows across the road.

"Are you spying on us?" she asked, stunned to find him there.

"What the hell?" Jake growled.

"Just keeping an eye on Mr. Donovan, as requested by the Jefferson County Sheriff's Department. Looks like it's a good thing I'm around."

~ ♪ ~

JD Donovan was overly cooperative, making Devon even more suspicious. "A woman you are responsible for is stabbed while on tour with you, you have a known stalker, and yet you show up on Colleen's door, putting her in the direct line of danger."

"It's not like that," Colleen insisted.

"And you," Devon growled, turning his attention to where she sat next to Donovan on her couch. "Why didn't you tell me about the message as soon as you got it?"

"Take a pill, detective," she snarled. Devon bit back his amusement. He loved her spunk but didn't want to encourage it. "You are not my keeper. You're not my anything. I got a one-word message from a number I don't recognize. It's not Armageddon."

"It is now that your friend here has brought the trouble to your doorstep."

"We don't even know if it's connected. Hell, Devon, for all I know, it could be from your wife."

"Wife?" Donovan turned on Colleen. "You slept with a married guy?"

"Oh, get off your righteous horse, Jake. Like you've never slept with a married woman."

"I'm not proud of my past, Coll, but you're better than me, better than that."

"She didn't know I was married," Devon confessed, not sure why. He didn't owe this jackass an explanation. Maybe he owed it to Colleen though. Hell, maybe it was just the opening he'd been waiting for. "Sarah doesn't know about us and we're legally separated now so I'm confident the messages aren't from her."

Colleen pinned him with a fierce stare. "Exactly, you left her and she's out for vengeance. Simple, even predictable."

Maybe for someone else, but not for Sarah. "She left me," Devon clarified because he wouldn't lie to Colleen again, not if he wanted a second chance with her. "Plus, this is a Phoenix area code. Sarah isn't manipulative. She'd never purchase a pay as you go phone and register it in the same city where your friend here recently had a show."

"You haven't read or seen *Gone Girl*," Colleen said.

"Excuse me?" Devon replied.

"It's a book turned into movie. Never mind." She turned to Donovan. "Were the messages Margot received from a Phoenix number?"

"Seattle," Devon and Donovan said together.

Donovan turned his attention to Devon, his brow raised in question.

"Deputy French sent the case file. I read through it." Then he'd called his brother Campbell, a PI living in Seattle, to have him check out the number and dig up whatever he could on one Jacob Daniel Donovan. Not that Devon didn't trust the Jefferson County Sheriff's Department to do their job, but they had to follow rules and protocols. Campbell wasn't restricted by such things and worked fast. Devon might not be able to present anything Campbell dug up as evidence, but it could give him some leads to pursue on his own. If the chief questioned his source, he'd chalk it up to intuition.

"Phoenix and Seattle are pretty far away from each other. We're looking into where the phones were purchased. If they were purchased in a store and not online, that narrows the suspects down to people associated with the tour. Crew, staff, musicians."

"Stalkers," Jake added.

"Says here Ms. Islynn Gray has an alibi. So does your drummer."

"Maybe she's not working alone. Didn't you say women don't use knives?" he asked Colleen who nodded. Then he turned back to Devon. "Maybe she slept with Marky to give herself an alibi while her accomplice — a man — attacked Margot."

It all seemed a little too clean. Yes, some crimes were obvious, but even the obvious ones weren't always clean. Donovan was too eager to accept the stalker and a potential accomplice as the culprits. Devon's gut told him to keep digging.

"Colleen, I'd like to take your phone so we can monitor the incoming messages. I'd also like you to come down to the station and respond to one of the messages while we are monitoring. We have a tech guy who does some pretty amazing work with phones."

"You can't have my phone. I'll come down and do whatever, but you can't keep my phone."

"You can get a temporary until this is resolved," Devon suggested.

"No. I have my life in this phone. I know that sounds ridiculous, but …"

Her breaths grew shallow and rapid. "Breathe, Coll," he urged, hoping to talk her down before the panic attack took her. He knew, however, that was unlikely. Each time he'd witnessed one, there was no stopping it once it started.

Donovan put his arm around her and pulled her body into his.

"She needs space," Devon demanded, but Donovan just glared at him and pulled her closer.

"I've got you, Coll. It's all right, baby. Just let it go."

Hot blood surged through Devon. He fisted his hands, ready to punch something, someone. He'd never understood his attraction to Colleen. It'd been the most powerful thing he'd ever experienced. Devon wasn't the type to cheat and Colleen had been his only extramarital affair. He'd let her go because of how much he'd hurt her, because she deserved so much more.

With Sarah leaving him and filing for divorce, hope had sparked that maybe Colleen would give him a second chance. Devon had planned to wait. He owed it to her to be divorced before he asked — even begged — for another chance. Seeing her in the arms of another man, particularly one who was under suspicion for attempted murder, made Devon mental.

Colleen clung to Donovan, her breathing slowing steadily. The sobs never came and before Devon knew it, she was breathing in and out with slow, deep breaths.

Donovan had managed something Devon had never been able to do. Didn't that just boil his blood even more.

~ ♪ ~

Jake wasn't a morning person, never had been and never would be, but Colleen was worth the sacrifice of his much-needed sleep.

It's not like he'd slept a wink anyway, not on the uncomfortable air mattress in her guest room and not with her just feet away, warm and soft and smelling like an ocean breeze crossing a mountain field.

Colleen had to be to work by 4:45. It was an insane schedule, but the morning show had always been her dream. Even when Jake visited and they stayed up late talking, she was still eager to get to the studio.

Jake didn't usually get up with her, but this wasn't a normal visit. She didn't want to talk about what happened last night. She'd forced the detective to leave, promising to stop by the station this afternoon with her phone. Then she'd uncorked the wine they had started that afternoon and insisted on reviewing the business plan for Jake's Internet station.

He hadn't worked up the nerve to ask her to come work with him. After the text messages and Detective Taggart's inquisition, it just didn't seem like the right time. Plus, he wanted her approval of his plan before he offered her the job. When she offered advice on what qualities to look for in a station manager and technical staff, Jake knew he had a solid plan.

"Coffee smells good," she said, coming into the kitchen all showered and dressed in jeans and a short-sleeve pink shirt that boasted *Girl Power* right across her chest. Jake's knees went a little weak.

Nola was glued to Colleen's side.

The Keurig in the kitchen made sense since she lived alone, but Jake was particular about his coffee and brought his own stash as well as his beloved coffee press.

He poured a cup from the press and handed it to her. "Thanks," she almost moaned, breathing in the nutty aroma and making Jake a little nutty in the process. "You didn't have to get up."

"I wanted to see you off. Believe me, I'm going back to bed."

"I'm going to skip out early, as soon as the show is over. There shouldn't be anything pressing happening. I'll be home at 10:30."

"I might be up by then," he joked, unsure if he'd be able to go back to sleep. Now that the threats were targeted at Colleen, he didn't want to leave her alone, but she insisted she'd be fine at work. "Actually, I thought I could give you a ride in, pick you up when you're done. You know, be your personal chauffeur."

"I'll be fine. No one knows you're here. The text messages are just a coincidence."

"Rebekah knows I'm here. Deputy French and the Jefferson County Sheriff's Department know I'm here. Your friend Detective Taggart knows I'm here."

"Devon isn't my friend."

"He hurt you," Jake sighed.

"He did and I've moved on. It was a long time ago and it didn't even last that long."

"No matter. He hurt you. That makes him a bad guy."

"You're sweet," she said, giving his shoulder a quick squeeze.

He grabbed her hand. "Coll, what happened last night?"

"What? Nothing. I just freaked out a little bit. It's not a big deal, really."

"Not a big deal? You were hyperventilating in my arms."

"It was just adrenaline," she pulled her hand away and went to the fridge to dump some flavored creamer in her coffee.

"The detective acted like it's happened before."

"You worry too much. Listen, I gotta run. I'll see you around 10:30, k?"

Jake didn't like it. He didn't like that she was blowing him off and he didn't like that the detective knew something about Colleen that Jake didn't.

"Let me take you."

She laughed, putting her coffee down and leaning her forehead against his. "I love you, Jake. You're my best friend, but you're making a big deal out of nothing. Let it go."

He wasn't going to let it go, but he would let it rest, at least until she got home from work. "Call me when you get to the station and when you're leaving," he insisted.

She gave him a quick peck on the cheek. "Nag." She detoured to the living room and grabbed the little purple pistol out of the monkey, clipping the holster to her pants before blowing him a kiss and heading out the door.

"Wait," he called, stopping her on the porch. "You're taking Nola?"

"I always take Nola. She's the station dog. I think I'd be fired if she didn't come in." With that she stepped off, leaving him standing in the doorway and watching the two of them hurry to her car.

Jake finished his coffee and climbed into Colleen's bed. There was no chance of him being able to sleep on the inflatable mattress in the small guest room, but with any luck, he'd pass right out on her memory foam mattress.

The room smelled like her, an ocean breeze and a field of wild flowers. The smell was even stronger as he fell onto the mattress, his body responding with an aching need.

This wasn't going to work.

He wondered if Detective Taggart had ever spent the night here. Obviously, Colleen couldn't have gone to his place, but did he just stop by for a quick roll or did he sleep here, Colleen wrapped up in his arms?

Jake punched the mattress and bolted off the bed. He was going to go insane, either thinking about Colleen with another man or thinking about how she wasn't there. He went into the living room and flipped the switch on the radio in the corner. The radio was already tuned to The Wave, and Colleen's laughter echoed throughout the room.

"So the big news today is JD Donovan has canceled his next five shows," her co-host said when the laughter settled.

Shit. Of all the things they'd talked about, they never talked about how Colleen would handle this inevitable news over the air.

"Actually, the shows have been rescheduled to the end of the tour, so all tickets will be honored on the new dates."

Good girl, he thought. She was sticking to the facts.

"We all know you and JD are close, CC. You must have some inside information about the tour."

"As we know, Margot Potter, the opening act for the show, was injured. I don't know any details, just that they are scheduling a new act to replace Margot while she's recovering."

"Those are going to be big shoes to fill," Seager said.

"Absolutely. Margot's one of the hottest acts in country right now. I wouldn't be surprised if they pull in another one of the hot new acts from Old Red Barn Records. JD has always had a unique sound. His biggest influences come from blues rock, and some of the new acts coming out of Old Red Barn carry that same influence."

"Kind of like this guy," Seager added as Greg Felton's *Hollow Heart* faded in.

Holy shit, she was good. Not only did she shift the focus, she'd promoted the hell out of Jake's label while she was at it.

Damn, did he love that woman.

♪ Chapter 6 ♪

"THANKS AGAIN for that, Seager," Colleen said to her morning show partner as she logged off and stowed her laptop for the day. Kyle Seager had been the *Drive at Five* evening show host for years. Two years ago, he made the leap to the morning when the early show became *The Morning Drive with Seager and CC*.

"Anything for you, love." She'd taken Seager aside as soon as she'd arrived to strategize how they'd handle the JD Donovan story. It had yet to break, which gave them an advantage. Even though Colleen knew more than she was willing to share, Seager trusted her and was willing to go on a little faith. She owed him big time.

"I'll see you in the morning," she said, patting him on the shoulder.

Seager grabbed her hand. "Sure thing, but hey, Cece, if your friend happens to be in town and happened to sign a CD or, I don't know, say a guitar, that'd be some great promotional material for us."

Colleen smiled. "If I happen to see him, I'll mention it. You're the best." She loved working with Seager. He wasn't just a colleague, he'd also become her friend.

Seager gave Nola a quick scratch behind her ears and they were on their way. Colleen couldn't wait to tell Jake how they'd handled it without gossiping and just hoped he didn't mind that she'd run with it. It wouldn't take long for the story to break, not with the Kansas City show scheduled for two days from now. They'd have to announce the new date soon.

Broken Strings

Her phone beeped and Colleen cringed, not wanting to see another SLUT message. She checked it in case Jake messaged her.

At the top of the stairs she stopped. The new message was from Devon, reminding her to stop by the station. God, he was a nag, worse than Jake.

There were two new SLUT messages, along with another number she didn't recognize.

Meet me at Boardwalk Brew. -Rebekah.

Great. The ice queen was in town. Colleen wondered if Jake knew.

Colleen ignored Devon and the slut messages and responded to Rebekah. *Can't. Have my dog.*

Lame. Boardwalk in five.

The boardwalk was a mile long, but Boardwalk Brew was only a couple blocks south of the station, so with Nola at her side, Colleen crossed the road and headed in that direction.

"You really do have the dog," Rebekah muttered when Colleen found Rebekah on the boardwalk across from the trendy coffee house.

Colleen didn't bother to respond because they both knew Colleen would come up with any excuse not to see Rebekah. She'd only caved because it was the lesser of two evils. She did not want her old college roommate showing up at her house and Rebekah was nothing if not relentless.

"What do you want?" Colleen asked.

"Nice to see you too." Rebekah's sneer gave away how she felt about seeing Colleen.

"There's no point wasting our breath or time on pleasantries. You wouldn't want to meet unless you wanted something from me."

"You're right. You need to get JD back on the road. We can't get around rescheduling Kansas City, but we can still salvage St. Louis, Des Moines, Minneapolis, and Chicago."

"Aren't you worried that whoever attacked Margot will do it again?" Colleen asked.

"All I care about is keeping JD on schedule. Margot getting stabbed has nothing to do with the tour and everything to do with her own issues. Her last single tanked and she's just trying to stir up publicity."

Colleen had met Margot a couple times. She was a quiet girl who was focused on her music. She'd confessed to Colleen that she wished she hadn't slept with Jake because she worried it would ruin her career. Margot admitted Jake's charms were difficult to resist, but she was glad their relationship had settle on platonic friendship.

It wasn't the first time Colleen had heard that story — the part about resisting Jake's charms. No woman had ever worried it was going to hurt her career though.

Margot didn't strike Colleen as the type of person to get herself stabbed for publicity's sake. Not that Colleen was a great judge of character. If she was, she'd never have slept with a married man.

"I'll pass on your message," Colleen said, turning back the way she'd come.

Rebekah grabbed her shoulder, giving Colleen a shove. When Colleen turned back with both hands fisted, she took a deep breath instead of decking Rebekah.

"It's not about delivering a message," Rebekah huffed. "You're the only person who can talk any sense into him. You need to get him back on the road." Her words were soaked with a thick coating of desperation.

"Why is this so important?" Colleen asked.

"I know you don't understand the importance of my job, but I keep everything running. Pushing five shows to the back of the tour messes up the studio schedule and that puts JD's contract at risk. You wouldn't want him to be in breach of contract, would you?"

"Recording studios shift schedules all the time. It's the nature of the business."

"Don't pretend to know anything about *the business*, CC." Rebekah rolled her eyes and used air quotes to frame *the business*. "You work at a radio station. That doesn't make you a music expert."

Colleen was willing to bet she knew more about 'the business' than Rebekah, but she wasn't going to argue. That would just make Rebekah even more crazy and Colleen had seen Rebekah's crazy side. It was why they weren't friends.

"You seem a little desperate." Which was Rebekah's MO, but Colleen felt obliged to point it out.

"It's my job to be desperate. That's what I get paid to be."

Rebekah let her go and stomped down the boardwalk. Just as Colleen was about to walk away, Rebekah turned with dramatic flair. "Just get him back on the road. Please."

Colleen headed back to the station, crossing the road and strolling straight down H Street to the parking lot behind the building. She noticed her back tire was flat and as she got closer, realized the front was flat too. She slid her hands over the rubber, finding a large gash on the side. She inspected the front tire and found the same thing. And again on the other side.

Someone had slashed all four tires.

And Rebekah the psycho just happened to be in town.

Hmmm …

The police station was visible from where Colleen parked. Either someone — cough, Rebekah — was awfully bold or just plain stupid.

Of course, psycho and stupid did have the same number of letters.

Colleen called Jake. "Hey, I'm having car trouble. Can you come down to the station and get Nola?"

"What kind of car trouble?" he asked.

"The bad kind."

"Oh, hell, Coll."

"Just come get Nola and bring her home for me, then you can do your protective alpha man thing, k?"

"I'll be right there. You call the police yet?"

"That's next on my to-do list."

She hung up with Jake and gave Nola a cuddle. While Nola had never seen slashed tires before, based on her quiet whimpers, she knew something was wrong. "It's alright, baby. Our guy is coming to get you."

Nola snuggled back and Colleen took a deep breath as she hit

Devon's number. He'd insisted she add him to her contacts last night and she'd agreed only to get him to leave.

Dark clouds moved in, making it seem late in the day rather than late in the morning. Nola didn't like storms. She would need Jake to stay home and sit with her so she didn't feel abandoned while Colleen dealt with the tires. That would work out well anyway. She didn't need Jake there defending Rebekah, which she knew he would do. He always did.

"Devon, it's Colleen. I'm standing in the parking lot behind the station and all four tires on my car have been slashed."

~ ♪ ~

Colleen didn't believe in coincidence. Rebekah shows up in town on the same day all four of her tires are slashed. No way was that coincidence.

Devon had been at the station when she called, so he arrived ahead of Jake.

"Rebekah Charles is Jake's personal assistant. She was also my roommate our senior year of college," she explained.

"She's a friend?" Devon asked.

"No."

"Roommates but not friends? Why is that?" Devon asked as Jake's car came to a screeching halt behind hers.

"Circumstances. I won't talk about it in front of Jake, so don't ask any questions until he takes Nola."

Jake ran from the car and gave her the brotherly once over before pulling her into her arms. "Are you hurt? What happened?" He let her go, looking at the car. "Jesus, did someone slash your tires?"

"All four," Devon said. "Where have you been all day, Mr. Donovan."

"You're accusing Jake? Are you insane?" Colleen barked.

"Just asking a simple question."

"I've been at Colleen's all day, waiting for her to come home from work."

"Alone, I suppose. With no one to verify your story. Again."

Jake got in Devon's face. "It's not a story, ass hat. It's the truth."

Colleen stepped between them. "Oh for crying out loud, Devon. Jake is my best friend. Why would he slash my tires?"

"I don't know," Devon shrugged, not taking his eyes off Jake. "Why would he stab Margot Potter?"

"I wouldn't," Jake growled.

Colleen stood there, her hand on both of their chests, her elbows locked, waiting for them to end their alpha stand-off. When her shoulder started to ache, she dropped her arms and reached inside Jake's coat, finding his keys on the first try. Score!

"Come on, baby," she said to Nola.

"Where are you going?" they both asked. For two men who didn't like each other, they sure did act alike.

"You two want to have a stupid stare down, be my guest, but a storm is rolling in, so I'm taking Nola home before she freaks out."

"I'm going with you. You shouldn't be alone," Jake insisted, stepping toward the car.

"I've been alone all my life, Jake," she reminded him.

"I still have questions for you, Coll." Devon insisted.

Jake took the keys and opened the back door. "Nola, come," he said and Colleen wasn't surprised she obeyed. She worshiped the man, and who could blame her since he had rescued her from who knows what kind of fate.

"Come on, Colleen. Come to the station so we can finish this up and I can figure out who did this to your car."

"I'll bring Nola home and meet you there," Jake said.

"No. You can't leave her alone, not during a storm."

"I brought this on, Colleen," Jake snapped, his frustration thick. He rarely used her full name. "I'm not going to let you deal with it on your own."

Colleen rested a hand on Jake's arm. "I'm fine. It won't take long and I can call Seager to give me a ride home. I really need you to stay with Nola. You know how scared she gets during a storm."

Jake peered over his shoulder to where Nola was looking at them out the window, already shaking. "Okay, I'll stay with Nola." Then he pointed at Devon. "You bring her home and make sure she's safe."

Colleen rolled her eyes again, but couldn't deny she loved Jake's possessiveness. She kissed his cheek and stepped back, giving him space to get in the car.

After he started the car, Colleen knocked on the window. "I almost forgot, Rebekah's in town."

Jake muttered a string of curses that made Colleen chuckle despite the situation. "I told her not to come here."

Giving him a sympathetic smile, Colleen shrugged. "She wants you back on the road."

"Of course she does," he mumbled, shaking his head. "I'm sorry, Coll."

"Not your fault. Go. I'll see you soon."

Jake nodded as he put the window up. He pulled out much more slowly than he'd pulled in and Colleen waved at Nola.

"We going to do this in the rain?" she asked, a heavy drizzle coating her skin. She kept a raincoat in the back seat of her car, but Devon wouldn't let her touch it.

"The team is on their way over," he said, showing her a text message that read *En route*. "Once the scene is secure, we can head over to the station and you can tell me why your former college roommate isn't your friend. Wait in the Tahoe if you want to get out of the rain."

Ten minutes later, as Colleen sat in the front of the cop-mobile, Devon's team, which consisted of both uniformed and non-uniformed personnel, had erected a large pop-up tent over her car and were opening up tool boxes. Devon was talking to a petite woman Colleen didn't recognize but who had an air of authority that far outweighed her size.

Colleen's phone beeped, and even though reluctant to read the text, she put her fears aside and opened it.

Jake. *U ok?*

Colleen wasn't okay, but Jake didn't need to know that. *Fine. Waiting 2 go 2 PD.*

He wasted no time responding. *I can b there in a few.*

No. Stay with Nola.

I AM SO SORRY, COLL. Colleen could feel his regret, but Jake hadn't asked for any of this.

NOT ur fault.

Her phone went silent after that. She half expected another SLUT message from the Seattle number, but there was nothing.

She startled when Devon climbed into the SUV next to her. "I've got a conference room waiting for us at the station."

When they reached the station, the metal detector beeped as she walked through. She showed her gun and Devon assured the officer manning the entrance that it was fine, she had a permit to carry concealed. They took the stairs to the second floor, straight to the same conference room where Devon had questioned her over a year ago.

"I hate this room," she murmured.

"No one is going to hurt you in here," he assured her, just as he had that first time. It had been raining that night, too.

"I could use a coffee," she said, focusing on her breathing. Deep breath in, and release. Deep breath in, release. Lather. Rinse. Repeat.

"Coffee is on it's way."

"As is a female officer, I'm assuming." Since she'd been through the rigmarole before, Colleen knew the Granite Beach PD liked to have a female officer present when questioning a female witness. Plus, being alone with Devon was dangerous.

"Detective Paige is on the other side of the glass, but she can come in here if you'd be more comfortable."

"I'd be more comfortable in my living room with a glass of Merlot, Lady Antebellum on my iPod, and Nola snuggled up next to me."

Based on his poke face, Devon didn't find her statement amusing. She hated that even through his bland expression he oozed sex, his short beard and faded cut that was longer at the top begged to be fondled. Colleen pushed aside the impulse and the memories of how his beard felt against her skin.

"What about JD?" Devon asked.

"Oh, for crying out loud."

Before Colleen could launch into a rant about Jake being her best friend and Devon's jealousy ridiculous, a woman dressed in business casual slacks and shirt came in with two cups of coffee. "Anything else, detective?" she asked.

"No, thank you, Kate." Devon turned to the glass. "Detective Paige, why don't you join us in here."

Less than a minute later, Detective Paige was flipping a switch near the glass and taking a seat at the end of the table. Devon sat across from Colleen.

"The speakers are off, so no one in that room can hear us," he assured Colleen. "Tell me about Rebekah."

"She was a commuter but decided to live on campus our senior year. My planned roommate was pregnant and opted not to come back, so they put Rebekah with me. We got along fine, had meals together, went out. We weren't the closest of friends, but we got along fine."

"And you knew Mr. Donovan in college too?" Devon asked.

"Devon, you have to promise me that Jake won't find out about this."

"Colleen," he warned.

"Promise me, Devon, or I don't say a word."

♪ Chapter 7 ♪

DEVON CONTINUED to study her with that bland expression. His nickname ought to be Switzerland he was so neutral. "He doesn't know what happened to you, does he?" Devon asked.

"No. He doesn't. I want to keep it that way." Colleen knew Jake. He would blame himself and he'd look at her with the same pity he looked at Rebekah with. Colleen couldn't handle that and didn't want him to accept blame. What had happened wasn't his fault.

"How does Rebekah play into this if you two aren't friends?"

"Rebekah was attacked a few weeks after I was, except she wasn't so lucky. She didn't get away before he raped her." At least that was Rebekah's story. Colleen still doubted Rebekah was attacked at all.

"You and your roommate were both attacked, a few weeks apart?" The last time Devon interviewed Colleen in this room, she'd been reluctant to tell him about the attack in college, but doing so made her feel a little less crazy after the panic attack he'd witnessed. She hadn't told him about all the other attacks, though, because it didn't seem relevant.

"Along with three other girls on campus."

Devon slammed his fist on the table and Colleen could practically see the smoke coming out of his ears he was so pissed.

"Did they catch the perp?" Detective Paige asked.

"Yes. Ex-boyfriend of the resident assistant on our floor."

"Spencer Mardin," Devon said to his partner.

Colleen's chest rose and fell with the rapid beat of her growing panic. Yes, she'd gotten away before he'd raped her, but that didn't mean she ran away unscathed. To this day, it was the most terrifying event of her life and every time she was reminded of it, the panic consumed her.

"Breathe, Coll," Devon said, his hand reaching across the table to caress hers.

She withdrew, still fully aware it was Devon. His affection wasn't welcome.

"What does she need?" Detective Paige asked.

"She just needs to breathe. Colleen, look at me. You're in the PD You are not on campus. No one here is going to hurt you."

Her eyes shot up to his. "You hurt me," she said before she could think better of it.

Colleen focused on her breathing and on the hate she had for Devon that she just couldn't seem to let go. It helped. Hate was a lot less painful than the horror she'd survived.

"What happened after the attacks?" Devon asked, ignoring her stab. "You told me once you testified against him. Did Rebekah?"

"No. She refused. We had a support group with a counselor, but she wouldn't go. She started inviting guys back to our room, having sex with them when she thought I was sleeping. I asked her to stop. She wouldn't, so I reported her. She was put on probation but still wouldn't stop and eventually got kicked out of the dorms. She didn't come back to school after spring break."

"So how did she end up as JD Donovan's personal assistant?" Devon inquired.

Colleen never told Devon about Jake. Men didn't tend to like it when their girlfriend's best friend was a guy. Given Jake's reputation, people had a tendency to assume Colleen was one of the many notches on Jake's guitar. With Devon, as with the few other men she dated, Colleen had talked about her best friend without specifying name or gender.

"She contacted Jake a couple years later. She'd graduated with a degree in marketing and convinced him he needed a personal assistant to manage his affairs. I warned him not to hire her, but Jake has always had a soft spot for a damsel in distress and Rebekah is a master in that role."

"Did she sleep with him?" Detective Paige asked.

"No."

"How do you know for sure?" Devon asked.

"Because Jake tells me about all his women and he's a horrible liar. I've asked him on more than one occasion and he's always said no. I believe him."

"He could be lying," Devon added, going all Switzerland again.

"To what end?" Colleen asked. "He tells me about all of them and I approve of none of them. He would have no reason not to tell me if he slept with Rebekah."

"Maybe he's playing you?"

"Is that the detective talking or the—" Colleen caught herself before she gave away more information than Detective Paige needed. "I trust Jake. He's one of the few people I trust. He's not playing me."

"Okay," Detective Paige cut in. "JD hired Rebekah and you don't think he's ever slept with her. What makes you think she's involved in the incident with your tires?"

Colleen took a deep breath and chose her words carefully. Just because Rebekah was a psycho didn't mean Colleen had to act like one. "She likes people to think she's more important than she is. She's his personal assistant, but her business cards and voice mail label her JD Donovan Enterprises Executive Director."

"What does Donovan say about that?" Devon asked.

"Jake doesn't care. She has somehow managed to get him out of some pretty tight jams with women and alcohol and she keeps his schedule straight, so he lets her call herself whatever she wants."

Rebekah was high maintenance, but she played her part so well that if you didn't know her, you wouldn't peg her for a drama queen. Jake tolerated it because she kept him out of the tabloids, at least some of the time, but Colleen didn't fall for the act.

"So you say she's here in Granite Beach?" Devon asked.

She scrolled to the text message and handed her phone to Devon. "She sent me a text and I met her on the boardwalk. She begged me to get Jake back on the road."

"Why?" Detective Paige chimed in.

"She claims she's worried about the schedule and studio time and his contract. I don't buy it."

"Why not?" the woman asked.

"Because it's Rebekah. She has a self-serving agenda. If she wants Jake on the road, it's because it somehow benefits her. I don't know how, but that's how she rolls."

Detective Paige looked skeptical and Colleen got it. She sounded like a jealous girlfriend. Maybe she was. Not that she was Jake's girlfriend, but he was the person she cared about most in the world and Rebekah was a person who wouldn't think twice about hurting him. Jake didn't see that or at least chose to look past all of Rebekah's flaws. She was quick to pull the woe is me card. She had guilted him into hiring her, and Colleen was sure she used that tactic whenever it suited her.

"I know what you're thinking," Colleen said to the female detective. She was a pretty woman, tall and slender, but the straight leg khaki slacks and dark blue button up shirt with the flak jacket underneath didn't do anything for her appearance. Add to it the tight French twist of her hair and stern expression and she definitely looked the role of the cop. "Me not liking her has nothing to do with Jake. She uses people. She's manipulative and selfish."

"And she gets to spend every day in close proximity to your man." The detective hit a sore spot Colleen couldn't deny. She would trade the world to be able to spend her days with Jake. There was just one small problem.

"Jake isn't my man, he's my best friend. We're not romantically involved."

"Have you ever been?" Detective Paige asked.

Colleen thought back to that one kiss, that night when everything changed. She wondered what would have happened had she not been attacked on her way to his show. "No, never."

"Have you ever wanted to be?" the detective followed up.

"No," Colleen said firmly, hoping the two detectives bought the lie.

"I think it's time to make that call to your admirer," Devon said, wiggling her phone. "Let's head up to the Tech Center."

~ ♪ ~

"She's the one, isn't she?" Leah asked as they watched Erik get his equipment ready for the call. Devon and Leah were remanded to the observation room so they didn't make any detectable noise while Colleen sat in a chair at the big workstation in the Tech Center.

"The one?" Devon played dumb.

"The one you had an affair with."

He liked working with Leah. She always got straight to the point and did a good job of keeping him from losing his temper when he was frustrated with a witness or perp. He didn't however, like being the target of her inquiries.

Leah had let him borrow her car enough times when he wanted to take Colleen on a date that he knew she had suspicions, but she'd never voiced them. He should have known she was too good a detective to not figure it out.

"Yeah," he admitted.

"You sure it's a good idea that you're the lead on this case?"

"We aren't involved anymore."

"But you want to be," she said without accusation. Her translucent reflection in the mirror portrayed Leah's casual-as-always demeanor. With hands in her pockets, her posture was as loose as it could be with the flak jacket beneath her clothes.

"I know how to compartmentalize my personal life. Whatever intentions I may or may not have regarding Colleen won't impact my ability to work this case."

Leah laughed then. "I'm not the captain, Devon. I'm trying to be your friend."

She was a good friend, always had been. They'd been through the academy together, rode patrols together, and worked their way to detective at the same time. He liked working with Leah. She was focused and confident, and pretty damn insightful.

"I care about what happens to her," he admitted. When Sarah asked for a divorce three months ago, Devon was floored but not at all hurt. She'd finally worked her way through the depression after losing the baby, but all the therapy in the world couldn't save their marriage. Devon knew he was to blame but he didn't think his affair had any bearing on the outcome. Sarah had left him emotionally long before she made the decision to physically leave. He'd gotten over that hurt long ago.

But he hadn't gotten over Colleen.

"We're set in here," Erik said.

They'd coached Colleen on what to say when the perp answered. Erik would need 90 seconds to triangulate the receiving cell phone. With any luck, the perp would want to engage with her. Given the number of text messages Colleen had received, Devon was hopeful.

Colleen called the number. It rang twice and stopped.

Devon held his breath waiting for the person on the other end to say something.

"Dammit," Erik cursed. "He didn't answer. Based on the rings, I'm guessing he hit ignore."

"Try again," Devon commanded into the microphone that let them communicate from the observation room.

Colleen did and Erik swore again when the computerized voice stated the person did not have voice mail set up. "He must have turned it off."

Jake was ready to strangle Rebekah. While she'd worked miracles for him for most of his career, he was beginning to think she'd outlived her purpose in his life.

"I came here to get away from the drama, Chuck. If I wanted you here, I would have invited you."

Rebekah sat on the edge of the chair in Colleen's living room, a black spaghetti-strap top barely keeping her breasts contained. She was pretty, with straight blonde hair and hazel eyes, but she never smiled, just like now. Jake always thought of her as tragic, even before she'd been attacked in college. "You need to get back on the road. Taking time off makes you look guilty."

"How so? I'm cooperating with the police." He didn't want to cooperate, at least not with Detective Taggart, but that had more to do with the way the man looked at Colleen than anything.

Rebekah's phone rang, causing her to utter a string of expletives that almost made him blush. She reached into her pocket and silenced the phone.

"Deputy French said you didn't have to cancel your shows."

"Rescheduled, not canceled," he corrected.

"Don't get technical with me. I manage your schedule, I understand the logistics. *Rescheduling*," she said with a thick layer of sarcasm and air quotes for effect, "makes a mess of the studio time we have planned for the end of the tour. You're so eager to record the next album. I'm surprised you'd delay it."

"I don't want anyone else to get hurt because of me," he said. He had spoken with Margot earlier and she was being discharged tomorrow. Jake had offered his RV instead of the bus Margot road with her crew, but she said her parents were there and she was flying back to Virginia with them.

"Margot didn't get hurt because of you, you dufus."

"I'm the one with the stalker and she didn't start receiving threats until she went on the road with me."

"She made the *proverbial bed*," more air quotes, "she has to sleep in it."

"So you think because she slept with me, she made herself a target?"

"Makes sense to me. Are you sleeping with CC?"

"That is none of your business," he warned.

"Everything you do is my business, JD, everything. If I'm expected to clean up your messes, I need all the details."

Jake didn't like to think of Colleen as a mess. In fact, he was hoping she was the one thing he got right, but hell, he'd already made her a target just by coming here. "No, I'm not sleeping with her."

"Good. You need to keep it in your pants until this is all sorted."

Like that was a problem. He'd stopped sleeping around a year ago and it had been almost two years since he'd been with Margot. Once she'd agreed to sign with his label, he kept the relationship professional. Margot was one of the few people who knew the label was his. Rebekah didn't even know.

"So is there anything else you need, Chuck?" he asked, using the nickname she hated just to rile her up. "Because I have things to do."

"What things?"

"The none of your business things."

"Fine, but can I borrow your car? I took a bus from the airport to save you money and I have some things I need to do that require me having a car."

Jake went to the front door, Rebekah hot on his heels, and grabbed his keys out of the glazed gourd bowl on the small table. His grandmother had made the bowl — she had made dozens of them — and Jake had given this one to Colleen when Nana died. "Call me when you're done and I'll come get it. When is your flight out?"

"When is your flight out?" she countered.

"I don't need you here, Rebekah. Any work you need to do can be done from Tennessee." She kept a small apartment in Nashville since that was where they had set up headquarters when not on the road.

"Where you go, I go. You know that."

Which was one of the reasons he was eager to let her go. He just had to get through this last album and then he was breaking free not just of the tight reign Southern Rebel had on his music, but also of Rebekah's tight leash that he no longer needed.

~ ♪ ~

When Colleen climbed down from the cop-mobile, she breathed in the ocean air. The rain had stopped, but it was still dark and gray, as if the ominous sky warned of more horror to come.

The driver side door slammed shut. Colleen stepped it out, hoping Devon would take the hint and leave. As his footsteps plodded along behind her, she stopped at the bottom of the porch steps and turned, pinning him with a fierce look.

He stood there undeterred. "When this investigation is over, will you have dinner with me?" he asked. The alpha cop was gone, the empathetic man she once cared about making another appearance.

"No," she said sternly, not allowing herself to soften under his charms.

"Coll—"

She held up a hand. "Devon, you lied to me." She was more calm now than she'd been when she first found out he was married, but time had only dulled the pain and anger, not killed it.

"I didn't tell you I was married—"

"It was a lie of omission," she interjected. "That doesn't make it forgivable."

Devon stood his ground, looming over her in that dark suit. Colleen's body betrayed her, warming under the alpha cop's affectionate gaze. "I never lied about the way I felt about you."

Shaking her head, she looked away, grasping for an ounce of self-preservation. "We had great sex. That's all it was."

"You know that's not true, Colleen. What do I have to do to convince you to give us a second chance?"

The hurt in his voice almost did her in, but he was the one who had hurt her, not the other way around. "I don't give second chances. You know that."

Devon shook his head. "Is it because of Donovan?"

"Jake?" she asked, a little confused by the question. "No. He's my best friend."

"He doesn't look at you like a best friend."

Colleen wished that were true. "He's protective, that's all."

Devon chortled, the affection gone and the alpha cop taking over. "He's trouble. Best friend or not, he's hiding something. He is somehow involved in all of this and I'm going to find out. Don't protect him out of some sense of loyalty."

Colleen wasn't sure Devon understood loyalty. How could he? He'd cheated on his wife, betrayed his marriage vows. Jake might play around, but he avoided commitment, so he was allowed. Aside from his reputation, he truly was a good guy. "Jake couldn't hurt a fly. If you think he's the one behind all this crap, you're delusional."

Devon continued to scowl. "I want you to come back in tomorrow so we can try that number again from your phone."

"Yes, sir," she said, giving him a quick salute.

As she turned to head up the steps, Colleen realized Jake's car was gone. The hesitation gave Devon the opportunity to grab her hand, weaving his fingers between hers before caressing her thumb with his.

"I'm sorry for hurting you."

The regret in his voice sent an arrow to her heart, but Colleen's default defense mechanism was to hold a grudge, so Devon's betrayal was only ever a thought away. A piece of her heart still beat for him, however, and she didn't want him to continue to hurt over it. Turning, she plastered on a brave smile. "I'm over it, Devon. You need to move on too."

"If you're over it, give me another chance," he pleaded.

Colleen shook her head. "I'm over the hurt. I'm not over the betrayal. What you did is unforgivable."

"Forgiveness is a choice, not a death sentence."

Broken Strings

She tugged her hand away, wiggling her fingers to rid them of the warmth of his touch. "So is betrayal. I may have thrown myself at you that first night, but you chose to pursue me after that. You chose to cheat on your wife. You chose to not tell me you were married."

She'd never forget the horror when she discovered his lie. Colleen had done things in her life she wasn't proud of, to the point she didn't even speak of them. She had not however, ever wanted to destroy a marriage. "I'm not that woman, Devon. I never wanted to be, and your choices turned me into something I'm ashamed of." And broke her heart in the process.

Devon lifted her chin with one finger, forcing her to look at him. "I'm not proud of what I did, to you or to Sarah, but dammit, Colleen, you made me feel. You made me want and need like I've never wanted or needed before."

His words were another arrow to her heart, because Devon had made her feel too, for the first time since before she'd been attacked in college. Feeling wasn't enough, though. Trust was an essential component of any relationship. So was loyalty. She didn't see how she could ever trust him, but beyond that, Colleen reminded herself after she'd kicked him to the curb, he'd stayed with his wife. He admitted Sarah left him, not the other way around. What kind of man cheated on his wife and then stayed with her? "I wish you well, Devon, but you and I have no future together."

♪ Chapter 8 ♪

COLLEEN WAS not impressed to find her front door unlocked. She jumped out of her skin when she saw Jake sitting on her couch.

"Jesus, put that away," he said, sitting up straight from his slouched position.

"I could have shot you," she warned, trying to catch her own breath. "Why is the door unlocked and where the hell is your car?"

Jake let out a long breath. "I let Rebekah borrow it."

"The ice queen was here? In my house?" Colleen snarled.

"I know you like to ignore things in hopes that they'll go away, but you know Rebekah isn't like that. Plus, she works for me. I wouldn't be a very good boss …"

"Letting her in my house isn't being a very good friend. Don't do that again," Colleen warned.

Jake shook his head. "I saw you out there with Detective Ass Hat."

Great. She'd traded one jealous alpha for another. "You were spying on me?"

He shrugged, as if it wasn't a big deal that he was violating her personal space with careless behavior and stupid jealousy. "It looked like you two were having a tender moment, so I came and sat down. The last thing I need to see is you making out with that ass-hole."

"I didn't make out with him." Colleen dropped her keys in the bowl and put Tania back in the holster clipped to her pants.

"You ever going to tell me why you carry a gun?" he asked.

"I like to think of Tania as more of a wingman than a gun," Colleen said, giving the weapon a gentle pat.

"Tania?" he chuckled. "From *Enemy at the Gates*?"

"Who else would I name my wingman after?"

Jake raised a brow but didn't say anything. If there was one movie Colleen would never forget, it was that one. They'd watched it in the Campus Center just as they had watched countless other movies: cuddled up on the overused couch at the back of the room. It was a common hangout for them since Jake had two roommates who constantly played video games and Colleen roomed with Rebekah, who at that time had a ridiculous crush on Jake.

With his arm around her shoulder, they'd each held their breath during the intense love scene and Colleen had been more than relieved when the guns started firing again. That scene had quite an impact on both of them because before Jake headed out to get ready for his show that night, he had kissed her in the shadows of the fountain in the Campus Center courtyard.

Her toes still curled remembering that kiss.

Jake tossed the pillows on the floor and patted the cushion next to him. Colleen poured herself into the small space and Jake's arm moved around her shoulders as it always did. She was happy the drama was over for the day. The police still had her car, not that she needed it. She could walk to work if she had to, but if she needed a ride, Seager could swing by on his way in. Tomorrow she'd sort out the tire situation.

"You've put her in a coma," Colleen said, eying Nola who was passed out on her back next to Jake, her white-furred belly exposed as Jake rubbed it.

"I love her. I'm glad you two worked out for each other."

Colleen wasn't sure how she'd lived without the dog in her life. She made bad decisions about men, but the one thing she'd done right in her life was adopt Nola.

"Coll?" he murmured.

"Yeah?"

"Is that a gun on your hip or are you just excited to see me?"

She should put it away, but she still needed to head out for her afternoon run.

"I hope this doesn't bruise your ego, but it actually is a gun." She pulled the clip off her pants and set the weapon on the table at the end of the couch.

"Oh, thank God, because if you were just happy to see me, we were going to have to have a talk."

Jake always made her laugh. Colleen didn't realize how much she missed him when he wasn't around until he was there, just chilling with her, fitting so perfectly into her life just like Nola did. He was so easy to be with, having no expectations and needing nothing from her except that she be herself.

"I need to go for a run. Want to join me?"

"Are we running from the Zombie Apocalypse?" he asked.

"No. Running to stay in shape," she patted his stomach and found nothing but rock hard muscle. "Some of us have to work harder than others."

"You should skip it. We can hang here and watch a movie."

That was appealing but she knew how she'd feel later if she didn't do her daily run. "I can get three miles in and be back in 40 minutes." She pushed off the couch, but Jake grabbed her hand to stop her from walking away. Colleen's heart lodged in her throat and she swallowed, pushing it back into her chest where it belonged.

"Stay, Coll. Hang out with me."

Maybe if Jake wanted something more from her, like to relive that kiss, she'd give in to his plea — bad idea or not. They may have remained best friends, but that didn't extinguish the longing Colleen had always felt for Jake.

She leaned down and planted a quick kiss on his cheek. "We have all evening to hang out." Her fingers slid from his and she made her way back to the bedroom where she changed into a pair of navy blue spandex shorts, black sports bra, and a torn up black t-shirt that bragged *Can't*

Touch This in hot pink letters.

As she came out of her bedroom, Jake came out of the small guest room across the hall wearing running pants and a t-shirt.

"So the couch potato can run," she chuckled.

"You're getting text threats and your tires slashed. No way am I letting you run by yourself."

She loved his protectiveness even though it wasn't necessary. "You're much better company than Tania," she joked.

"You're going to leave that little squirt gun behind, right?"

"I never leave Tania behind. The only one here equipped with a little squirt gun is you."

Amusement widened his eyes. "Nice. I see how it is."

Colleen clipped the holster inside her shorts, positioning it so her arm wouldn't brush the gun while she ran. Colleen preferred to have the gun holstered at the front of her left hip so that it was an easy grab with her right hand, putting her immediately into firing position. It didn't matter that she'd never shoot it at a person.

As they reached the front door, Jake grabbed her hand again and pulled her body flush with us. He was solid and warm, his mischievous smile as sexy as the heat in his blue eyes. "I can promise you one thing," he said before licking his lips. "If my not-so-little squirt gun was poking you in the hip, it would absolutely be because I was happy to see you."

~ ♪ ~

When Colleen licked her lips, Jake took it as an invitation.

His mouth covered hers and he wrangled every ounce of willpower to keep it gentle. She kissed him back and his relief was replaced with the longing he'd lived with for years.

Jake's hand slid into Colleen's silky waves. He was testing the waters, but she didn't back away.

Her lips were soft, welcoming, and even though every male part of him was ready to dive in head first without a life jacket, Jake focused on just enjoying the moment.

It was their second first kiss and it was so much better than he remembered.

Colleen dipped her head, her breaths shallow. Jake continued to kiss her, first her cheek and then her temple. He was working his way to her sexy lobe when she asked, "What are we doing?"

"Kissing," he whispered across her ear.

Colleen turned into his face, taking away his access to her ear and giving him a sideways glance. "I got that, but—"

"No, buts. Come on Coll, we both know that was long overdue."

"We've kissed before," she reminded him.

"Once. Eight years ago and never since."

"Jake—"

His mouth covered hers again, this time not so gentle. He pressed her against the front door, showing her exactly how much she affected him. She didn't fight him. When he pushed his tongue into her mouth, hers thrust forward and she clung to him, practically climbing up his body.

She felt so good. She was strong and fit, but still soft like a woman should be.

When they came up for air, her hands pushed against his chest but he didn't budge. Most of the time he gave her space when she asked for it. Doing that now wouldn't help his cause.

"We are not having sex," Colleen said, looking at his feet.

He lifted her chin and once their eyes met, held her there. "That's not what this is about."

"Then what is it about?"

"Us." For Jake, it was that simple.

"You're going to have to be more clear, Jake, because I'm not willing to risk our friendship for something that's going to blow through town faster than a hurricane."

"I'm not willing to risk our friendship, either. I want you in my life. Every day. Every part."

"I …" but her words trailed off. She rubbed her eyes as though she had a headache. "Is this because of Devon? Because you don't have to worry, I'm not involved with him and I don't want to be."

"I'm glad you don't want to be with him. You shouldn't be with someone who isn't willing to put you first."

"Jake—"

His fingers brushed her cheek, pushing a rogue wave off her face. Her skin was as soft as her hair. Jake could touch her all day, but he knew she was overwhelmed and if he pushed her too hard, she would shut down. "Let's just go for your run. I know it clears your head. We can talk when we get back."

~ ♪ ~

Run? He wanted to go for a run after kissing her like that?

Colleen's legs were Jell-O in a cracked mold. If she tried to move, the mold would break and she'd be Jake's for the taking.

Jake could kiss.

Holy shit, could he!

If memories of their first kiss made her toes curl, this kiss made her entire body quiver.

Colleen stepped aside, trying to give herself a little breathing room. If there was one thing she excelled at, it was making bad decisions about men. Jake could turn a girl to melted chocolate with just a kiss but she had been broken for so long, she wasn't sure he could put the pieces back together. To give him a fair shot, he had to know what had broken her.

Sobering up, she grabbed the running pouch and strapped it around her waist. She checked the pouch for the house key and forced a smile — not that the smile was hard. He'd just kissed her giddy.

"Let's run," she said.

"Is Nola coming?" he asked, giving a quick glance over his shoulder.

"Nola only runs when a ball is involved. We can take her to the dog beach later." The dog beach was one of the perks of living in Granite Beach and was a short walk, just half a mile north of the bluffs. "The police kept my phone. Do you have yours?"

Jake crossed the room to grab his phone and Colleen slid it into her pouch. She locked up, double-checked the doors, and they were off.

It was a mile on a slight downhill before the boardwalk started. Colleen's routine involved running to the end of the mile long boardwalk and back for a total of four miles.

When they reached the end of her street, Colleen stopped to stretch. The downhill was her warm-up, but she got serious on the boardwalk.

Jake took up position beside her, grabbing his ankle to stretch his quad. "Give a guy a break, would ya? A treadmill isn't quite the same as the real thing."

"That's a lame excuse," she called over her shoulder, not slowing. Colleen would have been fine running by herself, but he insisted on joining her, so he was going to have to keep up or eat her dust.

Occasionally she glanced over her shoulder to make sure Jake hadn't fallen too far behind. The blood pumped like pistons in an engine pushed to full speed, sweat rolling even under the mid-day clouds. Colleen felt good for the first time since she'd seen Rebekah's text that morning.

The busy boardwalk created plenty of obstacles, but she kept to the running track in the middle. Colleen always took in her surroundings, a result of being caught unaware in college, so she noticed people on the beach and on the sidewalk across the road. No one seemed interested in her until she reached the beachfront casino. The man in the hooded sweatshirt lurking in the shadows made her heart and feet screech to a halt.

She'd bet the bank it was the same man she'd seen yesterday.

As if on autopilot, Colleen pulled Tania from the holster and gripped her with both hands. She kept the gun pointing at the ground as the man disappeared into the casino.

"Coll, what the hell?"

"Did you see him? Under the stairs?"

"See who? There's no one over there."

Colleen preferred the adrenaline rush to the aftermath of the surge. The shakes came on with no amount of subtlety and her chest seized up as though someone had placed a cement block on it.

"Jesus, Coll, come here." Jake pulled her into his embrace as her whole body shook. She couldn't breathe. Her eyes stung with unshed tears. God, she hated this.

"Call … Devon," she managed and Jake stepped back enough to open the running pouch and retrieve his phone.

"This is Jake Donovan," he barked seconds later. "Colleen just saw someone down here on the boardwalk who has her freaked out … I don't know who."

"Spencer Mardin," she gasped. "Tell him I saw Spencer Mardin."

♪ Chapter 9 ♪

SPENCER MARDIN … Spencer Mardin …

Jake chanted the name over and over in his head, trying to turn the distant familiarity into something tangible. He came up with nothing.

Colleen was too busy hyperventilating to explain what was going on. Jake paced the boardwalk, repeating the name in his head with every step.

Ten minutes after the call, Taggart arrived, the SUV screeching to a halt in front of Jake. A woman climbed down from the passenger side. She wore tan slacks, a white shirt, and a soft scowl, possibly from pulling her long hair into a tight ponytail.

"Is she all right?" Taggart asked as stormed around the SUV to the boardwalk. Jake had managed to get Colleen to put the gun away but she hadn't said a word, not even when he asked who the guy was.

"She's not even close to being all right," Jake snarled, blocking the detective's path. "Who the hell is Spencer Mardin?"

Taggart looked over Jake's shoulder at Colleen. Jake turned to find Colleen giving the detective a piercing glare and subtle shake of her head.

What the hell?

"Can you give me a minute alone with her?" Taggart asked, his voice losing a lot of the edge Jake was accustomed to.

"I'm not leaving her alone with you," Jake growled, turning his attention back to the detective. Taggart might be a cop, but Jake didn't trust him, especially not with Colleen. "Does this have to do with the stabbing and the texts and her tires?"

Taggart sneered. "I don't know. I need to talk to Colleen before I can draw any conclusions on that."

Jake wanted to hit something, someone, namely the guy who had scared Coll, but he wasn't opposed to letting out his frustration on the detective.

"Why don't we take a walk and you can tell me what happened?" the woman suggested, her scowl gone.

His protest came up short when Colleen's hand rested on his shoulder. "I'm fine. Let me talk to Devon."

Shaking his head, Jake turned, taking Colleen's hand and pressing it to his mouth. "Talk to me," he pleaded.

Her forced smile broke his heart. "You're not a detective. You can't help with this."

Pain shot through him as though he'd just been stabbed in the gut. As the non-existent knife turned with slow precision, Jake choked on his argument. He wanted to help, wanted to be the man Colleen needed right now, but he couldn't do that if she didn't trust him. Telling him whatever secret she was keeping was one thing, but since she wouldn't even make eye contact with Jake, it was obvious she didn't trust him.

When the hell had that happened?

They'd been best friends since college, shared everything with each other. There wasn't anything he couldn't talk to Colleen about, from his fears of failure to his playboy exploits. Jake had thought it was the same for her. She was private, always had been, but she still talked to him, trusted him.

"I don't like this, Coll, you keeping secrets from me," he whispered, not wanting the detective to think he had an upper hand.

"This has nothing to do with you," she said.

"I'm not just some guy passing through your life. We're supposed to be best friends. We tell each other everything. How can I be a part of your life if you won't trust me?"

Colleen shook her head, tears pooling in her eyes. "I trust you and I need you to trust me. Let me talk to Devon."

A lone tear trailed down her cheek. Jake wiped it away with his thumb, cupping her face in his shaking hand. She looked so sad, even scared, and it wrecked Jake. He couldn't protect her if he didn't know what to protect her from.

"I won't be far," he conceded. A somber smile passed her lips for a brief moment before she turned away and stepped toward the detective.

~ ♪ ~

"Hey. You okay?" Devon asked, his hand resting on Colleen's shoulder. Her body shook under his fingers, stirring up the memories of the first night they'd met.

"Don't be nice to me," Colleen muttered, shrugging off his hand.

Devon sighed but kept his hand to himself, his posture stiffening as they stepped down the boardwalk. "Where did you see him?"

"He was in front of the casino, under the stairs. I know you think I'm crazy. Maybe I am."

"I don't think you're crazy. I think you saw a man who looks a lot like the guy who attacked you in college and that has you freaked out."

"Just like last time," she sighed.

They had found the man who tried to take her purse fourteen months ago. Under the shadows of a cloudy night, and with the attack in college clouding her judgment, the man looked enough like her prior attacker to justify her reaction. Devon had no doubt the same was true now.

He wanted to pull her into his arms and hold her until the demons stopped haunting her, but she'd made it clear earlier where they stood. Devon kept a professional distance between them, just to keep his impulses restrained.

"I'll run a check on Mardin to see what he's up to these days. In the meantime, can you describe what he was wearing? What he was doing?"

"He was just standing there, like a ghost." She buried her hands in her face, shaking her head. "Oh my God, I am crazy."

"You're not crazy, Coll."

"I wish you wouldn't call me that," she whispered. She'd once told him the only other person who called her that was her best friend. Most people called her CC because of her radio station persona. Her closest friends and family called her Colleen. Only Devon and apparently JD Donovan — the best friend, the man putting her in danger — called her Coll.

"Just because you don't think we have a future together doesn't mean I don't care about you," he pointed out.

She tugged the band from her hair, releasing the wild waves before pushing her hands through them. Her posture stiffened, as if she'd dug deep for the strength to survive this alleged near-miss. "Don't make this harder than it has to be."

Maybe she was posturing to keep distance between them. Devon didn't like it, but what could he do except his job. "Let's get back to the perp. Where exactly did you see him?"

She turned and pointed at the casino. "Under the stairs, in the corner. His hands were in his pockets. Jeans, he was wearing worn jeans and a dark sweatshirt, maybe black. It was the kind that zips."

Devon pulled out his notepad and scribbled the description.

"What about his hair? Long? Short?"

Colleen closed her eyes and held her breath as she tried to remember. "It wasn't short, but it wasn't long either. All one length, maybe, pushed back off his face. He might have had a goatee. It was hard to tell with him being in the shadows."

Which is why Devon doubted it was actually Spencer Mardin, but he didn't doubt the power of post-traumatic stress. Colleen had been through hell in college and survived it. She had every reason to get spooked, especially considering the bullshit Donovan had introduced into her life.

"What did he do when you saw him?" Devon probed.

"He was staring and all I could do was grab my gun. When I pulled it out, he bolted into the casino."

That damn gun. While he didn't begrudge anyone their constitutional rights, he'd seen too many situations that went south fast because someone pulled a gun. He'd prefer she carry pepper spray, but his repeated requests were always shrugged off. At least she went to the range regularly and had taken a gun safety course.

Devon opted not to repeat his request from yesterday to stop pointing her gun at people. "Where was Donovan this whole time?"

Colleen laughed, actual amusement coming through. "Eating my dust."

"Excuse me?"

"He's not used to running anywhere except across the stage or on a treadmill. He couldn't keep up, so he was fifteen or twenty yards behind me."

Devon had never run with Colleen, but there was a time when he'd park near the boardwalk and watch her run. She had a fast, consistent pace. He looked over his shoulder to where Leah stood with Donovan, jotting notes in the department-issued notepad. Devon had given his partner the lowdown on Colleen's college experience but left out the details of how he'd found out her history. Someone had to be objective in this case and Leah would be better equipped to be objective if she didn't know about Colleen's near-miss over a year ago. He did wonder, though, if Leah was telling Donovan about the college attack.

"You going to tell him?" Devon asked, turning back to Colleen.

"I'm going to try not to. I guess it depends on how much Detective Paige is giving up."

"She's just doing her job. You know that right?"

"This sucks, Devon."

Instead of putting his arm around her, Devon flipped through the notepad, pretending to review his notes. "I know. So you going to run home or do you want a ride?"

He expected her to put up a fight, so when she said she'd take a ride, he was floored.

Devon held the door for her and by the time he climbed into the driver's seat, Leah and Donovan joined them in the SUV.

Donovan sat in the back with his arm around Colleen. Devon did his best to keep his eyes on the road, but couldn't keep from glaring in the rear view. The whole best friends thing was bullshit. He'd never met friends of the opposite sex who sat that close. Is that why Colleen had said they didn't have a future, because she was already sleeping with her best friend?

"Whoa, stop the car," Donovan said after they pulled onto Colleen's street.

"What is it?" Colleen asked.

"Nola. She's out."

Colleen looked out the window as Devon started to break. He hadn't even come to a full stop when Colleen jumped out of the SUV.

~ ♪ ~

"How the hell did she get out?" Devon asked as he came around the cop-mobile.

Colleen had locked the front door, but she hadn't checked the back door when she got home. She turned to Jake. "Did you let her out back today?"

"Of course."

"Tell me you locked the door when she came back in," she pleaded.

Jake nodded. "Yeah. Maybe. I don't know," he admitted, shaking his head. "I think I did, but maybe I didn't."

Colleen wanted to strangle him. "You need to remember Jake. Did you lock the damn door or not?"

"I did." He didn't sound convinced.

"Get in the SUV," Devon commanded.

Colleen got Nola in the cop-mobile. Devon drove to the left when the road split, not his usual route. "Side gate is open," he pointed out as he eased to a stop in front of her house. Colleen's heart lodged in her throat.

"I did not open the gate," Jake said in defense.

Colleen would have remembered if it had been open when they left. Devon gave her a look in the mirror, very familiar with her cross checks. "It was closed when we left for our run," she affirmed.

"And the back door?" Devon asked.

"I was distracted," she admitted, remembering how Jake had kissed her just before they left. "I didn't check it."

"You three stay in the SUV — and it's not negotiable, Colleen. Leah and I will check the house. Give her your key."

Colleen didn't argue. Nola was safe, and after the events of the last couple days, she was not eager to face the unknown.

After handing Detective Paige the key, Colleen and Jake watched through the windshield as Devon went through the gate and Detective Paige went to the front door. After a brief pause, she unlocked the door and went inside, gun drawn.

"I'm sorry, Coll. I'm not used to being in a house. I might not have locked it."

Jake had people to do these things for him. When he was on the road, he lived out of his massive RV and was never alone.

In her world, leaving the door unlocked was inviting disaster — or at the very least, opening the door to another panic attack.

Nola sat alert between them. Colleen rested her hand on Jake's to reassure him. "Let's just be more vigilant about the doors, okay? You let Rebekah borrow your car. Did you take my house key off the ring?"

"Shit. No. I wasn't even thinking. But she wouldn't let herself into your house."

Colleen cocked her head. "She can be psycho, Jake. She would absolutely let herself into my house."

"Okay, she would," he chuffed, "but she wouldn't let Nola out or leave the door open."

Colleen didn't agree, but didn't argue the point. "You need to get your keys back."

Broken Strings

He'd kept his phone since the boardwalk. After giving Nola a few long strokes, he sent a text message. Colleen assumed it was to Rebekah.

Devon and his partner came out of the house, both of them strutting over to the SUV, looking all big-bad-coppish, even though Detective Paige wasn't all that big.

Devon opened Jake's door. "House is clear. The back door was open. I need you to do a walk through to make sure nothing is out of order."

Colleen took the key from Detective Paige and tucked it into the pouch as they approached the house. She was grateful Nola wasn't a runner. When Colleen worked in the flowerbeds on the front lawn, Nola had free roam of the neighborhood but she never went far. Regardless, her girl was getting steak for dinner tonight for sticking close to home.

While doing the walk-through, Devon hovered close to Colleen. Nothing was missing and Jake checked his things, also finding nothing missing or out of place.

That didn't keep the heebie-jeebies from racing up Colleen's spine. "I'll have a patrol car swing by here periodically. Take this." Devon handed her a flip phone. "It's not fancy, but it's all set up and ready to use."

She looked at the contacts and found his number, Detective Paige's number, and the station line programmed in.

"Anything out of the ordinary happens, you call 911, and then you call me. Understood, Colleen?"

"I'm not 12, Devon," she retorted to his alpha cop attitude. "I know how to handle myself in an emergency."

"Put your gun in the monkey. *Call* if there's a problem. Do not go for your gun."

She wasn't sure she'd be able to put *Tania* away for the night. Seemed smarter to keep the small pistol clipped right to her waist. "Thanks. I promise to call if there's a problem."

Devon looked at Jake. "Make sure she does."

The detectives left and Colleen went to the kitchen to get Nola a special dog cookie. As soon as she opened the narrow cupboard next to the microwave, Nola sat and started wagging her tail. "Yes, you are such a good baby. I'm not even going to make you work for it." She held out one of the flat, heart-shaped dog cookies and Nola snatched it up.

Jake sat on the couch moping when she and Nola crossed the open living space of her bungalow. "Stop beating yourself up."

"I shouldn't have come here, I put you in danger."

Colleen was happy to see Jake. Too much time passed since he last visited. The ghost she saw in the shadows had more to do with her past than the drama happening on his tour. "You don't know that."

With his piercing blue eyes and crooked smile, Jake played the playboy to perfection. This brooding guy sitting in front of her was a stranger she barely recognized. "None of this would have happened to you if I hadn't come."

"Jake, stop it. You are always welcome here. No matter what."

"I will never forgive myself if you get hurt."

His statement only reinforced why she hadn't told him about the attack in college or the one over a year ago.

She sat next to him, resting her hand on his leg. "I'm fine. No one was hurt."

Instead of putting his arm around her with that easy affection they'd always shared, he turned, pulling his leg away and putting space between them. "Who is Spencer Mardin, Coll? And why do you carry a gun everywhere?"

♪ Chapter 10 ♪

COLLEEN SHOULD have seen that question coming. The fact she hadn't proved how much the day's events messed with her head. "I don't want to talk about this right now. Let's order Thai and watch a movie."

"You're going to have to tell me eventually."

She had kept it from him for eight years. There was no reason to tell him now.

Except there was every reason. If things were changing between them, and based on that kiss earlier, they were, she couldn't keep the secret from him. The problem was he'd blame himself. Colleen didn't want him to take on that burden since it was her responsibility. She'd been the one to screw up, not him.

Was that really Spencer Mardin she'd seen? Was it a coincidence he showed up in Granite Beach at the same time as Jake? It had to be coincidence because Spencer Mardin would have no reason to sabotage Jake's career and life.

Maybe it was more about Colleen and Rebekah. If he was feeling vengeful, he might come after those who had put him in jail.

Of course, Rebekah had never identified him and didn't testify at his trial, so she hadn't played a part in putting the creep behind bars.

"How about we talk about us, then?" Jake asked, a crooked smile softening his expression.

Colleen had fallen for Jake long before he became a country playboy. That smile played a potent role in her fall, but it was everything else about Jake, the side of him the rest of the world didn't get to see, that had stolen her heart.

After the attack and with Jake's talent launching him into the spotlight, she'd given up the dream of *us*. The thought of them being together as more than just friends was so far from her grasp, she was afraid to even wade in the waters. "How about I grab a shower while you call for dinner?" she suggested steal some time. Leaning across the distance he'd put between them, she pressed a quick kiss to his cheek before giving a mocking sniff. "And then you should take a shower."

As she moved back, Jake grabbed her arm, holding her in place and setting her on fire with his piercing blue eyes. "We could save water and shower together."

Every inch of her body screamed yes, but Colleen had a habit of making bad decisions when it came to men. She was determined to not fall into that pattern with Jake. "Nice try, playboy," she joked, pulling away. Colleen headed straight for the bathroom before Jake could corner her again or make another tempting suggestion. Inside the bathroom, she leaned on the door, wondering whether to lock it.

This was Jake. Her college crush turned best friend turned best kiss she'd ever had in her whole life. Twice.

Self-preservation had her fingers resting on the lock. Would Jake be offended if he tried to shower with her and found the door locked? Would she be offended if she left it unlocked and he didn't try?

Self-preservation. She flipped the lock into place and stripped. The last time she thought Spencer Mardin lurked in the shadows, she fell into bed with Devon. Colleen wouldn't make that mistake with Jake, no matter how much his kiss had rocked her world.

If she was going to give in to her feelings, and that was a big *if* given her history, she would do it rationally, not while recovering from a panic attack, or because loneliness had her convinced she would die alone.

Turning the water up as hot as she could stand, Colleen tried not to think about Jake's proposition to save water. He was in shape despite not being a runner. She'd felt his solid abs when she'd teased him earlier.

Broken Strings

What would he look like naked? What would he feel like …

Okaaaaayyy. Down girl. Maybe she needed to turn the water to cold.

Focusing on the task at hand, Colleen squeezed a generous puddle of shampoo into her palm and massaged it into her scalp. She dug her fingers in, working out the tension and ignoring the growing desire Jake inspired.

She was doing well considering the events of the last two days. A full panic attack never took hold after the incident in front of the casino. It was some sort of major miracle and despite the fact her house may have been broken into, she was feeling … happy.

When was the last time she felt happy?

She wasn't even sure she'd found that with Devon in the short time they'd been together.

Jake was the reason. Happiness always swarmed when he came to town, but that kiss held possibilities she hadn't allowed herself to hope for. He wanted more. He wanted *us*. Colleen wanted that too.

With her hair rinsed and the sweat washed from her body, she turned the shower off and wrapped her crazy hair in a towel before drying off. After wrapping the big towel around her body, Colleen hoped to make it across the hall to her room without attracting any attention.

She almost dropped the towel when she opened the door to find Jake standing there.

"You make it hard for a guy to take a shower when you lock the door." He gave her a slow perusal that nearly made the towel burst into flames. Then he shook his head. "This look doesn't suit you at all."

"No?" she laughed. "What would you suggest?"

His finger hooked into the knot, that wasn't hiding her cleavage. "You'd look a hell of a lot better with that towel on the floor."

Colleen fisted the knot, catching his finger before it loosened the towel. She wanted the *us*, but she wasn't ready to jump into the deep end. "Jake …"

He tugged his finger from her grasp and caressed her cheek. "I know. I don't want to rush things, but damn, Coll." He shook his head again and stepped back to give her room.

"I've made a lot of bad decisions," she admitted, hoping he would understand she wasn't pushing him away.

Shoving his hands in his pockets, Jake dropped his head and seemed to take a new interest in his sneakers. "Me too."

Jake's feet swept back and forth on the floor as the air thickened between them. Colleen's mistakes were a lot to deal with, but so was Jake's reputation. What the tabloids reported wasn't off the mark. Jake had always been open and honest with her, sometimes too much so.

His feet stopped and he looked up, that sexy smile pushing aside what she suspected was regret. "No looking back."

No looking back. It sounded like a dream, but then, Jake had always been the dreamer. Colleen was the realist, even before she'd been attacked in college. Back then, she had no doubt Jake would launch into stardom, but when time became a problem, she'd sold her soul to be sure of it.

She didn't want to look back either, but the realist knew you couldn't run from the past. She'd been trying to for eight years and had gotten nowhere.

Maybe all she needed was Jake. She smiled and gave a single nod. "No looking back."

~ ♪ ~

After a long night of tossing and turning, with a little bit of staring at the ceiling just to mix things up, Devon was grateful for Leah's coffee addiction. Boardwalk Brew was only a four-block walk from the station. Leah despised instant coffee, so made the trek several times a day.

As she entered the war room, a coffee in each hand and looking well rested, Devon wished he could be more objective about this case.

"You're good at puzzles," Devon said as Leah handed him one of the paper cups.

"So are you," she said.

"Thanks — for this," he said, holding up the cup before taking sip. "The puzzle thing — I need eyes that might be a little more objective than mine."

Leah moved around to the other side of the table and smiled as she sat facing him. "Objectivity isn't always the most powerful weapon in the investigative arsenal."

"I could still use some." He slid the file he'd compiled across the table.

"What are we looking at?" she asked, flipping open the manila folder.

"Spencer Mardin and the five women he attacked at Hawthorn State College eight years ago."

"You think it's related to the JD Donovan case?"

"If I was being objective, I'd say no and conclude Colleen's PTS is making her see a man who isn't there. *If* I was being objective."

Leah smiled again. "Well, I am being objective. The PTS is something we have to keep in mind, but twice does not a trend make. The stress from the text messages and tire slashing might have conjured up her nemesis, but I'm willing to give her the benefit of the doubt. Run me through it."

"Mardin was a student, living in the same dorm. Each floor was split, half male, half female, a common area in between. Everyone with a key card for that building had access to the whole dorm. Mardin was seeing the female resident assistant, Hannah Carlson, at the start of the school year. We can assume he chose his room based on her RA assignment."

Leah studied the summary of bullet points Devon had put together. "So he was on the same floor? And all five girls, they were on the same floor?"

"No. Colleen and her roommate Rebekah Charles were the only ones on that floor. In fact, they were the only ones in that dorm." Once he'd given up on the tossing and turning, Devon spent the morning twilight hours studying the Spencer Mardin case. There were a lot of gaps and he didn't know if it was because Mardin was caught and four of the women identified him as the attacker or if because it was poorly investigated. He supposed it didn't matter since the guy was convicted.

"So did he pick them at random or did he somehow know them?" Leah asked.

Devon shook his head and shrugged. "That's what I want to figure out."

Leah spread the profiles of the girls out on the table. "Who was first?"

"Colleen."

"And who was last?"

"Rebekah."

Devon listed out the other girls in the order of attack and Leah arranged the papers. "So did he come full circle or was that coincidence?"

It was another question Devon couldn't answer. "I don't know."

"Let's start by trying to connect the girls," Leah suggested.

Devon had tried to do that since dawn, but he asked Leah for help, so worked through the exercise with her. They ruled out hair color, dorms, classes, extracurricular activities, and boyfriends.

Two hours later, they had nothing.

"All we have is data from that semester," Devon deduced. "Maybe the connection between them goes further back. We should have Marie pull records for previous semesters, too."

"Or maybe we're looking at this from the wrong perspective." Leah looked at each of the profiles, tapping the papers like she did when trying to find a solution. "We're trying to connect the girls to Mardin. What if the connection is the girlfriend?"

"There was nothing on her in the case file. She wasn't attacked and they weren't together when it happened. According to the file, they didn't even interview her."

Leah smiled as if she'd found the answer they were looking for.

"Okay, let's pull that up. Any word from the Jefferson County Sheriff's Department on the case?"

He hadn't heard a thing since that initial call. "You work on the ex-girlfriend. I'll give Deputy French a call and see if Marie has had any luck finding Spencer Mardin. I'll check with Erik, too to see if Tech came up with anything."

"You hear anything from your girl this morning?" Leah asked as she gathered the papers.

"She's not my girl and no." Devon heard her on the radio on his way to the station. Colleen sounded her usual, snarky self, but he knew from experience how well she compartmentalized her trauma.

"Her car has been processed, so she can have it back," Leah informed him.

"Thanks. I'll let her know."

Devon stopped in the break room and grabbed a cup of sub-standard coffee. As he choked the caffeine down, he sent Colleen a text, hoping she had taken the phone he gave her. He didn't expect to hear back from her until after ten when the morning show ended, so he was surprised when she responded immediately.

If you need help with the car, let me know, he texted back.

Thanks. Will call Mike's 4 a tow.

Mike's was a local garage at the north end of town, a few blocks west of the beach. Most of the locals went there for service. They were good guys and would take care of Colleen.

Devon wanted to help, but Colleen wouldn't ask and if he offered, she'd hand him a dozen excuses. Devon opted to save them both the trouble. It was best to focus on the case.

He stopped by Tech first. "No more SLUT messages," Erik announced as Devon walked in. "But she got a colorful new one from a different number." Erik had the cell phone connected to the computer and brought the message up on the large monitor. *Lying Cunt.* According to the time stamp, the message came in minutes after the incident on the boardwalk yesterday.

"You able to track it?" Devon asked.

"It's another disposable phone. Callie traced the sale of the first one to Phoenix," Erik explained. Callie Forsythe was new to the department, but in the short time she'd been there, she'd proven herself efficient. "The phone was purchased with cash at Rite Aid. We'll need a court order to get the store's video feed around the time of purchase. She's working on tracking the sale of this one right now."

Erik handed him a printout of the data on the first phone and Devon tucked it into his file. The phone Margot Potter received calls from had also been purchased in Phoenix. Devon needed to talk to Donovan and find out if something happened there to trigger the events.

His next stop was Records and Research. Marie Galvin was a research genius, fast and efficient. Most detectives were convinced if Marie couldn't find it, it couldn't be found. Devon knew that wasn't true. Marie was clever, but restricted by department regulation. If Marie came up short, Devon called his brother. He didn't know how Campbell did it, but he never came up short.

"Spencer Mardin is in the wind," Marie said with a snarl. "He served his time at Bridgewater State Penitentiary and worked for a couple years at various jobs: McDonald's, then a diner in Fall River, first as a bus boy, then as a cook. His last job was at a cell phone Kiosk in a mall. He reported to his parole officer as required until he wasn't required to anymore. That was a year ago. There's no trace of him after that. No employment records, no hits on his SSN, nothing on his license."

"You got his PO's info?" Devon asked. That was as good a place as any to start.

"Of course. It's in the file along with contact info for each of the jobs."

"Thanks. Any luck on Hannah Carlson?"

Marie snickered and rolled her eyes. "You realize Leah just gave me that five minutes ago, right? I'm good, but I'm not that good."

Devon winked at her. "You are that good, Marie. Don't ever think otherwise."

"Flattery won't make it happen faster," she responded with a smile. "I can only work as fast as the search engines allow. I tasked Eddie with pulling up the complete school records on all five girls, Mardin, and Carlson."

"Great. We'll take it as it comes in."

Marie nodded. "I figured. I have you on speed dial."

Devon went back to the war room and started putting everything up on the bulletin board.

He needed to question Donovan. Devon was convinced something happened in Phoenix. To figure out what, he had to go to the source. That also give him an excuse to give Colleen a ride home.

~ ♪ ~

Jake had been torn between guarding Colleen's house and guarding her. He figured she had plenty of people looking out for her at work, so he stuck around the house waiting for Rebekah to drop his car off, and waiting for anyone else who might want to cause trouble.

Sitting down with his old guitar, Rêver, Jake couldn't keep from smiling. Rêver had been his mother's guitar. She had named it when her father first gave it to her on her fifteenth birthday. Gramps had handcrafted the guitar for his daughter, who dreamed of being a musician one day. Rêver, the French word meaning to dream, was the perfect name for such an elegant instrument.

What made him smile even more was how Colleen had named her gun. Jake was only ten when his parents died, but he was sure his mother would have loved Colleen.

Strumming a chord, Jake hoped to make sense of the lyrics bouncing through his head. All morning he struggled to focus on the words, but they wouldn't string together. There was a fine line between fantasy and art, and he was straddling it. After seeing Colleen wrapped up in that towel last night, he didn't think he'd ever need help with inspiration again, yet he was coming up empty.

He caressed the small gouge on the edge adjacent to the bridge. It was one of many scars, every single one of them holding a memory of Jake's journey. This particular one came from Colleen, the day of his first paid gig. It was an outdoor party at a lake. Jake rolled the sound equipment on a hand-truck along the narrow path through the woods. Colleen carried his guitar, strumming it as they walked, making up silly lyrics to distract him from the nerves wound tighter than his guitar strings. When she tripped on a root, she did her best to keep the guitar safe, but it still suffered the one ding.

Jake was more worried about Colleen, who had cut up her knee. She ignored her own injury, apologizing over and over for hurting his guitar. To appease her, he asked her to kiss the guitar's bruise to make it better. He'd always been attracted to her, but in that moment, Jake wanted to abandon the gig and take her right there in the woods.

He'd felt the same last night, but just like that day in the woods, he pushed his impulses aside.

Last night hadn't been what he expected. After he'd grabbed a shower, they'd settled in for Thai food and a movie. The last thing he'd wanted to do was watch a movie, but it was important to take things slow, so he put the brakes on what he wanted and let Colleen take the lead. Even though she'd sat close, her hand on his leg, his hand around her shoulder, he'd felt the distance. She was good at distance, always had been, but Jake's super-power was perseverance. He wasn't about to give up. His world began and ended with her.

♪
Began with her touch.
Ended in her eyes.
♪

He strummed a chord, hoping that would keep the inspiration flowing.

♪
Began with her touch, began with her touch ...
The beat of his heart began with her touch.
♪

No, that wasn't quite it. Jake let his fingers play across the strings. He closed his eyes, allowing the music to take the lead. Lyrics didn't always come easy to him, but somehow the chords brought out the words they needed. He just had to let go, clear his head, embrace the feeling.

Jake focused on Colleen, picturing her in his head, the easy smile, snarky wit, her strength. She was beautiful. There was nothing about her he didn't love.

♪
The end began with your touch
From the start, I knew it was too much.
Baby you stole my breath then you stole my heart.
My heart ... my heart.
You stole my breath and broke my heart.

The end began with your smile.
From that first moment, if only for a while.
Girl you robbed my senses and you made me beg.
My heart ... my heart.
You robbed my senses and broke my heart.
♪

"Not your best work." Rebekah's raspy voice pulled him out of the moment.

Jake cursed under his breath, wondering when she'd snuck into Colleen's house. "I haven't been at it long. You know I write and rewrite and rewrite again."

"I know," Rebekah said, not an ounce of sympathy in her voice. "I've been there from start to finish and I can tell you, it's not your best work. Maybe you should drop it and move on to something else."

It wasn't his best work. He knew it but he didn't want to hear it. Sometimes you had to wade through the shit to get to the gold.

Jake noticed the keys dangling from Rebekah's finger. "Do you need a ride back to your hotel?" he asked, not in the mood to deal with her attitude.

"No, I've got it covered. Thanks for use of the car."

It wasn't like Rebekah to be gracious, so the comment took him by surprise. "Anytime. Oh, and just so you don't think I'm leaving you out of the loop, I'm planning to head to the farm for the weekend."

Rebekah raised an eyebrow. "Just the weekend?"

"Yeah. Then I'll be back here until it's time to head to Detroit."

"You taking Princess Perfection to the farm?" Rebekah sneered.

"I plan to ask Coll to join me, yeah."

Rebekah shook her head. "My ride's waiting."

She turned to leave. "Chuck, don't go showing up at the farm."

Turning back in a huff, she pinned him with the stern expression that earned her the nickname *Ice Queen* from Colleen. Colleen also liked to refer to Rebekah as Ruler of the Underworld. Sometimes Jake had to agree, especially when she demanded more of Jake than he was willing to compromise on. "JD, it's my job to keep you out of trouble. I can't do that if we're in different states."

"I'm laying low. There's no trouble. You need to get used to that." There hadn't been trouble at all this tour, not until Margot was threatened and then stabbed.

"Right. Trouble is your Siamese twin. You can run from it, but it always finds you."

He didn't believe that was true. He stirred up trouble because it was easier than facing the loneliness of his life. Maybe it was called growing up, but he'd finally acknowledged he wasn't happy. The women, the drinking, it had stopped being fun. Recording, the road, all the shows, he wasn't enjoying any of it anymore. There were things he wanted that he couldn't have so long as he kept doing the same old song and dance.

"Why don't you head to Detroit? Meet the trucks, make sure everything's in order." There was nothing to check, nothing to do, but if she took the bait, she'd be out of his hair for a week.

"I go where you go. That's how this works."

Jake wasn't sure when Rebekah had started not just running his life, but commanding it. It was his fault. Letting her handle everything was easy, but part of his new plan included taking back control of his life. He needed to let Rebekah go and that was going to be like lighting a match over an open can of gasoline.

She set the keys in the red bowl on the table next to the door and stomped out. Rebekah stomped a lot. She seldom smiled, was way too serious about her job. Since her job was Jake's life, he had to cut those ties sooner rather than later. Maybe Rebekah would find happiness too.

Jake got up to lock the door after it slammed shut. Nola looked at him like he was a fool.

"I know, girl. I'm not too bright. Come on. Let's get some fresh air."

Grabbing Rêver and the notepad he kept close when writing, Jake headed to the back. Maybe he'd find inspiration with the rhythm of the crashing waves creating some ambiance.

♪ Chapter 11 ♪

THE FRONT door was unlocked. Colleen reached for her gun, but Devon put his hand on her arm. "Easy there, Wyatt Earp."

"Last time my door was unlocked, my dog was wandering around the neighborhood."

"Yeah, but Donovan's here. Isn't that his car?"

"I'm going to kill him if he forgot to lock the door," Colleen muttered.

Devon took the lead, not because Colleen wanted him to but because he eased by her without giving her a choice. The low whimper of Jake's guitar hummed from the backyard, luring them through the house to the back door. Colleen pushed past Devon, forcing him to stop as she stood at the door.

Jake sat on a large rock near the edge of the yard where a narrow path wove down to the shore. He looked at home, his eyes closed, the guitar resting on one thigh as his fingers danced across the strings, words just a whisper across his lips.

♪
Deep in my veins
Thick in my blood
The pulse of your love
Is never enough
♪

"Donovan," Devon called through the door, his harsh and abrupt voice cutting through the beauty of Jake strumming a new song.

Jake's eyes flew open, his fingers no longer making sweet music.

"You're an ass-hole," Colleen mumbled over her shoulder as she stepped onto the patio. "Sorry, Jake. That sounded good."

"Still working on it," he mumbled.

"Always so modest." The melody leaned to Jake's soulful side rather than the country he'd been performing for the past eight years. It was reminiscent of the music he had written in college.

"I would have picked you up," he said, gripping his guitar in one hand as he pushed off the rock.

Colleen had planned to get a ride with Seager, but as they left the studio, she found Devon waiting in the parking lot. "Devon has some questions for you," she said when Jake stopped in front of her. Her breath caught under the power of his smile, the one with all the promises he had yet to speak.

She had to remind herself to breathe. "I'll make coffee," Colleen announced, trying not to trip over her own feet as she headed back to the house.

"Use the press," he called after her. "None of that instant crap."

"Snob," she retorted. "Come on. Let's move this to the kitchen."

She pushed by Devon, who continued to loom in the doorway. She refused to acknowledge another alpha stand-off between the two men, so continued on to the kitchen. By the time she got the kettle going, Devon and Jake settled at the table, once again scowling at each other.

"Colleen received a message from a different number," Devon stated. "We were able to track the sale to the same store in Phoenix where the other phone was purchased."

"Wait, Colleen received another message. What was it?"

"It's not appropriate to say in mixed company," Devon said.

"I'm hardly mixed company," Colleen pointed out.

"Let's just say the perp called you a liar."

"A liar?" Colleen asked, resting her hands on her hips. "What the hell am I lying about?"

"I don't know," he said, never taking his gaze off Jake. "What I'd like to know is what happened in Phoenix?"

"What do you mean?"

"It seems like Phoenix was the catalyst for all this. That's where the cell phones were purchased. Did you fire someone on your crew? Sleep with the wrong woman?"

Colleen looked up from the French press. Jake claimed he hadn't slept with anyone in a year. She wanted to see how he responded to Devon's question ... and hoped he hadn't been lying.

"Nothing happened. There was no woman and no one was fired."

"Any big changes? Change in schedule? Someone's mother died and you wouldn't let them go to the funeral?"

"My crew is my family. If someone's mother died, of course I'd let them go." Jake chewed on his lip, a telltale that he was contemplating something.

"What are you thinking?" she pressed.

"My contract with Southern Rebel. It wasn't Phoenix, it was Austin, a week earlier. We were there for four days. Rebekah gave me the new contract but I told her I wasn't signing with Southern Rebel again."

"You're not staying with your record label?" Devon asked, taking out his notebook.

"It's not *my* record label," Jake corrected. "It's the label I signed with. And no, I'm not staying with them."

"That's got to piss a few people off," Devon drawled.

"I told Rebekah I would deal with it, but apparently Paul Curran harassed her because he showed up the next day."

Colleen shivered at the name of her former boss. Paul got his start in radio and moved on to Southern Rebel Records after Jake's first top ten hit. His radio marketing expertise landed him in the promotion department, but Paul worked his way into management.

Despite her preference for the Keurig because it was fast and easy, Colleen managed to get the French press all set up. She brought three

Broken Strings

cups and the press to the table before grabbing milk and sugar.

"Who is Paul Curran?" Devon asked, scribbling in his pad, as Colleen took a seat adjacent to both of them.

"He's the director of the arts and repertoire department," Jake explained. "That's where contracts originate. He doesn't work directly with artists unless there's an issue getting someone to sign."

"And you not signing is an issue," Devon finished.

Jake nodded before giving Colleen a quick glance. He knew there was no love-loss between her and Paul, but he didn't know the true reason. Colleen intended to take that secret to her grave. "Paul helped launch my career. He was a radio show host and played my demo during his Emerging Musicians show. I was offered a deal not long after that."

"What radio station?" Devon asked

"A country station out of Boston. It was difficult to get him to play demos. I'd been trying for months." Jake gave Colleen another quick glance, as unsettling as the last one. "Then Colleen did her internship under him and convinced him to give my CD a listen. He liked it."

Paul loved it, but he leveraged his position to get Colleen into bed. She didn't know how many other interns had suffered the same fate. She thought he was bluffing at first and blew him off, but when he didn't play Jake's demo, she realized he was dead serious. Colleen loved Jake, but she wasn't willing to compromise herself. Jake would find another way.

Then circumstances changed. Jake's grandmother died and his Gramps was going to lose the farm. Jake needed money and fast. He had more talent in one hand than most people possessed in their entire body. He would eventually make it through the red tape, but without a big break, it could take years. Gramps didn't have years, so Colleen broke her number one rule and slept with her boss. Jake's quick success made it worth it, even if it did taint her career.

Colleen had gotten past it and now Jake was on the verge of making music his way. She couldn't be more proud.

"What did Curran say when you saw him in Austin?" Devon asked.

Jake shook his head and fisted his hands. "He wasn't happy. I'm the biggest selling name for them, so they stand to lose a lot when I leave."

"They'll still retain the rights to the albums you've already recorded though, right?" Devon asked.

"Yeah, but I'm on the up-slide. No label wants to lose someone on their way up."

"Is Margot Potter with your label?"

Jake pounded his fists on the table. Colleen held her cup, but the other two jumped, coffee sloshing over the edges. Neither man seemed fazed. "I told you, Southern Rebel isn't my label."

"Semantics," Devon mumbled, but Colleen imagined he was deliberately winding Jake up. "Who does Margot record with?"

A smirk lifted one corner of Jake's mouth before it disappeared. "Margot is with Old Red Barn Records."

Devon wore his cop-face, but Colleen had no doubt he'd caught Jake's smile. "What do you know about that label?" Devon asked.

"It's new, small, but growing fast." Jake stated simple facts available to anyone.

Devon raised a brow. "Is that who you plan to sign with?"

The question hung between the two men, Jake clearly contemplating his next move. Colleen wondered if he'd tell the truth. Devon could keep a secret. He'd proven that when he hadn't told Colleen he was married. Jake's secret, however, might not serve Devon's purpose. He wouldn't have any reason to keep it confidential unless it helped the case.

"I haven't made any decisions about my next album yet," Jake stated.

Not the truth. She understood he wasn't ready to reveal his connection to the label, but he had to know Devon could dig that information up.

Devon stared at Jake who stared right back. The alpha stand-off between these two bordered on ridiculous. Did Devon suspect Jake wasn't telling the whole truth?

"Anything else, detective?" Jake asked before taking a drink of the coffee Colleen labored over.

Devon pushed away from the table, his coffee still untouched. "I'll be in touch if I have any other questions."

Colleen followed him to the door. Devon left without even the courtesy of a good-bye. She didn't slam the door, but made no effort to close it lightly, nor to be subtle about turning the deadbolt. She also slid the chain into place, just to satisfy her own angst. "This is how you lock the door," she snarled as she turned back to Jake.

"I know how to lock a door," Jake snapped.

"Knowing and doing are two different things," she said, stepping across the room.

Jake moved to the sink, grabbing a dish towel and returning to the table where he mopped up the coffee. "I locked it after Rebekah left."

Colleen took a seat and a long sip of coffee. Yeah, the French press coffee was definitely better, even if it was a bit more work than the pre-packaged cups. "The door was unlocked when I got here."

After tossing the towel across the room, where it landed in the sink, Jake took a seat. "I swear, Coll, I locked it."

She didn't want to argue about the stupid door. She couldn't explain the importance of personal security without revealing why it was so necessary, so she let it go and focused on the investigation. "Why didn't you tell Devon about Old Red Barn Records?"

"Why don't you tell me why you carry a gun?" he asked, the angst thick in his voice.

"I carry a gun for personal safety," she explained, shrugging it off. "Lots of women do, just like locking the front door. This is the live free or die state, after all."

"Yeah, right. So this whole gun thing has nothing to do with you and Paul?"

Colleen's stomach lurched. "What do you mean?" He couldn't know. Paul was slime, but he wouldn't go public ... would he?

"What do I mean?" he chuffed, abandoning the dirty cups and crossing the small kitchen until he loomed over Colleen. "You slept with him."

Choking back the bile, Colleen shook her head but couldn't find any words to deny the accusation because it was the truth.

Self-preservation kicked in. "You," she emphasized, "are withholding information in an investigation."

"I don't see how me owning Old Red Barn Records has anything to do with the investigation. No one knows about it."

Colleen stood and crossed her arms. "Are you sure about that?"

"Positive." Jake stepped back and dropped his head, as if he was too ashamed of what Colleen had done to even look at her. When he raised his head, the hurt in his eyes shattered her heart. "Why'd you do it, Coll? Why'd you sleep with him?"

If the look in his eyes hadn't done her in, the disappointment in his voice would have. She swallowed hard, unable to find any words to defend her actions.

~ ♪ ~

Colleen's eyes glassed over as she looked away. Jake wanted to take back the question and the accusation in his voice. Hurting Colleen wasn't his plan, but she had secrets, too many of them. Whatever happened in the past didn't matter now, but he had to know the truth, not Paul Curran's version.

"You owe me for your success," Paul had said when he showed up in Austin. *"I only played your demo because your girlfriend made me an offer I couldn't refuse."*

Jake didn't want to believe it, none of it, not what Colleen had done, nor the other horrible things he had said about Colleen.

The truth was written all over her face. The fact she tried to change the subject proved her guilt even further.

Jake's chest ached. He wasn't so naive that he didn't know Colleen had been with men, but a man like Paul Curran, and only because she wanted the man to play Jake's demo? "You shouldn't have done that,

Coll. I would have worked my way into the industry, if I had talent enough."

"You have the talent," she insisted, the guilt replaced with the resolve he had always respected. "You just didn't have time."

The time? What the ... "Because of the farm?" he asked, remembering what a bad year that was. His grandparents had sacrificed everything to put Jake through college. Grams died before he even came close to success. Gramps was a good farmer, but he didn't have a clue how to manage the finances. He'd fallen behind on everything and was ready to let the bank take the farm. Jake couldn't let that happen.

With only a month left of college, dropping out wouldn't have helped financially. Jake started looking into jobs when his demo got some play the weekend before graduation. A whirlwind struck after that. "We would have found a way. Dammit, it was bad enough that I sold out, but I made you sell out, too."

Signing with Southern Rebel records was a desperate move. He knew their reputation, knew he wouldn't be able to play his own music, but money and fear had driven him to sign.

"You didn't make me do anything," Colleen snapped, anger rolling off her. "Maybe it was stupid and maybe I was naive to think it wouldn't have repercussions, but given the same circumstances, I'd do it again."

That struck a chord. "Was he the only one?" Jake asked, because according to Paul, Colleen had slept her way up the ladder. It was hard enough to believe she'd slept with Paul to help Jake's career, but to sleep with others to advance her own career? No. No way was she that kind of person.

Colleen crossed her arms, clearly disgusted by the question. "Is that what he told you? That I screwed my way to the morning show?"

Jake nodded because he couldn't put words to Paul's accusation.

"He's a liar," Colleen fumed. "He's cruel and manipulative and a liar." The tears spilled down her cheeks. Jake felt like a first class asshole for making her talk about it.

"I'm sorry," he said, pulling her into his arms. Her whole body shook with each sob. "I'm sorry, Coll."

"You didn't do anything wrong," she managed, pulling back to look at him. "I slept with him. I made the choice. It was all me."

He wouldn't let her take the blame. "But only because of me. If I hadn't been so desperate ..." she cut his words off by placing her fingers over his lips. Her skin was soft and smelled like lilacs.

"It was a long time ago. I've moved past it. I never wanted you to know for this reason."

Jake wanted to kill the guy. He knew from experience that Paul had no integrity, but Jake never imagined the ass-hole would take advantage of a young woman like that. He wondered how many other innocent girls Paul had conned.

Her fingers slid across his cheek until she was cupping his face. "Let it go," she urged.

Jake sucked in a deep breath. He wasn't sure if he could let it go, but he had to at least get past it for Colleen's sake. "No more secrets," he demanded.

"No looking back," she whispered.

He kissed her forehead, grateful for the reminder of his own personal motto. "How do you feel about heading to the farm for the weekend? I can show you the studios and we can get away from all this investigation crap for a couple days."

The smile returned to her face, kicking Jake's heart into high gear. "I would love to see the studios. When do we leave?"

"As soon as you're packed."

♪ Chapter 12 ♪

To Viper:

Moving things to the farm.

From Viper:

C U in VT.

♪ Chapter 13 ♪

DEVON DIDN'T mind a stakeout and watching Colleen's house to make sure she was safe wasn't a hardship.

When Donovan packed a couple suitcases and two guitar cases in the trunk of his car, Devon was ready to wish the guy good riddance. With him leaving town, maybe he'd take this mess and the danger he put Colleen in with him.

Maybe with all of this behind them, Colleen would give Devon another shot. It was a fool's hope, but Devon held it close, just like he wanted to hold Colleen close.

The door opened again and Nola trotted out. The dog headed straight for Donovan who opened the back door. The dog jumped right in.

Colleen didn't go anywhere without Nola, nor would she let the dog go anywhere without her. Devon's stomach turned as Colleen stepped out of the house and locked the door. His anger surged when Donovan met her at the bottom of the steps and kissed her.

It wasn't the kind of kiss best friends exchange.

It was the kind lovers share.

The SUV shook with the force of his fist meeting the dashboard. Devon scrubbed his hand over his face, trying to gain some control, or at the very least some perspective. He'd hurt Colleen. He didn't deserve her love, but hell if he wanted this country singing ass-hole to have it.

He snatched his phone from the dashboard clip and hit Colleen's number. She stepped back from Donovan and answered.

"Where are you going?" he demanded before she even said hello.

Colleen turned, scanning the street until she spotted his SUV. "Are you spying on me?"

"I told you an officer would be posted outside your house," he reminded her.

"You're a detective, not an officer."

Donovan took his turn scanning the street, his arm going around Colleen when he found the SUV.

"I took a shift," Devon offered. "You look like you're leaving town."

"Not that it's any of your business, but yes, we're heading to Vermont for the weekend."

Donovan's home or record was Vermont. "What's in Vermont?"

"I defer back to my first comment — none of your business."

Devon was ready to climb out of the SUV and shake some sense into her. "Until we have the perpetrator of these threats in custody, you are my business. Everything you do is my business."

Her sardonic laugh echoed in his ear. "Do you want to know when I go to the bathroom?"

Devon expected the snarky comment. Colleen was nothing if not predictable. "If it means keeping you safe, yes."

"Oh for crying out loud." She turned out of Donovan's hold and away from Devon, heading for the passenger side of the car.

"What's in Vermont, Coll?" Devon asked.

"Jake's farm," she snarled as if the answer was obvious.

"Donovan has a farm?" How did that not come up in the background check?

"It was his grandparent's and now it's his. No one knows we're going there. We'll be safe."

"Don't go," Devon pleaded, starting the SUV and putting it in drive. She didn't say anything, just held the phone to her ear as he drove up. When he parked behind Donovan's car, she closed the phone and put it in her pocket, moving toward the SUV.

"Devon—"

"Don't go, Coll. Please," he begged as he climbed out.

"Are you begging because of the case or is this personal?" she asked.

"Yes," he answered, knowing it was something she would have said.

Colleen shook her head and crossed her arms, closing him off. "I told you there is no future for us."

"You never gave me a chance to explain. You ended things and before I had a chance to blink, you were gone."

Dropping her arms, anger took hold. "And you were back with your wife where you should have been all along."

It was Devon's turn to shake his head. "You have no idea what was going on in my marriage, so before you judge my decisions, hear me out."

"What if I don't want to? I never wanted to be the other woman, Devon. That's not who I am."

"Please," he pleaded. "Just hear me out." Devon had never begged, not even to Sarah. He supposed that right there said a lot about his marriage.

"It's not going to change anything," Colleen sighed.

Maybe it wouldn't, but he had hurt Colleen and at the very least owed her an explanation.

"Sarah was pregnant," he stated, cutting right to the chase before she put up more of an argument. Colleen's eyes went wide with shock, maybe horror. "No, wait. Listen to the whole story."

Pulling a confession from a perp wasn't just part of Devon's job, it was a part he loved. Offering his own confession felt like swallowing razor blades.

He kept his personal life private from the people he worked with and he kept his work private from his personal life. That had included Sarah, which was part of the problem.

"We hadn't told anyone yet. She'd had a miscarriage before and I wanted to wait to be sure this baby was okay because the first time was so hard on her. Then her mother died. Sarah and her mother were close and she was devastated, not just at the loss but for not telling her mother about the baby. She blamed me because I insisted we not say anything.

"Two days after her mother's funeral, Sarah …" he took a deep breath, feeling the ache in his heart all over again, "she miscarried again."

"I'm so sorry," Colleen said. He could see the sadness, maybe even pity in her eyes and he hated it. This was why he hadn't wanted to tell anyone about the baby.

"Sarah hated me at that point. Blamed my job, everything. I just thought she was depressed, I even suggested counseling. That only made her hate me more."

Sarah hated him to the point she was cruel. Devon was used to being called names. It was part of the deal when you were a cop. He'd never expected it from the woman he loved.

"She had asked me to move into the spare bedroom and I did. I thought it would help. It didn't. We reached a point where she wouldn't even speak to me anymore."

Colleen shook her head. "And then I threw myself at you."

"It's not your fault, Coll," he interjected. Devon didn't blame Colleen. This was all on him. "I cared about you. I wanted to leave Sarah and tell you the truth, but I just didn't know how." Sarah had threatened to kill herself on more than one occasion. Devon thought for sure if he left her, it would throw her over the edge. So, he continued to live the lie that was his life. It was a relief when Sarah asked for a divorce.

"I was," Colleen paused, shaking her head as if trying to shake the words out. "Dammit, Devon. I'm sorry for all that happened to you, but it doesn't change anything."

"Is that because I hurt you or because you're with him now?" Devon nodded at Donovan who watched them from the other side of his car.

Colleen looked over her shoulder and Donovan's expression softened. "I need to get going."

"Don't go with him." The way Donovan looked at her, the way they had kissed, Devon knew what the guy had planned. Hell, they might have already slept together. If Devon could keep Colleen from spending a weekend with the guy, maybe there was still a chance. "He's a wild card. You know that. With everything that's going on right now, you're going to get hurt."

"It's time for you to move on," she said and turned, stepping away and not looking back.

~ ♪ ~

Ninety minutes of silence put Jake over the edge. He tried to respect Colleen's privacy and feelings, but a man could only take so much. "You want to talk about it?"

"Talk about what?" she muttered, still staring out the window.

"Detective Dipwad upset you." It felt like pointing out the obvious, but he had to start somewhere.

Colleen leaned back in the seat, closing her eyes. "I wish you wouldn't call him that. His name is Devon and he's a person with feelings just like you and I."

Well crap. What the hell had that ass-hole said to her back the house? "I'm sorry. Are you okay?"

"I'm not the bad guy here. *He* was married. *He* lied."

"Did he blame you for something?" Jake asked, ready to turn the car around and tear the guy apart.

"It's just, I mean, what the hell am I supposed to do? It's been a year since we broke up. I got over him. Ov-er."

Colleen rambled when she was angry and confused. She wasn't talking to Jake, nor asking for input even though he was ready to give it. First and foremost, he wanted to have a nice long talk with Detective Taggart, one that started with Jake telling him he was an ass-hole and ended with Jake's fists telling the guy the same thing.

Instead of turning the car around, Jake put his hand on Colleen's,

Broken Strings

giving it a gentle squeeze.

"I'm sorry," she sighed. "I'm ranting."

"Don't apologize. He hurt you, I get that."

"I can't talk about this with you," she said, her head flopping to the side to look at him. He gave her a quick glance.

"Come on, Coll. You talk to me about everything."

"That was before," she said.

"Before what? Before we kissed? Because I'd like to remind you that we kissed once before and you still talked to me about everything." Of course, the kiss in college didn't have the potency the ones now did. They weren't unsure kids anymore, trying to wade through hormones and expectations and the struggle of drifting somewhere between living life and growing up. They'd both made their way in the world, found success in their careers, and lost at love. It was time for that last part to change.

She smiled then and he had to remind himself to focus on the road. "I was going to say before you saw me in nothing but a towel."

"Actually," he smirked, "I've seen you in a towel before."

She slapped his arm. "You have not."

"Yes, yes I have," he nodded, the memory a portrait in his mind.

"How? Wha— when?"

"Start of our last semester. We were going to the Kenny Wayne Shepherd concert. I was excited so I showed up early. You were just coming out of the bathroom." Thank God for dorm bathrooms that required residents to walk down the hall with their shower gear. In their co-ed dorm, most girls wore robes, but sometimes a guy got lucky and spotted all that wet, glistening skin. "I saw you in the towel and nearly passed out."

"But, you were late picking me up for that concert," she reminded him.

"Yeah, well, I saw you in a towel. Your hair was all wet, dripping down your back. You were barefoot. The towel didn't even reach mid-thigh and didn't quite come together on the side. If I didn't take a breather, we weren't going to make it to the concert."

He dared a glance and found her looking at him with one eyebrow raised. "That's a pretty vivid memory."

Jake smiled and wished they were at the farmhouse where he could act on his driving need for her. "It was a pretty vivid reality."

That moment was a turning point. Jake realized Colleen wasn't just his best friend, she was a woman he wanted. It took him two months to work up the courage to kiss her. At the time, that kiss had been worth the wait, but he always wondered if he hadn't waited so long if things would have been different.

She squeezed his hand. "It's not fair, you know. I've never seen you in a towel and you've seen me in one twice now."

"To make it fair, we should just skip the towel. I could pull over right now." If memory served, there was a rest area coming up on Interstate 89 soon.

"What? A little I showed you mine now you'll show me yours?"

Jake was good with that. "And you can show me yours again, without the towel this time."

Colleen laughed. "Maybe you should watch the road, Speed-racer."

Jake looked at the road only to realize the car straddled the centerline and the speedometer pushed eighty. While drifting back to the right side, he let off the accelerator.

Colleen seemed more relaxed now. Jake was anything but. He had an erection so hard it could crack concrete and the temperature in the car rivaled that of the sun's surface even with the A/C cranked. He couldn't get the fantasy of Colleen naked and underneath him out of his head.

For reasons Jake didn't want think about — like maybe she was still thinking about that detective — Colleen seemed unaffected.

Wasn't that one way to soften the hammer.

"Penny for your thoughts," he said after a few minutes of her staring out the window again.

He was rewarded with another laugh. "You are such a girl sometimes."

"What, because I care about what's running through your head?"

"Because you insist on talking about it."

Jake sighed. "You used to be a lot more open. Now you're like a closed book with a lock on it."

~ ♪ ~

Colleen had been accused of being aloof, even cold. One man even told anyone who would listen that she was downright frigid. None of that had bothered her, especially after her affair with Devon when she'd discovered it only took the right man to set her passion free. Jake's accusation of her being locked up tight somehow cut deeper than any other she'd endured.

She shrugged in an attempt not to let it bother her. "It's been kind of a crazy week. First you show up and then the text messages and my tires, and …" Her words trailed off. Colleen didn't want to think about what happened on the boardwalk, let alone talk about it.

"The incident on the boardwalk," Jake added. Of course he wouldn't let it go.

"Yeah, and then someone being in my house."

"We don't know for sure anyone was in your house. I might have left the door unlocked. Your tires could have been a freak occurrence, a case of mistaken identity. Fords are kind of a dime a dozen around here."

"And the incident on the boardwalk could have been my wild imagination," she sighed, because she couldn't even count the number of times she'd been told that. The man was alive as far as she knew, probably out of jail by now, but she'd been seeing his ghost ever since the attack in college.

"You ever going to tell me who Spencer Mardin is?"

She didn't want to, but it was becoming clear she was going to have to tell him everything, if only to prove she wasn't crazy.

Where would that leave them? Jake would still blame himself and it would change nothing.

"Do we get to see Gramps this trip?" she asked, a not-so-subtle attempt to change the subject.

"He'd never forgive me if I brought you to town and didn't bring you by."

Colleen adored Jake's grandfather. He was the wisest of the wise old men, weathered by hard work and a love of life that could inspire countless country songs. He was a charmer, like Jake, and incredibly handsome for a man pushing seventy-five. He had married Jake's grandmother, Nola, when they were just eighteen, a marriage that had lasted 47 years before she died. When Jake rescued the dog, he named her after his grandmother.

Jake and his grandparents had the kind of family Colleen envied. Growing up, it was just her and her mom. Brenda Cooper had gotten pregnant right after high school. Since Brenda never spoke of Colleen's father and he wasn't on her birth certificate, Colleen had no idea who the sperm donor was. Her grandparents had died before Colleen was old enough to ask questions. Brenda worked hard to keep them afloat. Even though Colleen didn't get to spend much time with her mother while growing up, she loved her and appreciated all her mother sacrificed. After Colleen graduated from college, Brenda moved from New Hampshire to southern California, trading cold winters and humid summers for the warm, dry climate. Colleen missed her, but that wasn't anything new. Even as a child, she always missed her mother.

Colleen's thoughts shifted from family to the men in her life. She didn't want to think about Devon or Spencer Mardin or how nervous and anxious she was about being alone with Jake at the farm. Not even the music on the radio could sway her thoughts, though. Devon's story had ripped her heart to pieces. She never told him, but she had been in love with him. Seeing him with his wife had been a fluke. Colleen had taken herself out to lunch at an Italian bistro at the southern tip of Granite Beach.

It was a pricey place, but that morning she'd found out she and Seager received a Country Music Awards nomination for Personality of the Year. Colleen had just gotten into her car when she saw the cop-mobile roll up. Devon had insisted on being discreet because of his job, so she waited to see if he was alone. Before getting out to talk to him, he helped the woman out of the SUV. Colleen's heart sank, forming a pit in her stomach that she still got every time she saw him.

At first, Colleen tried to convince herself he was working a case, but she recognized the intimacy between them, the way he rested his hand at the small of her back as they strolled across the parking lot.

She had waited to confront him, not wanting to make a scene at the restaurant during a lunch hour rush. Since Devon hadn't seen her sitting in her car, his reaction that night was one of genuine surprise. When he admitted the woman was his wife, humiliation sent Colleen running.

His confession today cut even deeper. Colleen believed in love and respected the sanctity of marriage. Being the other woman brought a shame she'd never felt before. Forgiving Devon had never been even a remote thought. Now she felt she'd judged him too harshly. He had said forgiveness was a choice. He was right. Holding the grudge against him was a heavy burden to carry. Forgiving him would free her from that weight.

It seemed like a lifetime later when Jake maneuvered down the long dirt driveway to the farm. The house and barn had both received a fresh coat of paint. The barn still had its rustic appeal, but there were modern additions, such as the skylights in the roof and the French doors that had replaced the big old barn doors at the front.

"I want the tour," she said as they pulled up in front of the house.

Jake wore a proud smile that warmed Colleen's heart.

He took her hand and led her to the barn, Nola trotting along at Colleen's side.

Colleen had been in the barn many times. It was where Jake liked to play guitar and unwind. All the hay was gone and the surfaces were cleanly finished with a rustic theme, maintaining the integrity of the structure.

"This is beautiful," she said. The open space now looked like a lounge, large enough to host a party while maintaining an intimate feel. The wooden furniture and burgundy cushions suited the space.

"Let's go upstairs to the recording studios," he said, giving her a tug.

They took the open staircase to the second floor, where they stopped in a hall that crossed the middle of the barn. Two walls of glass divided the space.

"There are two studios, one at each end. The sound rooms are connected from the inside." Colleen followed Jake into one of the studios. The equipment was high tech and the walls were adorned with framed posters of Jake's favorite musicians, everyone from blues to southern rock to country. There were even posters quoting literary figures.

"This is fantastic," Colleen marveled.

"Wait until you see upstairs," he dragged her out of the room, up another set of open stairs and through a door that led to the open space of the third floor. "There's an office back there for privacy, but I thought the open concept would be the most comfortable. The skylights let in natural light during the day, but there are blinds to block the sun. You should see it at night. It's magnificent."

Colleen marveled at the equipment. She had worked in radio stations that used such equipment, but had given up the high tech to work the morning show at The Wave.

"It's like a little taste of heaven up here," she said, brushing her fingers over the laptops and large screens. "Whomever you hire is going to love this place."

"Do you love it?" he asked.

"Of course I do. It's fabulous. It's almost like you built it for me."

"I did," he said.

She turned, a little surprised by his words.

"Wait, what?"

"Coll, I want you to run the station. You can plan the playlists, travel on tour and interview fans, pick the interview clips to broadcast, everything. You will be the voice of JD Donovan's Rock and Soul."

Broken Strings

With trembling hands, she grabbed Jake's arm. Dizzy with excitement, she glanced around the large room, taking in all the equipment, the concert posters, the furniture, looking out at the blue sky through the large skylights. It was perfect, a dream job. To be a host and producer, to make all the decisions.

Jake had taken her dream and molded it into his dream.

When she faced him, she could see the excitement in his wide smile and gleaming eyes. She jumped into his arms, kissing him as he spun her around.

When he put her down, Colleen's adrenaline spiked. She walked around, touching the equipment, picturing herself working there, compiling song lists, editing interviews.

She'd be going on tour with Jake. They'd be together.

It had been a long, lonely road to the morning show. Colleen had compromised herself more than once on the climb, but she had earned the spot on the morning show by proving herself. It was the first position she'd held that wasn't tainted with rumors and lies thanks to her unscrupulous behavior with Paul Curran.

Her relationship with Jake was no secret. She'd even made it into the tabloids a time or two, an affectionate picture spun into a seedy story that would sell papers. Colleen never cared all that much because the rumors helped her move up in radio, but it had always bothered Jake.

The adrenaline plummeted as Colleen faced the facts of a future with Jake. With her reputation finally clean, she wasn't sure she wanted to put herself in a situation to be tabloid fodder again. She didn't want to be the woman who got the job because she was sleeping with the boss. Based on Jake's reputation, those old rumors would surface again, once again tainting her reputation.

"Tell me what you're thinking," Jake said, caressing a hand over her back. Her body was on board with every touch, desperate for that physical connection with him, desperate for more. Her heart was even on board, racing with anticipation and excitement at all he had to offer. Her head, however, reminded her of the mistakes she had a habit of making when it came to men.

"I'm not sure I'm qualified," she said. "I've never managed a station, Jake. I'm just a morning show host."

"You're more than that. You've worked your way up to the morning show, as an intern, a producer, a program assistant, a host. You've done it all, Coll. You are more than qualified."

She had done it all. She had been in radio since her early days in college and had gotten her big break two years ago when The Wave's longtime morning show host decided to move to marketing. They had wanted to give the radio a fresh sound, that's why they moved Seager and hired Colleen to co-host. She loved working with Seager, loved The Wave. It had been her dream to do the morning show. What Jake offered, though, was like asking for the moon and being handed the universe.

Rumors and repercussions aside, she'd be a fool to turn him down. "I, I don't know what to say."

He pulled her against him, cupping her face in his hands. Awareness shot through her, like being poked with a lightning rod, but so much better.

And worse.

Taking the job meant stopping what was happening between them. It was the smart decision, one that would protect her from industry gossip and backlash.

"You're freaking out, aren't you?" he asked.

"A little."

"You don't have to make a decision now. No pressure. Take your time. But, you know, if you want to say yes now, I'm good with that too."

She laughed, wrapping her arms around him and resting her head against his chest. She could hear the beat of his heart, a sound so simple it made her wonder when her life had gotten so complicated.

There was a time when she had imagined a future with Devon, had dreamed of it. Even after she'd discovered his secret and walked away, she still fantasized about it. There had also been a time when she'd imagined a future with Jake but that had always been more of a dream than anything else.

Now, the only two men she had ever loved were both asking for a chance.

♪ Chapter 14 ♪

SOME WALLS had been knocked down during the farmhouse renovation, opening up the rooms so the kitchen, dining room, and living room were one large space. It allowed Colleen to see where Jake sat on the stool near the fire, his music stand propped up in front of him, the fire in the old stone fireplace blazing behind him.

Nola slept in front of the hearth. It wasn't cold enough to need a fire, but Jake insisted, said the ambiance helped him write.

Colleen kept busy in the kitchen, making chicken Alfredo lasagna because it required plenty of prep and would give her time to think.

Time to think about what Jake had offered and what it could mean for her professionally.

Time to think about Jake.

Focused on the music, Jake strummed some chords, trying to find a melody that worked with the words. He took notes on the notepad laid out on the music stand, sometimes chewing on the pencil as he experimented with notes. He was the serious musician, the one she had fallen in love with and ran away from all those years ago. Now he was giving her a chance to reclaim what they might have had.

She almost cut off her finger chopping the chicken, not paying attention. Colleen moved everything to the opposite counter, turning her back to the living room.

Was Jake offering her the job because of their relationship or did he truly believe she was the perfect fit?

She couldn't take a job based on charity. She'd lived with that reputation for too long and even though it hadn't been true back when she started, it wasn't something she wanted to live through again.

Paul Curran was a disgusting excuse for a human being. Yes, Colleen had sold out by sleeping with him as an intern, but it wasn't for her own career. Jake had the talent and would have made it without Paul playing his demo on the radio, but the farm wouldn't wait. Jake's grandfather was going into foreclosure and Colleen did what she did to move things along.

Paul had wanted it to continue. Colleen soon realized he was the type of man who could ruin someone's life. As soon as Jake signed with Southern Rebel, Colleen ended her unscrupulous arrangement. There was nothing Paul could do to hurt Jake, but he seemed to enjoy ruining Colleen's career.

No one wanted to hire a radio show host who had slept with her boss. The lewd rumors Paul had told fueled the fire burning her reputation. She'd had to start all over, working as a producer and then program assistant before she'd proved herself worthy of being on air. It took years and working at several different stations, but she'd finally left it all behind.

Colleen had worked hard, earned her place in radio. Jake needed someone he could trust to run the station, so yes, it was personal for him, but he never would have asked her if she wasn't one hundred percent qualified.

"The girl in my kitchen has the sweetest ass in the world," he sang, his voice all twangy as though he'd been drinking.

She turned to find him smiling at her, one corner of his mouth angled up in that sexy way that melted panties.

"You're distracting me," he said, strumming a chord.

"I'm making dinner."

"And giving me an inspiring view. However, it's not the kind of inspiration that requires a guitar."

He offered an inspiring view too, one that coaxed her into believing they had a future together. She smiled, ready to dive head first into the unknown, ready to tell him yes.

A flash from the corner of her eye caught her attention. "What is that?" she asked, going toward the window next to the fireplace. As she approached, the sight paralyzed her. "Oh my God," she gasped.

Jake joined her by the window, but only for second. "Oh shit. Call 911," he yelled, running for the door.

Before she could respond, he was outside running toward the blaze. Colleen grabbed the phone off the counter and dialed as she ran after him.

"911. What's your emergency?"

"There's a fire. The whole barn. The fire is, oh, God, the whole barn is on fire!"

~ ♪ ~

Devon shouldn't have been surprised to see Leah circling the table in the war room. "It's Friday night," he said as he walked in. "Don't you have a date or something?"

"I never have dates when I'm working a case," she murmured, only giving him a quick glance.

"Then you never have dates," he added, coming around the table to see what she was looking at.

"Hazard of the job," she said with indifference. Leah was a dedicated detective. She was young, had worked her way to detective faster than most. Devon hoped she wasn't sacrificing personal happiness for the job the way he had. "I talked to Hannah Carlson. She's now Heather Malone, living in Albany, New York."

"Get anything of value from her?"

Leah handed him a page with bullet point notes. "She broke up with Mardin after walking into his room and finding him getting a blow job from a blonde."

"Classy guy. Who was the blonde?"

"She doesn't know, said she didn't hang around long enough to find out and didn't want to know."

"I find that hard to believe." Devon had seen enough domestics to know a woman scorned didn't just walk away.

"Me, too. She said it was humiliating enough without knowing. If it was one of the residents on her floor, she'd have to face her every day and she'd prefer not to be in the know."

Sounded reasonable, but Devon still wasn't buying it. "How'd she react to him attacking all those girls?"

"She said he could be aggressive at times, but she never thought he could hurt anyone. She claimed she was shocked."

Devon put the sheet down and went to the bulletin board. It was a puzzle still, with too many pieces missing. "Have you been able to piece together a connection between the girls?" he asked.

"Not yet, but we haven't gotten all the school records. The school won't release them without a subpoena. The grand jury won't be in session for another month, so I pleaded our case to Captain McKinley and he agreed to go to the judge on Monday for a court order for the school records and cell phone records for these two phones."

"You've been busy," he said, impressed, as always. This was how Leah had worked her way to detective so quickly. She was dedicated, smart, always on task.

"You get anything from Mr. Donovan?" Leah asked.

"He's not signing a new contract with his current label. We need to dig up whatever we can on Paul Curran." Devon wrote the name on a note card and stuck it on the board under Donovan's name.

"Who's he?"

"He signs musicians for Southern Rebel Records. He was also Colleen's boss at one time. That's too much coincidence, if you ask me." Colleen and Jake hadn't shared much information about Curran, but based on Colleen's reaction to his name and the way Donovan looked at her after explaining she had worked for the guy, Devon was sure there was more to the story. "Forensics come back with anything on the car?"

he asked.

"They said the knife was serrated. Doesn't match what was used in the Margot Potter stabbing."

No surprise there, but he'd been hoping for a break. "Rubber is a lot harder to cut than flesh." The Jefferson County Sheriff's Department hadn't recovered a weapon, but the medical report stated it could have been a kitchen knife, something large with a straight edge.

Leah studied him for a moment. "I thought you were watching the house?"

Devon grunted, trying to hide his frustration. He thought if he confessed everything to Colleen she would understand. Instead, it just opened old wounds. "They went to Donovan's farm in Vermont for the weekend."

"I'm surprised you didn't follow them," she chuckled.

"I was tempted, but I couldn't justify it. I called the state police over there, told them Donovan is a person of interest, asked them to let us know if anything out of the ordinary happens while he's in town."

"Good. Maybe some distance from Ms. Cooper will give you a clearer perspective on the case," Leah suggested.

Devon grunted again. As long as Colleen was involved with Donovan, Devon wasn't going to be clear on anything.

~ ♪ ~

Jake watched his dreams go up in smoke. The irony wasn't lost on him. He was sure those were the words to a country song, if not more than one. He'd probably covered it at a bar at some point in the early days of his career.

He stood there helpless as the flames lit up the building like it was kindling. Colleen had pulled him back, away from the heat, away from the smoke. Now they watched from a safe distance as the firefighters did their thing. Jake knew without a doubt the whole thing was destroyed.

Destroyed. Just like that.

Broken Strings

"Do you want to keep standing here?" Colleen asked. He appreciated that she didn't urge him to go inside or leave altogether. She just held his hand in both of hers, standing there with him watching the destruction.

"I can't not watch," he admitted. It sounded so dumb, like he was watching a train wreck. Wasn't that the story of his life?

His parents had been killed by a drunk driver when he was ten. Jake had spent a week in the barn after the funeral. Grams brought him meals and a blanket. Gramps brought him his dad's guitar. They were devastated too, losing their only daughter, but they hid their anguish so Jake could survive his.

Grams had died from pneumonia while Jake was in college, before he even had the chance to make her proud. He'd been excused from classes that week, but Colleen skipped all of hers to go to the funeral and just be there for him. They'd spent countless hours in the barn, reassuring Grams' horse Ray that he wasn't alone. That was the first time Colleen had ever ridden a horse. Ray had fallen in love with her. So had Jake.

When Gramps was on the verge of losing the farm, he sold Ray and the other horses, along with the other animals. Gramps claimed he was too old to continue farming, but Jake saw through the rough outer layer to the hurt inside. He was determined not to let Gramps lose the farm.

He'd succeeded at that, but somehow lost Colleen. He still wasn't sure why.

Maybe she'd been right, that they were better as friends, that their lives were going in different directions and he needed to sow his wild oats. He'd done just that, not because he felt like he needed to, but because he was trying to mask the pain of being alone.

If one thing always held true, it was that he ached for her. Even now, with her standing there holding his hand, the empty feeling in his chest was like a black hole, ready to swallow him up. He knew the only way to soothe that ache was to make her his, to move beyond the friendship.

Colleen had always been the one for him, from that first moment when they'd both auditioned for the campus radio station. The producer said they had great chemistry and while he was referring to on air chemistry, Jake knew it didn't end there.

"I should call Gramps," he murmured, using Colleen's favorite distraction of changing the subject, even if it was only in his head. News had probably already reached the retirement community where Gramps rented an apartment, but he'd want to know no one was hurt.

"I can do it if you want," she offered.

Jake was tempted to let her. It would be easier to let her make the call than to deal with it himself, but that was how JD rolled. Rebekah handled all the unpleasant tasks that Jake didn't want to deal with. He'd been taking responsibility for all of that and despite Colleen's offer, he couldn't fall off the wagon. He didn't want to be the guy who took the easy way.

"Thanks, but I should."

They walked up to the porch and sat on the swing as if they were watching a movie. The flames seemed smaller, but Jake wasn't sure if that's because they were further from the barn or because the firefighters had it under control.

He dialed Gramps' number because it seemed easier than looking for it in his contact list. "Hello?" Gramps answered after half a ring.

"Hi Gramps."

"Oh, thank God. Are you all right?"

"Yeah, but the barn is destroyed."

"It's stuff, Jacob," Gramps insisted in his firm voice. "You can replace stuff. As long as you and Colleen and Nola are all right, that's all that matters."

"We're fine. We were in the house." Maybe if they had been in the barn, they would have caught it earlier and his dreams wouldn't be blowing away like smoke on the warm breeze.

"You remember that, son. Life is important."

Jake agreed, but that barn not only held a future, it was a gateway to the past, to his childhood memories. "Aren't you even upset? You worked in that barn your whole life."

"I did. That barn held a lot of memories but those memories live in my heart. There was nothing in there that can't be replaced. It's why you buy insurance."

Jake grunted. This project had been in the makings for two years. It had cost him a fortune.

"Are you safe there at the house? No danger of the fire spreading?" Gramps asked.

"The smoke is blowing east," Jake explained. The house sat about a hundred yards north of the barn. "The fire chief isn't worried about embers hitting the house, but they are keeping an eye on it anyway."

"Chief Jameson knows his stuff. You can trust his word."

"I guess," Jake sighed. Luckily, he and Colleen hadn't been told to leave. That was a battle Jake wasn't sure he had the energy to fight even though he couldn't see himself stepping foot off the property.

"You'll rebuild, Jacob," Gramps said. "It's a roadblock, not a dead end."

When Jake didn't say anything, Gramps bellowed, "Say it with me, son. It's a roadblock, not a dead end."

Jake repeated the words even though it felt superficial. He had lost everything. Rebuilding would take a lifetime. The light at the end of the tunnel had been getting bigger and brighter. Now it was just a flicker, threatening to burn out with the last flames.

"I love you, Gramps," Jake said, ready to end the call.

"I love you, too, Jacob. I'll be by in the morning. There's no point in my coming out there now and getting in the way."

That was good. As much as Gramps was putting on a brave front over the phone, Jake knew there would be pain on his face and right now, he couldn't deal with that.

Colleen rubbed his back as he leaned forward, his elbows resting on his knees, his face in his hands. The flames were smaller now but the barn was beyond salvageable.

"He's right," Colleen whispered as she rested her head on his shoulder. "This isn't a dead end."

His arm went around her shoulder, pulling her closer. With the warmth of the fire no longer reaching them, he clung to the warmth of her body, letting it push aside the rage that had been brewing. Someone was trying to ruin him. First the threats, then the attack on Margot. Jake had made a mistake coming to New England. He should have kept this mess away from Colleen, away from the farm. Maybe if he'd just stayed on tour, the culprit would have given up. Instead, Jake had made the person he loved the most, as well as his future, a target.

♪ Chapter 15 ♪

From Viper:

Barn is toast.

To Viper:

Well done ;-)

♪ Chapter 16 ♪

JAKE HAD been in the shower for almost forty-five minutes. Colleen wanted to check on him but checking on him meant seeing him naked. Before the fire, she'd been ready to open that door, but after hours of watching the barn burn to ash and seeing the hope fade from Jake's eyes, she wasn't sure now was the right time.

She stepped across his large bedroom. The house still had all the charm of an old farmhouse, but with the renovations, it also had all the modern conveniences of a new home. The runner that covered the hardwood floor between the bedroom door and the master bath was soft under her bare feet.

The bathroom didn't have a door. A wall had been opened up and a small bedroom had been converted into the master bath. Colleen paused before turning the corner. The shower was still running but there was no other noise. Jake liked to sing in the shower, but obviously he wasn't up for that tonight.

"Are you okay in there?" she called out.

"No," he said sharply.

She wanted to go to him, tell him everything was going to be all right, that they needed to start planning the rebuild. If he was anywhere else, she wouldn't hesitate. The lack of clothes would make it awkward.

Peeking around the corner, Colleen found Jake leaning against the wall, his back to the door. The shower was open, no curtain or glass door. The tiled floor sloped down to keep the water contained. It was beautifully designed, elegant, yet functional.

Her breaths were quick and shallow, not unlike what happened when she was hit with a panic attack. While she might be panicking a little, it wasn't the same. Jake was naked. He looked good. Her sketchy breathing revealed her desire. She'd kept it at bay for years when it came to this man, but it seemed they had come full circle. Had she not been attacked the same night he'd kissed her, maybe they would have already taken the leap. Then again, where would they be? Because she wasn't with Jake, she had made the decision to sleep with Paul in exchange for him playing Jake's demo. She never would have done that if she were *with* Jake.

Colleen held her breath as she took in the beauty of him. If she took another step forward, there would be no turning back. Funny how Jake had spoken those words to her. It had become a promise, one she wanted to embrace.

She loved him, always had, and not just because of what he looked like standing naked under the hot spray. Jake was her soul mate, the one person in the world she trusted without question. Now he wanted more. There was no chance of rejection, no feeling like a fool.

Taking a deep breath, Colleen dropped the plush robe that had been folded neatly at the end of the bed in the guest room and stepped across the room into the shower.

"You shouldn't be here," he growled as her arms went around him.

She didn't say anything, just pressed her body to his, absorbing his heat. When one of his hands covered hers across his ribcage, her heart skipped into overdrive.

"It's not supposed to be like this," he whispered.

"Like what?" she asked, turning her head and pressing her cheek between his shoulder blades.

"I don't want your pity."

"Sympathy isn't pity," she assured him.

He wove his fingers between hers. His heart thumped against her palm, matching the intensity of her own heartbeat. "I want you to be with me because you love me, not because I lost everything."

"I do love you."

"As a friend or as a man?" They'd been saying the words to each other for years. It was as natural as saying hello and they never ended a call or a said good-bye without exchanging those three words. It had always been in the bonds of their friendship even though for Colleen it had meant more.

"Both. It's always been both."

He turned, his blue eyes filled with sadness, glassy with unshed tears. Her heart broke for him, for everything that had been lost in the fire.

"It's always been both for me, too." A smile broke through the sadness. It wasn't the sexy smile that could melt panties with just a flash, but the smile he reserved for only those he loved, the one that sang of his happiness. Colleen's heart beat a little harder at seeing it.

"I can't stand the thought of losing you, especially after losing everything else tonight."

How could he think he'd lost her? She stroked his cheek. "You didn't lose everything. This is a roadblock, but we'll rebuild, make it better than it was. You said there were things you wanted to do that you couldn't because of the structure of the barn. Now we can."

He cupped her jaw, his thumb stroking her cheek. "We? Does that mean you're all in?"

"Yes," she whispered. She couldn't let the mistakes of her past keep her from taking this step with Jake.

This was Jake's dream and he wouldn't offer her the Internet radio station just because they were friends. He needed someone he trusted and could depend on to make the station successful. If anyone else had offered her the job, it would have been based on her credentials and she would have said yes. She was suited to the job because of her skills, but she was the person to help bring Jake's dream to life because of their love.

She'd been about to tell him that when they discovered the fire.

Broken Strings

"All in, Coll. Everything. The new label. The radio station. Me."

"I'm all in, Jake." She turned into his hand, her lips brushing the wet skin of his palm. "Especially you."

His affectionate gaze shifted, his eyes leaving hers to give a full body perusal that threatened to turn her skin to flames.

"You are so beautiful," he said, his head dipping before his lips brushed hers. She held on to his waist for dear life. They'd been kissing a lot in the last few days, but there was something about being naked and wet that made it bone melting despite the gentle caress.

Colleen stepped in to him, their naked bodies coming together. Jake paused for a moment, but then his tongue pushed past her lips and the gentleness was gone. His hands moved from her face, his arms wrapping around her and his hands clinging to her waist.

His erection was hard and hot and so enticing pressed against her belly. She held on to him, feeling the muscles of his back flex and bunch.

Her hands wandered down, unable to resist moving over the smooth skin of the very nice ass she'd gotten a thorough look at when she first stepped into the bathroom. Jake growled and released his hold, punching the handle of the shower to stop the water.

"As enticing as the shower is, I want to take my time with you. We need to move this to the bed."

Colleen had no objections, so she gave him a quick nod, unable to form even the word yes in the haze of desire she was lost in.

Jake took her hand and led her out of the bathroom. When they reached the giant bed at the other end of the spacious bedroom, he pulled her into his arms again.

"We're all wet," she pointed out, stalling as doubt crept its way into her head. She'd never been good at the sex thing, less so after she'd been attacked in college. Paul had told the world she was frigid, the two men she'd been with after that hadn't been as cruel, but it had been obvious they'd thought the same thing. For whatever reason, Devon had broken the ice. She hoped that wasn't a fluke because the last thing she wanted to do was disappoint Jake.

"I don't care," he said against her mouth as he turned them around and eased her down to the mattress.

He braced himself over her with one arm, his free hand teasing her with a slow exploration of her body, his eyes following. "I've written songs about this, but I don't think a song could capture just how special you are."

Colleen didn't like being put on a pedestal. She'd been broken for so long, after the attack in college and the drama with Paul. Her relationships failed because she had intimacy issues. Devon had gotten through that barrier, and Colleen hoped now that she could be what Jake was hoping for.

"Don't set your expectations too high," she joked. "We might not have any chemistry at all."

"We've always had chemistry. I'm about to prove it to you."

His mouth captured hers before she could argue, not that she wanted to, but there wouldn't be any turning back. If they made love and it was terrible, they'd never recover from that.

Jake loved her, which ratcheted her nerves even more. Though she'd fallen in love with Devon, that hadn't been the case the first few times they were together and she never told him how she felt once she realized it.

Already, it felt different with Jake ... different in a good way, in the way she knew there would be no regrets.

He had the most amazing mouth and Colleen's naughty brain conjured up images of where she wanted it focused. He was still perched over her, one knee between her legs. His thigh brushed against hers, the course hair making her skin prickle with anticipation. He continued to caress and tease with his hand, circling her breasts but not touching them, passing over her hip, but not touching her where she ached.

She was ready to explode. Maybe he was right about the whole chemistry thing.

Starting her own exploration, she smoothed both hands over his pecs, letting her thumbs brush across his nipples, which stole a hiss from him. She traced the thin line of hair that ran down the center of his rock solid abs to where it thickened at his groin. Maybe she should have teased him like he was teasing her, but patience wasn't one of her stronger qualities. She ran her fingers down his hard length, this time drawing a moan from him. As his pleasure vibrated against her tongue, she didn't hold back, taking him into her palm and wrapping her fingers around him. His skin was hot and soft and he was so hard it made her even more aroused.

He abandoned her mouth, his hand cupping her breast before his fingers scraped across her nipple. A little whimper came out of her, a desperate plea for more. He kissed her neck, working his way to her ear where he nipped and tugged at her lobe.

"That feels so good," he whispered and, God, his voice, so rough and soft at the same time. "You have to stop. It's too good. You'll make me come."

He took her hand and pressed it to the mattress next to her head. His mouth moved south, sucking her nipple into the searing heat and making her gasp.

He played there, his tongue doing wondrous things and she felt the pull between her legs. When both nipples were thoroughly lavished, he kissed his way down her stomach. Her breaths grew shallow, a combination of eagerness and nerves that had her whole body shaking.

"Easy, Coll. You'll like this, I promise."

Of that, she had no doubt, but this was Jake. Her college crush turned best friend. She'd given up hope years ago that they would follow their hearts back to each other. Now here they were.

"Just, hurry-up," she pleaded, desperate for the anticipation to be satisfied.

He chuckled against her hip and when she thought he was never going to stop teasing, his mouth moved to that most intimate spot. Colleen's hips jerked as she cried out, the vibration of Jake moaning against her very wet flesh creating an erotic song.

He was slow, patient, taking his time, his tongue moving up her center before he teased that most sensitive spot. The sensation tingled all the way to her fingers and toes, every muscle tensing as she cried out her release.

If it hadn't felt so good, she might be embarrassed at coming so fast, but Jake was undeterred as he continued laving her sensitive flesh.

~ ♪ ~

Jake kissed the inside of her thighs, loving the aftershocks of her orgasm. He was aching to be inside her, but he wanted to take his time, explore all of her before he had his fill.

Not that he ever thought he would have his fill.

Her skin was so soft and smooth and she tasted like heaven. As he kissed his way down her leg, he even thought her knees were perfect.

"Don't you dare touch my feet," she warned. He knew how ticklish she was there, but he didn't want to miss a single inch of her. He took one foot into his hands and kept a tight grip as she tried to pull away.

"I won't tickle," he promised, keeping a firm hold.

"Don't tell me you have a foot fetish," she laughed.

"I have a Colleen fetish that includes every inch of you."

He rubbed one foot, using both hands to ease the tension from her body. As she relaxed back into the mattress, the tension knotting his muscles eased too.

"That feels good," she sighed and Jake hoped to hear those words cross her pretty lips when he was inside her. She propped herself up, smiling at him. "You are so hired. How are you doing that without tickling?"

Jake smiled back. "Magic fingers."

"Amen," she said, lying back on the bed.

He worked her left foot thoroughly before starting on her right foot and being rewarding with a deep moan of satisfaction.

When he just couldn't wait any longer, Jake released her foot and moved up her body. He started shaking as Colleen's hands moved up and down his arms. She was the one with magic fingers, just a caress undoing him, or maybe it was that he'd fantasized about this for so long he was terrified he'd screw it up somehow.

"I'm a little nervous," he admitted.

"You?" she chuckled.

"Yeah. I've wanted this for a long time, wanted you for a long time. I hope I don't mess it up."

She smiled as her hand caressed his cheek. "I'm nervous too, so if we mess it up, we'll just have to try again, right?"

"Hmmm. I like the way you think. I have to get a condom out of my suitcase." He hated to leave her, but he hadn't expected this tonight, not after the fire, so it hadn't occurred to him to put his stash in the nightstand drawer.

It was perfect, though, Colleen coming to him in the shower, telling him yes, she was all in. Making love to her had been a fantasy for years, but having her by his side as he embarked on this new venture made his heart beat.

He loved the way she watched him, her cheeks flushed, her lips stretched in a shy smile. She was never one to show her vulnerability and he loved this side of her because it showed she trusted him.

He tugged a condom from the package before tossing the box on the nightstand for later. After tearing the wrapper, he slipped the condom on and moved back over her body.

"I love you, Coll," he said before brushing his lips across hers.

Her arms went around him, her fingers sending a shiver of anticipation up his spine. "I love you, too."

Those words were sweet music in his ears. He was devastated about the barn, but Gramps was right, it wasn't a dead end and with Colleen loving him and at his side, there was nothing he couldn't do.

Jake held his breath as he slid inside her, loving her tight, slick heat. Her breath caught and she tugged at her lower lip with her teeth, keeping her gaze fixed on his. He moved slow, pushing all the way in and only taking a breath as he pulled out slowly. Colleen gripped his arms as he perched above her and he had to break eye contact to see where they were joined, to watch as he sank deep inside her again.

Nothing had ever felt this good or this right. He'd always known Colleen was the one for him and being with her now, he wished he'd never fallen into the bad-boy lifestyle. They'd missed years together.

"Jake," she whispered, pulling his gaze back to hers. He lowered his body, the skin-to-skin contact sending an excited chill across his body. Her hips met his with an urgency he couldn't deny. He wouldn't last long, but they had the whole night, a whole future together, so he gave into the passion, thrusting into her the way he'd dreamed of so often.

"Open your eyes," he pleaded when she closed them. He needed to know she was there with him. She opened them again, once again biting down on her lower lip.

Her legs wrapped around his, keeping his body flush against hers. He pulled one of her legs up, hooking his arm under her knee so he could drive in deeper. Her cry of "yes," spurred him on, quickening his pace, but it was when she said his name, his given name, not his stage name, all the blood rushed from his head.

He bellowed with his release, saying her name as he pinched his eyes closed, kissing her mouth until he was numb. She cried out against his tongue, her body tightening around him.

She was his, and he was hers, and this moment would be a song forever written in his mind, but one he would only ever share with Colleen, the only woman he'd ever loved.

♪ Chapter 17 ♪

"GOOD MORNING, Sunshine," Colleen chirped.

Devon loved the sound of her happy voice, but the fact it might be Donovan putting the happy there put knots in his stomach.

"Do you know this song?" Devon barked, getting right to the point. He played the recording Erik made of the tune delivered via text message to Colleen's phone last night.

"I can't say that I do. Why?" she asked.

"Put your boyfriend on," Devon demanded.

"Hello?" Donovan said a few seconds later.

"This is Detective Taggart. Do you recognize this song?" He hit play again and waited.

"What the hell?" Donovan snarled after listening to the first verse. "Is this some kind of sick joke?"

"I take it you know the song?" Devon asked.

"Yeah, I know it. Why are you playing it?"

"It was sent via text message to Colleen's phone last night."

Donovan's heavy breaths filled the long pause before he spoke again. "What time last night?"

"About seven o'clock. Why?" Devon asked as he placed the tablet on the table in the war room.

"Because the barn on my farm burned to cinders last night."

Shit. Devon didn't like the guy, but he sure wouldn't wish something like this on him, especially since he'd dragged Colleen off to that farm. "Anyone hurt?" Devon asked, trying to stay objective.

"No, but I don't like this."

"What color was the barn?"

"Red," Donovan said, the anger in his voice cutting through the phone.

"I'd say the text message and the fire aren't a coincidence. I want to talk to the fire chief. You two sit tight until I get there," Devon advised. He hadn't liked them going to Vermont to start with, but there was no legal reason to detain them in Granite Beach. The fire gave him an excuse to check things out in Vermont.

"Yeah, sure. See you soon," Donovan said. Devon expected him to put up more of a fight. Either the guy had nothing to hide or he was a cocky SOB. Maybe whatever he was hiding burned down with the barn.

Sliding the phone in his pocket, he realized Leah was standing in the doorway of the war room. Despite it being Saturday, she was dressed in her usual straight-leg slacks and tucked in shirt, two coffees in hand. "So, we're off to Vermont, then?" she said.

Devon nodded. He hadn't expected any new developments on the case, but after Erik notified him about the text message, he couldn't resist the urge to check in. Devon had opted for a more casual uniform of jeans and a t-shirt. He kept a change of clothes in his locker and another in the SUV, so he could dress the part of detective without going home when he needed to. He took the coffee Leah handed him. "The red barn on Donovan's farm burned down last night."

Her brow shot up. "And Colleen Cooper receives a message with a song about burning down a red barn. A coincidence would be stretching it."

"Which is why I'm heading over there to talk to the fire chief," Devon pointed out.

"You could just talk to him on the phone."

"I could, but there's more to this than Donovan is telling me. I need to get to the bottom of it."

Leah shook her head. "Did you ever stop to consider that maybe

Broken Strings

you're suspicious of him because of his relationship with Ms. Cooper?"

"Every damn minute," Devon admitted, "but my gut is telling me he's hiding something and my gut is never wrong."

Leah held the door as he walked past her. "You got the case file?" he asked, already knowing the answer. Leah was nothing if not efficient.

"I've plugged everything into the online file and I've downloaded it to my tablet, so we're good to go."

Devon was done with the coffee by the time they reached the SUV. He tossed it in the trash bin he kept in the back and grabbed a water out of the small cooler he also kept back there.

Leah studied her notes, which included listening to that song over and over. Devon's adrenaline seemed to pump harder the closer they got to Vermont. He mentally reviewed everything he had learned, trying to make a connection between anything. Burning down a barn was a hell of an effort, but he supposed it was no less risky than stabbing a woman and not killing her.

There had to be some sort of connection, but what was it? Devon had a feeling the answer was within whatever information Jake Donovan wasn't providing.

"Shit," he said. "Look up Margot Potter's record label."

"What are you thinking?" Leah asked as she scrolled through files on the tablet.

"Red barn burned down. Red barn song on Colleen's phone. I swear her label is Red Barn or something.

"Old Red Barn Records," Leah confirmed. "I'm looking them up now. Let's hope 3G holds up."

Both of their phones provided cellular hotspots the tablet could piggyback on, but even that required a cellular signal. They'd passed a tower just minutes before, and he hoped it wasn't the last one they'd see. Devon tapped the steering wheel and pressed the accelerator.

"Try to keep it under 80," Leah warned.

"You just do your thing and leave the driving to me."

"I'm thinking I should have done the driving. All right. Here it is.

Old Red Barn Records. There's not a whole lot of information on the dot com. The website features the musicians, including Potter, but says nothing about the label."

Of course it couldn't be easy. "Wikipedia have anything?"

A minute later she was shaking her head. "The only results that return fall under each of the recording artists' pages. The label itself doesn't have an entry."

Devon tapped the steering wheel with his thumb, hoping for a case-breaking revelation. He came up short. "Marie's on duty this weekend, right? Have her find out who owns it."

"Already on it," Leah said, putting her phone to her ear.

She gave Marie the details and when she disconnected the call, angled her head and gave Devon the look.

He glanced over, and shook his head, focusing back on the road. "I know what you're going to say."

"Do you?"

"Country music. Red barn. Pretty common."

"That's not what I was going to say at all."

"No?" he questioned.

"No. I was thinking it's too much coincidence and without any information regarding the company, well, that's suspicious."

It was nice to have somebody objective on his side. "Donovan told me yesterday he's not signing a new contract with his current label. I'd bet money he has something in the works with this Old Red Barn label."

~ ♪ ~

Jake chucked the phone across the room.

"What's going on?" Colleen asked, her gleeful afterglow burning off. She'd been making coffee before her phone rang and had since stood leaning against the counter.

"That's a good look for you," he said, admiring how his t-shirt looked better on her than any of those snarky, curve-hugging shirts she liked to wear.

"Ditto," she said, returning the slow perusal. He'd managed to put on a pair of jeans, but nothing else, hoping he could entice her back to the bedroom before Gramps showed up. "So, what was with the song?"

Crap, right, back to reality. "You got a new message on your phone. It was a song about burning down a red barn." Jake shoved his hands through his hair, grabbing two fists full and giving a hard tug. "This is out of hand."

"Oh my God. Do you think someone set the fire?"

"I wanted to believe it was a freak accident, but with everything else that's happened," he shook his head, unable to believe how quickly his life had taken a wrong turn, "no way is it a coincidence."

"This isn't your fault," she said, her tone sharp.

"Of course it is. Margot was my responsibility. So are you. So was the barn. I put you in danger."

"We just need to figure out who is doing this. It's clear someone wants something from you. My bet is on Paul."

Jake shook his head. "I get that Southern Rebel wants me to sign and stands to lose a lot if I don't, but they've lost big artists before. Not even Paul would stoop to criminal behavior to keep me on."

"Maybe not, but I wouldn't trust him. Who else has something to lose?"

Jake didn't have a clue. So few people even knew what his plans were, how was it possible that anyone would feel threatened? "I don't know."

She focused her attention on the coffee, but the view when she turned her back to him was too good to ignore. He stepped up to her, pressing his erection into her very fine ass. "Last night was nothing short of amazing," he said across her ear before breathing in the scent of her hair.

"It was."

"We can skip the coffee, go upstairs and get you out of my old t-shirt."

She laughed, a sound that tugged at his heart. "I thought this was a good look for me?"

"Yes, but it's not as good as naked. You look amazing naked."

He turned her around and claimed her mouth before she could object. Her arms wrapped around his neck, pulling him closer and Jake was sure he'd died and gone to heaven.

"Well, isn't this cozy," Rebekah drawled.

Colleen turned away from him and released her hold, trying to push him back, but Jake didn't budge. He wasn't about to hide his relationship with Colleen from anyone, especially Rebekah.

"Chuck, haven't you ever heard of the fine art of knocking?" he asked over his shoulder.

She was dressed in one of her power suits, a ridiculous getup given that they were in northern Vermont and it was a Saturday. Who the hell was she trying to impress?

"Knocking isn't in my job description. You two need to get dressed before the camera crews get here," she said, looking less than impressed by the situation.

"What camera crews?" Jake demanded.

"This fire is all over the news. It's only a matter of time before the news stations find out you are here and then the cameras will be all over the place.

"It's private property and you can't see the house from the road," Colleen pointed out.

"I'm well aware of that, CC," Rebekah snapped with a heavy dose of angst, "but don't think that will stop the paparazzi."

She was right, of course. On any given day, JD Donovan was the perfect fodder for tabloids and entertainment papers. On a day when the red barn on his property burned down, the paparazzi would be worse than vultures closing in on a rotting carcass.

"Go get dressed," he whispered across Colleen's hair, not missing how soft her hair felt against his cheek. "I don't want to leave Chuck unsupervised."

He was surprised when Colleen kissed him. He indulged for a few moments before giving her room to get by him. He didn't miss the scowls she and Rebekah exchanged as Colleen headed down the hall, Nola at her side.

"I told you not to come to Vermont," he admonished when they were alone.

"Oh, please. What would you do in, oh, say, two hours, when the vipers show up with their fangs dripping with venom?"

"I'd call the police because they are trespassing. How did you find out about the fire, anyway?" No way could it be all over the news. Maybe the fire was, but it couldn't be tied to him yet. The property was still owned by Gramps, who had put everything into a trust. Even though Jake was the sole beneficiary, that information wasn't public knowledge.

"I was at the diner for breakfast this morning because the sorry excuse for a motel in this town doesn't serve breakfast. Everyone was talking about it."

It didn't surprise Jake that it would be big news at the diner. He wondered what they thought of Rebekah. The locals didn't like outsiders and Rebekah more than looked the part.

He finished making the coffee Colleen had started and offered Rebekah a cup.

"This is so much better than that crude they served at the diner."

Rebekah was such a snob. It was amazing how alike she and Colleen had been in college and how different they were now. Where Colleen was easy-going and tolerant, Rebekah was uptight and impatient. He wondered if that was because of the attack Rebekah had survived in college. She never seemed the same after that.

"The crew is ready to head to Des Moines. They're anxious to get things rolling again. I talked with Derek at Roadshow Productions and he said the arena can still do the show. Nothing else is planned."

"It's not fair to the fans to keep changing the dates. Derek agreed to reschedule the five shows and that's what we're doing. You need to lay off, Chuck. Scheduling the shows isn't your job."

"No, but keeping you on schedule is. Paul is already pissed about you not signing a new contract. He's been threatening breach of contract if you aren't in the studio October first."

"I'll call my lawyer," Jake responded. He was sure there weren't specific dates in the contract and even if there were, there had to be contingencies for situations like this. "I talked to Margot yesterday. She says she'll be ready to perform in Detroit, so that saves us having to find a new opener."

"Paul found a new opener."

"No," Jake yelled, his fists slamming the counter. "That's not his job. Let him know everything is in order and the tour will resume in Detroit as planned."

Rebekah's sinister smile drummed up Jake's dread. "You can tell him yourself. He'll be here this afternoon."

♪ Chapter 18 ♪

COLLEEN'S STOMACH lurched. The last person in the world she wanted to see besides Spencer Mardin was Paul Curran. She could deal with one nemesis at a time, but to have both Rebekah and Paul around, not to mention Devon. It was going to be a hell of an afternoon. Maybe she'd drive up to Waterbury and hit the Ben and Jerry's factory. There was no reason for her to be here while Jake was dealing with the tour schedule and studio time. There was no reason for her to be anywhere in the vicinity when Paul was around.

"Can I borrow your car?" she asked when she decided it was time to stop eavesdropping. She'd slipped into jeans and a t-shirt that stated *Yeah I shoot like a girl. You want a lesson?* Jake smirked while giving her the once over as she walked into the kitchen.

"Sure," he said, pulling her against him. He was solid and warm and her body seemed to fit perfectly against his. "Where are you off to?"

Colleen shrugged, looking up at his sky blue eyes. "You have a lot to deal with today. I don't want to be in the way."

"You won't be in the way," he reassured her. The guilt stung a bit for wanting to run, but it seemed like a better solution than the possibility of being surrounded by men she had been involved with at some point in her life.

"It will be more productive for you if I'm not here," she whispered, not wanting to let Rebekah in on the conversation.

"All in," he reminded her. "I want you to be involved in

everything."

That was going to take therapy to survive. "I'm going to need ice cream," she insisted.

"Let me get dressed and we'll head up together."

That sounded like fun, but he wasn't thinking straight. "You want Devon and Paul showing up while you're not here?"

Jake's smile faded as reality took hold. "I don't want them showing up at all. Maybe if I'm not here, they'll go away."

If only it was that simple. "You should stay."

"So should you." He pressed a kiss to her temple, leaving a tingle in its wake that shot straight to her nipples. While she didn't mind Jake knowing how easily he got to her, she wasn't fond of their audience.

Looking past Jake, Colleen found Rebekah staring them down. "Can we go upstairs and talk?" she asked.

Jake looked over his shoulder. "Chuck, can you step out?"

Colleen choked the laugh back. Rebekah hated that nickname and Jake knew it, but he liked to rile her up. Rebekah rolled her eyes and stomped off, slamming the door behind her.

Jake kissed Colleen, on the mouth this time, his lips firm and warm. They were like a song she could lose herself in, forgetting about all the drama complicating their lives.

He pulled away too soon. Colleen kept her eyes closed, replaying the way his lips seduced her into a willing and wanton woman with just a simple kiss.

"Are you scared because Paul is coming here or because I know what happened?" Jake asked, snapping her out of the brewing fantasy.

She opened her eyes, his expression too serious, and the moment was lost, reality pushing its way back in. "I'm not scared. That man brings out the worst in me and I try not to put myself in those situations." He was a harsh, brutal man, one who thrived on hurting others.

"I want him to see us together. I want us to stand up to him — together. No looking back, Coll." His voice was so sure, like Paul didn't matter, like no one mattered, like together they could conquer the world.

Jake's confidence pushed aside Colleen's apprehension. He was right, Paul didn't matter, not if they stood up to him together.

"Okay, I'll stay, but then we go for ice cream."

"Deal," he agreed, pulling her in tight. She loved the sound of his heart beating against her ear. The heat of his skin reminded her of their night together, making her ache and want for him.

"I'm going to go for a run," she said. Running always cleared her head and gave her perspective. She was going to need a good dose of that to deal with Paul and Devon.

"You're going to leave me alone with Chuck?" Jake whined.

"She's your employee," Colleen reminded him. She still didn't understand why he'd hired Rebekah, except that he felt sorry for her. Jake was a sucker for a lost cause.

"Only until I'm free from Southern Rebel. We have a PR department built in to Old Red Barn, so I'll be doing everything through them and find a personal assistant who doesn't have the need to control every aspect of my life."

Colleen couldn't believe he was getting rid of Rebekah after all these years. "Does Rebekah know this?"

"Not exactly. I keep encouraging her to find something new, to go work for someone else, but she hasn't taken the hint."

This was just great. Once Rebekah found out Colleen was going to manage the radio station, she would blame Colleen for being let go. Not that Colleen couldn't handle Rebekah's wrath, but she preferred to avoid conflict whenever possible. "Jake, are you sure she doesn't know? Or suspect? Maybe she's behind all the threats and the stabbing and my tires."

"Chuck? You can't be serious?"

"As a heart attack." Rebekah had shown up in Granite Beach right when Colleen's tires had been slashed. She had Colleen's number. She was on tour with Jake, so could easily purchase cell phones in Phoenix.

"I know she can be a little bitchy sometimes, but she could never hurt anyone. You know what she survived in college."

Colleen knew all too well, having been a survivor herself. Unlike Rebekah, Colleen kept knowledge of her attack private. Rebekah used it as a way to get people to feel sorry for her and bend to her every whim. "I get that you have a soft spot for a woman in distress, but that was a long time ago. If she's still affected by that, she should be in therapy." Or carry a gun. That was as good as therapy and Colleen preferred to spend her money on bullets instead of a co-pay.

Jake shrugged. They'd had similar discussions about Rebekah over the years, but Jake always insisted he needed her. Colleen wondered if he really was going to let her go. She wouldn't make the decision for him, or even offer up an ultimatum — even though it was tempting — but if he didn't let Rebekah go, Colleen was going to have a hard time working with her.

"Do not feed Nola from the table while I'm gone," she advised, giving her dog a quick pat as she headed back upstairs to change into running gear.

She was aware Jake and Nola followed her. "Looking for a show, cowboy?" she asked over her shoulder.

Jake grabbed her butt before pressing her against the banister at the top of the stairs. "I could give you a workout right here. Get your heart rate pumping. You wouldn't need the run."

Her heart rate was already pumping, her body one-hundred percent on board with Jake's offer. As he backed her down the hall, opening her jeans and stripping her out of her shirt, Colleen couldn't find the will to stop him. He kicked the bedroom door closed behind him, unsnapping his button-fly jeans with a quick tug and pushing them down. Her stomach fluttered at the sight of his gorgeous erection springing from his pants. He hadn't put on underwear and for whatever reason, maybe because it was Jake, Colleen found that even more arousing.

"You make a tempting offer," she said, squeezing her thighs together to try to ward off the building ache between her legs. "But this house is about to be invaded by a whole bunch of people."

His slanted smile almost melted her resolve. "I'd rather just lock the door and hide out up here until they're all gone."

Another tempting offer. "You know that won't work. Now put your pants back on. You're making Nola blush."

~ ♪ ~

"You're giving her the radio station, aren't you?" Rebekah asked, the bitchiness in her voice reaching a new pitch.

"She's going to manage it, yes," Jake confirmed. They sat on the porch swing, looking at the cinders still smoking from last night's fire.

While he hadn't told anyone about Old Red Barn Records, the radio station wasn't a secret. Jake hadn't gone into the details with anyone, that it would be more southern rock than country, but keeping the whole thing under wraps, along with the record label had seemed too daunting. It also provided him a good cover story. Whenever he needed to disappear for Old Red Barn business, he could say it was radio station business.

"Where are you going to put it now that the barn is gone?" Her voice lost some of the edge, but Jake knew it was only a temporary reprieve. He liked Rebekah, but with the changes he'd already made in his life, he was ready to see her move on.

"We're going to rebuild." The plan was to get the station going at the start of year, but he didn't want to set it up twice, so it was going to have to wait until the rebuild was complete.

"You're putting her in danger, you know. With everything that's going on, she's going to get hurt."

Jake didn't want to believe that was true. Yes, she was getting those crude text messages, and it was possible someone had gotten into her house. Of course, he was to blame for that, having not locked the door, but as long as they were together, he could keep her safe.

What raised his hackles, though, was Rebekah's concern. For whatever reason, she didn't like Colleen. He always suspected it was jealousy. Rebekah had tried to be more than Jake's personal assistant, but he had kept their relationship professional. Whenever he met up with Colleen, whether while on the road or during a hiatus, Rebekah always tried to run interference.

Speaking of interference, the black SUV Jake recognized as Detective Taggart's rolled up the long driveway, parking next to his car on the side of the house. Taggart and his partner both got out, studying the smoking remains of the barn before approaching the porch.

"Where's Colleen?" Taggart asked.

"What, no hello? How are you doing this fine day? You're in Vermont, detective, people are friendly here."

"I'd prefer to skip the pleasantries and get right to business. Colleen?"

Jake chuckled. It was far too easy to annoy the good detective. With Colleen not there to run interference, he'd take as many shots as he could. "She went for a run." Jake looked at his watch, noting she'd been gone for almost forty minutes. "She should be back any minute."

"And you are?" Detective Paige asked, looking at Rebekah. It seemed she wanted to skip the pleasantries too.

"This is my personal assistant, Rebekah Charles," Jake said before Rebekah could utter a word.

The two detectives exchanged a glance that Jake didn't like. "Funny how you keep turning up every time something bad happens," Taggart said.

"I go where Jake goes," Rebekah snarled.

A scream sounded from the woods before the echo of one, two, three gunshots cracked the quiet afternoon wide open. The two detectives drew their guns and took cover behind the SUV. Jake launched off the swing and bounded over the porch rails, breaking into a dead sprint toward the woods. He heard his name, commands for him to stop, but Colleen was in those woods and that was her scream. No way was he going to hide behind a car while who knows what was going on in the woods.

Fear pumped through his veins. He never should have let her leave the house alone. Someone must have followed them here, maybe the same person who had stabbed Margot and was sending the crude messages to Colleen. The same person who had set fire to his recording studio.

Before he hit the tree line, Colleen bounded out of the woods. Her normal pace was fast; he'd learned that when running on the boardwalk with her a couple days ago. Now she was moving like her feet were on fire.

She went right by him, gun in hand, and he made a quick turn, watching her leap up the porch steps and disappear inside the house.

Jake sprinted in behind her. "Are you all right?" he asked when he found her in the kitchen, pacing around the large island.

"Snake," she breathed out. "Giant, venomous, snarling snake."

"There were gunshots," he said, trying to catch his own breath.

"I shot it. Pulverized it. But there could be others." She hopped up on the counter, bringing her knees to her chest and hugging them.

Jake raked a hand through his hair. "Christ, Coll. You gave me a heart attack. I thought you were hurt."

"Sorry," she said, a shiver shaking her whole body. "I really, really hate snakes."

He knew this. He had always known it. She didn't even like things that resembled snakes, such as eels. They'd once gone to the New England Aquarium and she'd gone ghost white when she saw an eel in one of the tanks.

"What happened? Is someone in the woods?" Taggart demanded. Jake turned to find him coming toward them in the kitchen while his partner stood outside the door with her gun clutched in both hands.

"It was a snake," Jake said.

"As in reptile?" Detective Paige asked from the door.

Colleen nodded. "It was big. Huge. Like a cobra or that snake on Harry Potter."

Taggart holstered his gun. Detective Paige came inside and closed the door behind her.

"They're more afraid of you than—" Jake started.

"You know I don't believe that, so don't even try it."

"You discharged your weapon three times, Colleen," Taggart admonished. He stepped by Jake and held out his hand. Colleen surrendered the gun and the detective cleared the weapon and ejected the magazine. He set the gun on the counter but slipped the magazine in his pocket.

"I'd do it again, too. That thing was huge. Don't think I didn't see you just steal my bullets, Devon."

"This isn't a joke, Coll," Taggart said, the veins in his neck so tight they looked like ropes about to snap.

"Do I look like I'm joking?" Her whole body shook, and aside from the flushed patches of skin, she was ghost white.

"Devon, why don't you wait outside," Detective Paige suggested. "The fire chief should be here any minute. Mr. Donovan, you too. You can tell Detective Taggart what you know about the fire. I'll stay in here with Ms. Cooper."

♪ Chapter 19 ♪

From Viper:

U said she wldn't shoot.

To Viper:

Did she shoot u?

From Viper:

Not the point. I m out.

To Viper:

All or nothing. U back out, u don't c a dime.

♪ Chapter 20 ♪

"You think I'm crazy, don't you?" Colleen said.

The detective smiled. "Honestly, I would have done the same thing. Did any of your shots hit it?"

"All three." Colleen pushed her shoulders back and lifted her chin, proud of the hours she'd spent at the range. "I've never seen a snake that big out in the wild."

"Do you think it was native?" Detective Paige asked.

"I didn't take the time to study it. What? Do you think someone might have *put* it there?"

"I don't know, but at this point, I'm not willing to discount it. Who knows you're afraid of snakes?" The detective put her gun away and pulled out a small notepad.

"I don't know. Everyone, I guess. We did a segment once on the morning show about ridiculous fears. Snakes were a recurring topic that day." She hadn't wanted to reveal her own fear because there were some sick people out there. Colleen expected to receive rubber snakes in the mail. If she had, someone ran interference before they ever got to her desk. The one encouraging thing about that segment was the number of people — both men and women — who called or texted in saying they were afraid of snakes.

"When was that segment?" Detective Paige inquired.

"About a year ago, I think. You can call Delia at the station. She can look it up."

"Seems pretty unlikely that our perp would have been listening to that segment. Did you mention it on air recently?"

Colleen tried to think, but she couldn't recall mentioning it. She disliked snakes so much she tried not to talk about them at all. "I don't think so, but all the shows are recorded. Someone could go back through the recordings if you think it's important."

"We'll table it for now. I think it's safe for you to come down."

She hadn't even realized she was still up on the counter. She hopped down and headed straight for the freezer. "Great," she groaned when she realized the freezer was empty, except for one thing. She pulled the bottle of whiskey. "This'll have to do. Want a glass."

"No, thanks."

Colleen grabbed a shot glass from the cupboard next to the refrigerator. "I wanted to go to Ben and Jerry's, but Jake asked me to stick around. I could use a pint of Cheesecake Brownie right now." She poured a shot and threw it back. Jameson was supposed to be a sipping drink, but Colleen just needed a little something to settle her nerves."

Friggin' snake.

She capped the bottle and returned it to the freezer, feeling the warmth of the whiskey come alive in her chest.

"I like the Chocolate Peppermint Fudge. Is the factory nearby?" Detective Paige asked.

"It's about an hour north on Interstate 89. We could blow this pop stand, me and you. Let the boys duke it out."

"Tempting, but I have to work with Devon every day. I don't want to listen to him whine about me taking off for ice cream."

"You could be following a lead," Colleen suggested.

"I like the way you think, but I need to be here when the fire chief shows up."

"All work and no play ..." Colleen gave her a wink.

"That seems to be my motto," the detective stated without a lot of emotion before nodding toward the door. "I see your friend Rebekah is here."

Crud. Colleen had forgotten all about the ice queen. "She's like a bad penny, just keeps turning up."

"Was she here last night?" Detective Paige asked, following Colleen into the living room where she sank into the sofa. The detective sat upright in the adjacent chair.

"She says she stayed at the motel in town and heard about the fire while having breakfast at the diner," Colleen explained.

"You don't believe her?"

"I'd bet money she knew about the fire last night and spent the whole night working up a plan to turn the events to her advantage."

"What do you mean?"

Colleen realized she sounded like a jealous girlfriend. Paul wasn't the only one who brought out the worst in her. Rebekah ran a close second.

"Never mind. I'm just acting like a lunatic. The snake thing has me a little on edge."

The detective sat back in her chair, but Colleen couldn't relax. She resisted the urge to fidget under the detective's scrutiny, doing her best to mirror Detective Paige's casual posture. Movement outside caught her attention and she saw an old truck pull up. Jake ran to it and when Gramps climbed down, the two shared an affectionate embrace.

"Who's that?" the detective asked.

"Jake's grandfather. He lives in a retirement community in town."

"Can I ask you about the attacks in college?"

Colleen's stomach did its usual lurch when that topic came up and she fought back the shiver of fear, but was unsuccessful. She eyed the freezer.

"I can grab you another shot if that'll help," the detective offered.

"I'm not much of a drinker. I really wish there was ice cream."

The detective smiled. "I'll tell you what. You answer my questions and I'll hit the convenience store and buy you their whole supply."

Colleen laughed. "A pint should do it. I don't want to have to run in the woods again to deal with the calories and guilt."

"Alright, pint's on me."

"Then fire away."

"Why do you think Rebekah didn't testify?"

That was an easy question and at least she didn't have to relive her own experience. "Rebekah claimed she couldn't identify him. Said he attacked her from behind, pinned her face down on the ground, and didn't say a word."

"I read the report. That's not what I'm interested in. I want to know what you think."

"Why? I wasn't there. Rebekah and I weren't even that close by then."

"But you were her roommate. You got to see a side of her no one else did, even if you weren't that close. I went to college too. I had some great roommates but I also survived a couple roommates from hell. I'm just interested in your perspective."

Colleen looked out the window. She couldn't see Rebekah, but could see the swing was still moving to and fro, indicating she hadn't vacated her spot there.

"She liked to be the center of attention. When we'd all hang out, she'd get bitchy if someone asked Jake to sing or play his guitar. Then there were all these attacks. I was trying to keep it quiet, but the resident assistant and resident director knew, and then there were the other girls who were attacked who would come by to talk. She'd get bitchy every time someone stopped by and she was forced out of the room. At first, I offered to go somewhere else, but she made a big production out of that too, so I stopped offering and just let her do her thing."

"And what about Jake?"

"He didn't know about the attack. I didn't want him to know because he would have felt guilty. We had ..."

God, she'd never told this story. She wasn't sure she wanted to now, but got the feeling the information was important to the case. "Jake and I had kissed the night I was attacked. We'd never done that before." Colleen left out the part of how amazing it had been, how she was floating after Jake headed out for his gig. "It was the start of something new for us. He left for his gig and I was supposed to meet him after the show. I never made it."

Colleen didn't want to tell the rest, but Detective Paige didn't relent. "What happened?"

She shook her head at the stupidity of her decision. "I didn't wait for the shuttle. My dorm was across campus, but the walkway was well lit. I wasn't paying attention. Spencer grabbed me, dragged me into the shadows of a building, behind some shrubs. I struggled to get away. He was bigger, so much stronger than me."

She'd given herself a concussion head-butting him, but it stunned him enough that she was able to break free, kick him in the nuts, and make a run for the campus chapel. There was a chaplain in residence who called the police.

"Breathe, Colleen. Deep breath in through your nose. That's it. And out through your mouth."

Colleen did as she was instructed, not even realizing she had been breathing so fast. "Sorry. I don't have any control over the panic."

"No apology needed. I understand. Your response is normal."

There was nothing normal about it, but Colleen focused on getting her breathing under control.

"I was under the impression that you and Jake were never romantically involved," Detective Paige inquired.

"We weren't. I was freaked out after the attack." She faked the flu for a week hoping that was enough time to get over the trauma, but it hadn't been. "He would come up behind me and I'd jump. I was embarrassed, I guess, ashamed — and yes, I know that is ridiculous, but again, it's not something I could control. So, I broke things off. Told him we were better as friends. It hurt, but it was better than telling him the truth and having him feel guilty for my stupid decision to walk back to the dorms."

The detective didn't say anything, didn't even write any notes. She just sat there, her pretty smile putting Colleen at ease. Colleen wondered if the detective was involved with Devon. He was single now, seemed like a fling with his partner would be an easy no-strings-attached relationship for him.

"So back to Rebekah," Detective Paige said as if she knew where Colleen's wayward thoughts had gone and didn't want them to go any further. "We know she claimed she couldn't identify her attacker. Do you think that's true?"

"Honestly?" Colleen asked, looking out the window one more time to make sure the swing was still moving. "I don't think she was attacked at all."

"The rape kit was negative for bodily fluids, but the clinic documented physical injuries, both external and vaginal."

"She was seeing someone. I don't know who, but it had been going on for weeks."

"How do you know?" the detective asked.

"She started staying out late, which wasn't like her. Some nights it was obvious she'd been having sex. Hair all mussed. Cheeks flushed. Stubble burn on her neck. Buttons missing." Colleen had been happy for her roommate and relieved Rebekah had her own reason to get out of the room.

"Do you know exactly when it started?"

"A couple weeks before I was attacked, maybe. It was eight years ago, so it's a bit of a blur."

"What about after her attack? Was she still seeing him?"

"She never left the dorm until spring break. Then she didn't come back to school." And then, two years later, she called Jake and asked for a job.

"So if her motivation was for attention, why not come back to school after spring break?"

"I don't know," Colleen said. Maybe she was just being judgmental, but she had never believed Rebekah's claims.

~ ♪ ~

The old man's timing couldn't have been better. Devon had wanted to question Rebekah for a couple days but hadn't been able to get a hold of her. She didn't answer her phone and didn't have voice mail set up, which he found odd. For someone who took care of a country superstar's business, you'd think she'd be easier to contact.

Now they were alone on the porch, Donovan leading his grandfather over to the smoking remains of the barn.

"What brings you to Vermont, Miss Charles?" he asked.

"I go where JD goes. It's my job."

"Where were you last night?" he asked.

"At that rundown motel in the center of town."

"Alone?"

"Are you asking me for an alibi? Because I didn't get into town until after seven. I stopped just before the Vermont state line for gas and dinner. I can't remember the name of the town, but you can check my credit card records because I charged everything. After I checked in to the motel, I called my mother and was on the phone for over an hour." She tapped the screen of her phone several times and handed it to him. "She'll verify that I was watching Shark Tank."

"You seem to have all your bases covered," he pointed out. It all seemed a little too perfect.

"You learn to cover your own ass when you spend your life making sure JD Donovan's is covered."

"Being his personal assistant isn't a bed of roses, I take it."

"Officially, I'm the executive director of JD Donovan Enterprises, and no, it is not a bed of roses. JD can't keep himself out of trouble, so I spend a lot of time getting him out of it."

Devon almost laughed at hearing her title. It was just as Colleen had explained. "Isn't that what a lawyer is for?"

"I'm the reason he doesn't need a lawyer."

"If it's such a crappy job, why do it?" Devon asked, curious about her motivation.

"I didn't say it was crappy. It's just demanding at times. JD is a great guy when he's not being stupid. The job pays well and for the most part, it's pretty good work."

"But you're on the road a lot. That must be exhausting."

She shrugged. "You get used to it."

"Any theories on who might be behind the stabbing and tire slashing and fire?" he asked.

"Tire slashing?" she asked and even though she seemed surprised, Devon's instincts lit up like fireworks on the Fourth of July.

"Never mind," he said. "What about Margot Potter?"

"Margot was sleeping with JD so I'm sure it was just a jealous fan. Islynn Gray isn't the only whack job fan out there. JD has an entire entourage of them."

She didn't pursue the subject of the tire slashing and that made him even more suspicious. "How long have Donovan and Ms. Potter been sleeping together?"

"You know, I shouldn't have said anything. This is JD's personal business and it's my job to keep it personal."

Was she falling back on her job or had she just deliberately fed him information while making it seem like an accident? More important, maybe not to the case but to Devon, did Colleen know about Donovan's relationship with Potter? "Donovan has been cooperating. I'm sure he wouldn't mind you telling me about what's been happening."

"Then you can question us together. Do I need to be worried about this tire slashing or the fire? I thought the fire was just a freak accident."

"Have you received any harassing text messages?" he asked.

"Nope, can't say that I have. Do you want to check my phone?" She held the smart phone out to him.

"I don't need to check it. I am curious though, why don't you have voice mail set up?"

"I get a lot of crazies calling me. If I don't recognize a number, I don't answer. Business calls are routed through a service and if I don't answer, they leave a message there."

"Can I have that number in case I need to contact you?"

"Sure," she said and pulled a business card out of the purse sitting at her feet. Devon checked the information. As he tucked it into his pocket, a Mustang convertible pulled into the driveway.

Rebekah laughed. "Well, this party is about to get interesting."

~ ♪ ~

"This isn't the end of the world, son. Remember that," Gramps said, patting Jake on the back.

Jake nodded, feeling sad again about everything that had been lost. Yes, he had insurance. The barn would be rebuilt and the equipment replaced. It would be better than before. Time, though, that frustrated him. He had invested so much time and was ready to launch the new Internet radio station at the start of the year. Now it was going to have to wait.

A black Mustang convertible skidded to a stop near where he and Gramps stood, throwing gravel in its wake.

Paul.

This day was just getting better.

"Hope you had marshmallows to roast over that," the jackass quipped.

"Who the hell are you?" Gramps growled.

"Paul Curran. A&R Director at Southern Rebel Records," Curran held out his hand. Gramps was polite enough to shake it.

"Sonny, Jake's grandfather."

"Ah, a pleasure to meet you."

"We don't joke about the fire, understood?" Gramps warned.

"Ah, yes, sir. Sorry."

Jake had never seen Paul cower, but he almost did under Gramps' stern admonishment.

Colleen came out of the house, the detective right behind her, apprehension written all over her. She took a deep breath in as she stood on the porch. Jake figured she was mustering the courage to face her old boss. With her head held high and her shoulders back, she stepped with confidence down the steps and across the yard.

She wore jeans and a t-shirt instead of the running clothes she'd been in when Jake came outside. With her hair down, the dark blonde waves fluttered around in the breeze. She looked like an angel, confident and determined. When she reached them, she gave Gramps a hug.

"Gramps, I've missed you so much."

"I've missed you, too, darling. You keeping my boy in line?"

"He's doing just fine on his own," she said, leaving Gramps' affectionate embrace and moving up against Jake. Her arm moved around Jake's waist and his heart skipped a couple beats at the contact.

She didn't acknowledge Paul except for an angry glare. Jake put his arm around her shoulder and pulled her tight against him.

"CC, what a pleasure," Paul drawled.

Colleen rolled her eyes.

"What are you doing here, Paul?" Jake demanded.

"Why don't we go inside and talk business."

"We can talk business right here," Jake said. No way was he inviting this bastard into his home.

"We need to talk about the new contract," Paul said, his voice switching from friendly to all business.

The two detectives had moved across the yard, along with Rebekah. They didn't join the small huddle, but they were close enough that Jake assumed they could hear everything.

"We talked about it. I'm not signing with Southern Rebel again."

"Rumor has it you're planning to record with Old Red Barn." He looked over his shoulder at what was left of the barn. "That's a little foreshadowing of what's going to happen to your career if you do."

"Are you threatening me?" Jake demanded, stepping away from Colleen to get in Paul's face.

"Just stating the facts, boy. I made your career and you know it. My reach extends far beyond the walls of Southern Rebel Records. I can be your best ally or your worst enemy. It's your choice and your little girlfriend spreading her sweet legs for me isn't going to help your cause next time you're in a bind."

Jake didn't realize he'd punched the ass-hole until the pain shot up through his hand and up his arm.

"Jake," Colleen pleaded, pulling him back before he could get another shot in.

Taggart held Paul back while Gramps stood between them. At six three, and 250 pounds, Gramps was a barrel of a man. Even at his age, he could take Paul, who spent his days in a leather chair behind a big desk. He kept in shape by going to the gym, but didn't have any real world experience.

Paul looked over at Detective Paige who had her gun drawn and pointing at the ground.

"You a cop?" Paul asked.

She nodded.

"Then arrest that son of a bitch for assault."

"Sorry," she shrugged. "This isn't my jurisdiction."

"Then call someone in this jurisdiction. I want him arrested."

"Are you out of your mind?" Rebekah yelled, getting into Jake's face. "What the hell was that?"

"He disrepected Colleen," Jake said, shaking out his hand and shrugging out of Colleen's hold.

"Sounds to me like she disrespected herself," Rebekah said.

"You did not just say that," Jake growled.

"Enough," Gramps bellowed. "Mr. Curran, you are no longer welcome here and since I own this property, I'm asking you nicely to leave. If you can't do that, I'll call my nephew, the county sheriff, and he'll escort you and your expensive suit all the way to the county line."

"I can escort Mr. Curran out," Taggart said, giving the man a tug toward his car.

♪ Chapter 21 ♪

COLLEEN COULDN'T fight the satisfaction racing through her after Jake punched Paul in the face. The guy was going to have a pretty shiner in a few hours, one that was long overdue.

If Rebekah didn't shut her trap, maybe she'd have a matching one, courtesy of Colleen's fist.

"I always knew you were a whore," Rebekah whispered as they headed for the house.

"Just like looking in the mirror, isn't it?" Colleen fired back as she picked up the pace.

Rebekah snickered. "So the rumors are true. You really did screw Paul Curran to get him to play JD's demo."

Colleen wasn't going to lie and deny it, but she wouldn't give Rebekah the satisfaction of admitting it, either. Jake knew the truth and as far as everyone else was concerned, well, it was none of their business.

Coming to an abrupt stop in the dirt driveway, Colleen spun around and grabbed Rebekah's arm. Before she could decide whether to deck her or shove her face in the dirt, Jake pushed between them. "Shut it, Rebekah," he demanded.

Rebekah snarled at Jake, her nostrils flaring with every breath. Jake turned to Colleen, his expression calm considering the circumstances. His arm went around Colleen's shoulder, a possessive hold that sent a thrill through her, and then he stepped off, leading Colleen to the house at a casual pace.

It only took a few steps before Rebekah was at Jake's side. "He's going to retaliate and there isn't anything I can do to stop it," she warned.

Colleen didn't doubt that Jake had just unleashed a monster. Paul was an egotistical, narcissistic son of a bitch. Even though he'd been knocked down a peg or two, he wouldn't stay down.

"Then there's no reason for you to be here," Jake insisted. "Seriously, Chuck, I told you not to come. You need to head back to Tennessee."

Colleen was sure she heard Rebekah mumble that she hated Tennessee. After they climbed the porch steps, she grabbed her purse from the swing and stomped off to her car, a Ford Fusion with New Hampshire plates that Colleen guessed was a rental. Rebekah spun out of the driveway much the way Paul had driven in.

Devon and Paul were standing next to the Mustang talking. Devon had his notebook out and was writing. She wondered what Paul could possibly have to offer to the case. He was a jerk of the highest order and if what came out of his mouth wasn't pure lies, it was cruel and self-serving.

"Why don't you two head inside," Detective Paige suggested from the bottom of the steps. "I'm going to call the fire chief and see what's keeping him. I think he's going to need some ice," she finished, nodding at Jake's hand.

It was red and swollen and when Colleen slid her fingers over his knuckles, he flinched. "Thank you," she said, taking his hand and kissing the bruises.

"I can't hit a woman, but Rebekah is on the short road to being fired," he said.

"She doesn't bother me," Colleen lied.

Cupping her face with his hands, he now looked like the weight of the world rested on his shoulders. "I'm not going to have people who work for me bad-mouthing you."

"I did what I did, Jake. I can't undo it. You keep saying no looking back." Colleen wanted that, but there were going to be hurdles and she needed Jake with her, not getting himself into trouble because of the decisions she had made.

"I mean it. That's why I don't want anyone talking that way about you."

Resting her hands on his chest, his warmth pushed the cold reality from her hands. Her fingers curled, desperate to grasp more of that warmth and hold it forever. "I'm a big girl. I can handle it," she assured him because it was who she was. Always.

"Yeah, well, you shouldn't have to," he sighed, clasping his hands over hers and holding them against his heart.

"I appreciate you defending my honor, but you can't lash out every time someone says something bad about me. I'm an on air personality. There are lots of people who don't like me or things I say." She stepped closer to him, moving on to her tiptoes to kiss his scruffy chin. "It's part of the job and if you think it's not going to happen when I work for you, you need to wake up and smell the manure, buddy."

"Are you saying my farm smells like shit?" he laughed and Colleen was glad the tension had eased.

"Actually, it smells a little charred."

Jake released her hands, his arms moving around her to hold her close. She loved the easy affection they shared. It was so natural, so right, and so much easier to embrace than to avoid. "So much for getting away for the weekend. I should have taken you to Jay Peak instead. We would have had a blast at the indoor water park."

"Disaster seems to be following you," she said, her hands going around his strong shoulders. "If we'd gone up there, something else would have happened."

A knock on the door had Jake sighing and Colleen turning. Through the beveled glass, she could tell it was Devon and his partner.

"We could ignore them," Jake suggested, "head out the back. I could call Gramps and have him pick us up over at the Miller Homestead."

The neighboring farm was owned by one of Gramps' cousins.

"Tempting, but Devon can be persistent. Probably best if we just talk to him now." She kissed Jake on the cheek and called for Devon to come in. His partner followed with Gramps behind her.

"I can see why you don't want to sign a new contract," Devon said, shaking Jake's hand. The gesture surprised Colleen. It was the first peace offering Devon had shown toward Jake. "That guy's an ass-hole."

While Jake settled on a bar stool, Colleen grabbed a freezer bag from the drawer and filled it from the ice dispenser before placing it over Jake's bruised hand.

"Thanks," he said, those blue eyes looking at her as if nothing else existed.

"Is it true, Coll?" Devon asked, ruining the moment. He was a master at that.

"That's none of your damn business," Jake said, pushing off the bar stool and getting into Devon's face.

Colleen stepped between the two men before they came to blows. "Calm down, Jake. He's just asking a simple question." Though there was nothing simple about it and Colleen didn't want to answer with an audience, especially with Gramps standing there.

She dared a glance at the man who was like a grandfather to her, too and received a sympathetic smile. "Where's Nola?" he asked, as if knowing Colleen needed him to leave.

"She's upstairs. She likes the window seat at the end of the hall," Colleen explained and Gramps headed toward the stairs.

"Did you sleep with that guy?" Devon asked more directly this time. "To get your friend here's career off the ground?"

"It's not that simple," Colleen said, "but yes, I slept with him. It was eight years ago, so can we please just let it rest?"

"I get the impression he's not the kind of man who is going to let it rest. You need to prepare yourself," Devon advised.

A pick-up truck pulled into the driveway, followed by a State Trooper. The place felt like Grand Central Station, but Colleen supposed it was routine after a fire like this. She was also relieved to escape Devon's inquisition.

"About time," Devon groaned, pinning Colleen with a look that spoke volumes to his disappointment in her decisions. She shouldn't care. He had cheated on his wife and lied to Colleen. He had no right to judge her.

Yet, the ache of disappointing him was a heavy weight on her chest. She was no better than him. She hadn't lied or cheated, but she'd sold out and was naive to think it was all in the past.

~ ♪ ~

The fire chief was responsible for investigating the cause of the fire, but after Devon called him that morning, Chief Jameson felt compelled to call in the Fire Investigation Unit. The fire safety investigator and the fire chief agreed the fire had started at the southwest corner of the barn where an accelerant, probably soaked onto some sort of material like a shirt or rag, was used to ignite the fire.

There was a lot of radio and recording gear. Devon didn't know much about that sort of equipment, but he figured it had to be tens of thousands of dollars. Donovan had explained he was setting up an Internet radio station that would be broadcast from the barn. Devon wondered if Colleen was involved.

Donovan and his grandfather tagged along while the fire chief and fire safety investigator inspected the rubble. Colleen stayed inside and Leah headed into town to see what Rebekah Charles was up to.

Devon was tired of listening to the speculation about the fire and was relieved and hopeful when Leah called.

"Tell me you've got something good," he pleaded.

"Marie turned up the owner of Old Red Barn Records." Her voice was chipper, as if whatever Marie discovered was good for the case.

"Do tell."

"A man named Toby Tibbs runs things. Marie looked him up and he got his start with Southern Rebel."

"Can't be a coincidence," Devon said, watching Donovan linger by the barn with his grandfather.

"Nope, but that's not all. Tibbs runs the label but the company is part of a trust."

"You're going to make me ask, aren't you?"

"This is a fun game," she quipped.

"Fine. Who's the settlor?"

"Harrison Miller."

Devon searched his brain but came up short. "If that's supposed to mean something to me, I'm missing it," he said.

"This is where Marie earned her paycheck. Harrison and Nola Miller had one daughter, Carrie Anne Miller who was killed by a drunk driver almost twenty years ago, along with her husband, Jason Daniel Donovan. They had one son."

"Jacob Daniel Donovan," Devon finished, piecing it all together. "Sonny must be a nickname."

"Right. Marie couldn't dig up the details of the trust but I'd bet my next paycheck that Jake Donovan is the sole beneficiary of his grandfather's trust."

"Son of a bitch. This wasn't just a radio station. It was a recording studio."

"Come again?" Leah asked.

"There's a substantial amount of recording equipment left in the rubble of the barn. Donovan said he was starting an Internet radio station. I've been inside The Wave and there's not that much equipment. I bet most of what's here was for a recording studio."

"Old Red Barn Records is located in Nashville," Leah added.

"Right, but for how long?" It made sense. Devon assumed the barn here was red before it burned down. "You on your way back here?"

"I am. Talking to Rebekah Charles was also interesting. I'll tell you about it when I get back."

"I already talked to Rebekah Charles," he reminded her.

"She's a woman. She's going to sing a different tune to a man than to a woman. Not unlike Ms. Cooper."

"I don't like you doubling back on my work," he growled.

"You admitted you're not objective when it comes to Colleen Cooper, so I'm doing exactly what you need me to do."

Devon didn't like it. Maybe he wasn't objective, but talking to Rebekah it was easy to see she didn't like Colleen. You didn't have to be objective to pick up on that.

"I'm hitting the store for some Ben and Jerry's. You want some?"

"Ice cream? No, I'm all set, thanks."

"Suit yourself, but don't be begging for any of mine. I don't share."

"Before you stuff your face, call Marie back. I want Jake Donovan's financials. His grandfather's trust may own the record company, but I bet Donovan's money is what pays for it."

~ ♪ ~

Jake sat on the leather couch with Colleen and Nola. He'd hoped after the fire inspector left the two detectives would hit the road too. Instead, they sat in the adjacent chairs while Gramps sat on the love seat across from the couch.

Colleen was digging into a vat of ice cream, moaning every time she took a bite and making Jake insane with lust. He wanted to be the one making her moan like that, just like he had last night. He could get to it, too, if all these people would leave.

"So, Mr. Miller, it seems you own a recording studio," Detective Paige stated.

Shit. Jake knew the detectives might figure it out, but he hoped it would slip through the cracks. He didn't trust them to keep it confidential. Now it was inevitable his involvement would be disclosed sooner than planned.

Gramps looked to Jake who gave him a nod.

"I do," Gramps confirmed. Jake almost smiled at the simple answer.

Gramps wasn't going to give anything more away than what was asked.

"Why?" Detective Paige asked.

"Seemed like a good investment. We have some talented young musicians recording on our label."

"Our?"

"It's a company. I have employees." Gramps matter-of-fact demeanor was perfect for this interrogation. Jake swallowed a chuckle and sat back to enjoy the show.

"Is your grandson one of them?" Taggart asked.

"Like Jake has time for that," Gramps said. "He's on tour and under contract to record an album with Southern Rebel."

"But when that obligation is finished, you plan to take over Old Red Barn Records," Taggart suggested, turning to Jake.

"I'm a musician. I plan to keep making music," Jake offered.

"Under the Old Red Barn Label?" Detective Paige asked.

Colleen gave his leg a squeeze. He didn't know if she was supporting him or encouraging him to tell the whole truth.

"Yes," he conceded because he wasn't about to lie.

"Why didn't you tell me this when I asked you?" Taggart's angst-filled voice raised Jake's hackles.

"Because I have a plan, a carefully thought out plan that includes when my involvement with Old Red Barn Records will be public knowledge. Southern Rebel isn't happy about me not signing a new contract and I don't need them stirring up trouble with my label."

"You're neck deep in trouble," Taggart said.

Jake couldn't deny that. "No one knows my affiliation with the label," he pointed out. "So whatever is going on has nothing to do with that."

The two detectives exchanged a look.

"It took our research analyst two hours," Detective Paige said.

"Right, to find out a man named Harrison Miller owns the company. Then it takes two sets of birth certificates to tie me to Harrison Miller and even then it's an assumption because beneficiary information is confidential and takes a court order." Jake knew if anyone dug hard enough they'd find his connection, but he didn't want to make it easy, hoping no one would be ambitious enough to do all that digging. He never anticipated being the person of interest in the stabbing of his opening act, or being the victim of arson.

"Why'd you lie?" Taggart asked, the judgment sharp in his tone.

"Because it has nothing to do with the investigation. Me and Gramps and Toby Tibbs are the only ones who know I'm moving to Old Red Barn. Well, and Colleen. You put it in your investigation and it becomes public record."

"Not until the investigation is done," Detective Paige said.

"I'm telling you, no one knows, so you need to find a new angle."

"Not even the executive director of JD Donovan Enterprises?" Taggart asked.

Jake shook his head. "Rebekah likes to think she knows everything about me, but I can assure you, she knows nothing about this."

"Is that because you intend to fire her?" Detective Paige asked.

Jake looked at Colleen, wondering if she'd told the detective of his plans to let Rebekah go when his contract with Southern Rebel was done. She shook her head.

"What makes you think I intend to fire her?" he asked.

"Because that's what she told me."

"What exactly did Rebekah say?" Jake demanded. She had a tendency to eavesdrop, which was why Jake took extra precautions when conducting business regarding his record label.

"She said once Colleen starts running the radio station she'll convince you Rebekah is no longer needed," Detective Paige explained.

Colleen snickered. "Of course she'd say that. She's going to put this all on me, just like she always does."

"Are you planning to fire her? Because if you are, it speaks to motive," Taggart said.

"Motive?" Jake shook his head. He didn't believe Rebekah was responsible for any of this. She could be overbearing at times, but wasn't capable of threatening people or stabbing them.

"Seems she has a lot to lose here," Detective Paige added.

"There are plenty of other musicians out there who can use someone with Rebekah's skills. She won't have any trouble finding a job," Jake explained. In fact, Owen Foster had mentioned he'd like to hire someone to take care of his business the way Rebekah took care of Jake's.

"Rebekah's been with me for six years. She's loyal and dedicated."

"Colleen, what do you think?" Leah asked.

Jake turned to Colleen, hoping for support. He didn't believe Rebekah capable of any of this. Colleen might not like her, but she couldn't believe her former roommate capable either. Her glance spoke otherwise.

"I'm sorry, Jake, but I don't trust her."

~ ♪ ~

"You owe me for this. Big time," Leah muttered.

Devon gave her a nudge. "At least it's not the middle of winter."

"First mosquito bite I get, I'm out of here and you can find your own way back to Granite Beach."

"You forget, I have the keys."

She grumbled something about stupid, jealous men and Devon took that as his cue to keep his mouth shut.

They sat in the old broken down truck near the edge of the woods watching the house as if they were at a drive-in theater with a movie was playing out in front of them. Devon had scoped out the truck earlier in the day and decided it was the perfect spot for a stake-out. He and Leah had no authority here, but even being outside his jurisdiction didn't turn off his instincts. He was worried Colleen was in danger and damn if the woman wasn't stubborn. She refused to head back to Granite Beach and Devon refused to let anything bad happen to her.

"Did you bring any popcorn?" he asked, trying to make light of the situation. Leah adamantly opposed the stake-out but was left with no choice since Devon was driving.

"I'm fresh out, sorry," she smirked and then reached into her bag for a bag of potato chips.

"And you're not going to share, are you?"

"You've been on stake-outs before. You should know better than to show up empty handed."

In truth, he wasn't hungry. Seeing Colleen with Donovan was enough to kill his appetite. Knowing what they were probably doing in that house right this very moment made him sick to his stomach. It should be Devon with her, not that pretty boy musician.

"I could be on a date," Leah sighed before crunching a chip.

"Really? With who?" She hadn't mentioned having plans, not that he'd intended this to be an overnight excursion.

"Anyone. Someone. This blows."

"The stake-out or not having a date?" Devon dared to ask.

"Both. I work too much. Most of the time it doesn't bother me, but then you see normal people together living their normal lives getting some normal nooky. I haven't had nooky in forever."

"We might be crossing the line of information you're supposed to share with your partner," he said, not at all comfortable with Leah's sex life, or the lack of one, or the thought of anyone, specifically Colleen, getting nooky.

"You make me do a stake-out in Northern Vermont on a Saturday night, you get to listen to me whine about being lonely."

"Fair enough," he mumbled even though he still wasn't comfortable with the topic.

"What are you hoping to see tonight?" she asked. "Because I bet the only thing going on in that house is some nooky."

He didn't need that reminder. "I don't know. Something was off all day and I couldn't put my finger on it."

"Your Spidey sense was tingling?" she jested.

"Something like that." It was still bugging him, yet everything was quiet. Maybe it was the calm before the storm.

"You think your girl might have contrived all this to land a dream job managing a big country star's Internet radio station?" Leah suggested.

"Colleen? No. She doesn't have a manipulative bone in her body." Now Rebekah, on the other hand, well, he could believe her capable of masterminding this whole farce. Devon however, wasn't convinced she would stoop to criminal behavior. If she wanted to manage the Internet radio station, which Leah had shed some light on after questioning Ms. Charles, why would she want the barn burned to ashes?

♪ Chapter 22 ♪

From Viper:

Pigs grazing at farm. Barking up wrong tree.

To Viper:

Hit the beach. Put eyes there.

♪ Chapter 23 ♪

COLLEEN WAS completely wired and totally tired all at the same time. She had made dinner for Jake and Gramps and then they'd had a proper visit where the three of them tossed around ideas for rebuilding the barn. Gramps said he would get the area cleaned up and all the rubble removed as soon as the insurance company would allow.

After Gramps left, Colleen washed the dishes and scrubbed the granite counters more than they needed while Jake took Nola out. Now she had nothing to do.

Nola came running in from the back door, circling Colleen and wagging her tail as though she'd been gone for hours.

"How's my girl?" Colleen cooed, giving Nola a scratch behind the ears.

"You say she's not a runner, but I'll tell you, once she decides to come in, she sure makes a run for it."

"It's the big open space. She's not used to it." Granite Beach wasn't a city by any means, but it was crowded and there weren't a lot of open areas like what the farm had to offer. Nola was going to love it here.

"Jake?" Colleen asked, realizing they hadn't broached the subject of living arrangements. "What's going to happen when I start with the station? Will I be living here?"

"I was hoping you would. I know you love living on the ocean, but I've got shares in a private island, so we can spend as much time there as we want." He stepped up to her, pulling her into his arms and making her feel all warm and gooey. "You can have your own room if you're more comfortable that way, but I was hoping you'd move in with me."

She did love the ocean, but she'd grown up in northern New Hampshire, in the heart of the White Mountains. While she wasn't a fan of winters, she did miss the beauty and tranquility of the mountains from time to time.

Things were moving so fast, but then they'd kept their feelings on the back-burner for the better part of a decade, so maybe they were just catching up. "You'll be here full-time? Not in Nashville?"

"This is where I'll be except when I'm on the road. Even then, I'm going to cut the tour schedule back to only four or five months every other year. I can't keep burning the candle at both ends."

Jake's tour schedule was about eight months a year, giving him only a few months to produce a new album every year. It was one of the things that had been keeping him from recording his own music. When he got to the recording studio, they had songs they considered marketable all demo'd and ready for him to choose and record.

"Are you okay? Is this moving too fast?" he asked, cupping her face, his thumb sending erotic sparks through her as it caressed her cheek.

"It's not too fast. I want to move in with you. It was just a bit of a crazy day," she admitted, relaxing under his touch.

"Are you still upset about what Paul said?"

"No," she scoffed, stepping away from him. She went back to scrubbing the sparkling counter. She had known Paul would say something because that was the kind of ass-hole he was, and she'd thought she was prepared. She'd thought wrong.

Jake put his hand on hers, stopping the incessant cleaning. "He can't hurt us. What happened doesn't matter."

She wished that were true, but Paul had hurt her. His hateful words cut deep and the wound still oozed. Colleen reminded herself she had no regrets. Jake had gotten his record deal and she had escaped the dark cloud of that decision and earned the morning show at The Wave.

"I'm glad you hit him," she admitted. "You know there are going to be repercussions."

"I don't care. I'll deal with it. He needs to know he can't say things like that and get away with it."

Jake had always been on her side. It was one of the reasons she had always loved him. She tossed the dishcloth in the sink and wrapped her arms around his waist. The loud thump of his heart against her ear pushed aside the anxiety.

"It's been a long day. How about we get in the shower?" he suggested.

God, yes. Wash away this day and replace it with a memory that was worth holding on to.

He took her hand and led her up the stairs, through the bedroom, and into the large, exquisite bathroom.

"I didn't get to undress you last night," he said, smoothing his hand over her t-shirt. As he grazed her breast, it shot a jolt of awareness all the way through her.

He gripped the hem of the shirt and practically ripped it over her head. With the same enthusiasm, he opened her jeans and pushed them down, leaving her standing there in her bra and panties.

"You are a vision," he said. "An inspiration."

"Do I get to undress you now?" she asked, stepping closer.

"No time," he said, pulling his wallet out of his pocket and retrieving a condom that he placed in her hand. Then with lightning speed, he tugged his shirt over his head with one hand and shed his pants.

Naked.

He was naked and a glorious sight.

"I'd say you're overdressed now," he said, stepping up to her. She ran a hand over his chest as he reached behind her and deftly released her bra. She shrugged out of it and he was quick to push her panties over her hips.

"So beautiful," he uttered before his mouth claimed hers.

All day, the kisses they'd stolen here and there had been sweet and affectionate, but now there was a demand in the kiss, a desperation that was contagious. Jake backed her up, hitting a button that turned the water on for all five shower heads.

With shaking hands, Colleen tore the wrapper open and rolled it over his thick length. Jake lifted one of her legs so her foot rested on a narrow lip she hadn't noticed before, his hand moving between her legs and teasing the very core of her.

She was wet — not from the water — and eager. Last night he had taken his time, making Colleen feel loved and cherished. Now in his haste, he made her feel like a woman, desired and needed.

With a loud grunt that echoed off the tiled walls, he pushed inside her. It felt so good to be with Jake like this, to no longer mask her desire. The tile was cold on her back but the heat from his body pressed against hers and hot water raining over them made her indifferent to the hard wall behind her. She lifted her leg around his hip to take more of him and was rewarded with a rumbly moan from him.

Next thing she knew he lifted her other leg. She locked her ankles together and clung to him, the hair of his chest scraping against her nipples as he continued to push inside her.

It was fast and hard and it stole Colleen's breath. She wanted more, more, wanted to be closer even though they were as close as two people could be. She rocked her hips and arched her back and the sensation of feeling him deeper made her toes curl.

With one hand on her breast doing delicious things to her nipple and the other gripping her ass, Colleen's entire body grew delirious with lust.

"Jake," she sighed as he kissed that magic spot right under her earlobe.

"I know," he whispered across her ear.

She'd never felt so connected to someone. It was amazing, freeing, as if she'd been locked in a cage her whole life and someone had broken the lock and she was free to be herself.

"I love you," she proclaimed. She'd never been one to get lost in the throes of passion, but this was Jake, the man she'd loved for as long as she could remember. She embraced the free fall, let herself feel, enjoy, rejoice in everything Jake offered.

~ ♪ ~

It was the best shower he'd ever had and their desperation for each other had continued once they made it to the bed. Colleen had drifted off a while ago, but Jake was too wired to sleep. Holding her like this was enough to make a man go insane. Her skin was soft, her body warm, and Jake was desperate to make love to her again.

"Coll," he whispered across her ear. He caressed her arm, up and down, hoping the subtle touch would wake her, but she only stirred. Moving up her arm once more, his fingers traced a path over her shoulder and across her chest. She sighed, still asleep but enjoying his touch. Her breasts were so soft and he couldn't resist the urge to cup one, to feel the heaviness of her awakening arousal in his hand.

"Coll," he said again, his middle finger brushing her nipple. God, even asleep she was so responsive. He wondered if she was wet already, or still.

He kissed her shoulder as his hand moved south. His erection was already aching for her, pressed against her butt. If he didn't need a condom, he could push inside her now. When his hand moved between her legs and he found she was wet, he lost it. He had to have her.

"Coll, baby," he said this time, not whispering. He rolled her onto her stomach, going with her so he could reach a condom on the nightstand. He knew the moment she woke up because her relaxed body stiffened beneath him.

She started wriggling. "Relax, baby," he said. "This will feel good, I promise."

She sucked in a deep breath and jerked her body. "Get off me," she demanded. Her voice wasn't playful. No, she sounded terrified.

"Coll, what's wrong?" he asked, rolling off her.

She bolted out of bed, turning the light on. Her eyes were wide, glazed with fear, her breaths erratic.

"Colleen, what's wrong?" he asked again. She looked at him and he realized her whole body was shaking.

She ran out of the room. Jake grabbed a pair of jeans out of his suitcase and chased after her as he tried to get them on. The light in her room was on and he went in to find her digging a shirt out of her suitcase.

"Colleen, baby, talk to me," he said, trying to keep his voice calm even though he was anything but. He had no idea what had happened or why she was so terrified. Had she been having a nightmare? "It was just a dream."

She shook her head wildly and stormed past him. She hit the switch at the top of the stairs to turn on the light there, running down the stairs. Jake followed, seeing the house illuminate as she ran from room to room turning lights on.

~ ♪ ~

"We've got some action at the house," Leah said.

Devon watched the house light up systematically. "Shit," he said, placing the iPad on the seat next to him and bolting out of the truck.

"What are you thinking?" Leah asked, moving in beside him as he ran toward the house.

"Something spooked Colleen," he said, drawing his gun.

"She's done this before?" Leah asked.

"Yeah," Devon confirmed, remembering the night she'd fallen asleep in his arms. She'd been relaxed, all soft, warm woman. He'd started touching her, trying to rouse her so they could make love again, only when she woke up, she panicked. She'd run around the house, turning on every light and grabbing her gun. It had taken him almost an hour to calm her down.

The door was locked when they got to it. Devon stepped back and pointed his gun at where the deadbolt was engaged.

Leah put her hand on his arm. "Let's not do anything drastic. Try knocking first."

Devon banged on the door even though he'd have preferred to knock it down. He could see movement behind the door's tempered glass, but no one opened the door. He banged again.

"What the hell?" Donovan said when he flung the door open. "I thought you left."

"What's going on?" Leah asked.

"Nothing. You need to go." He made to close the door, but Devon pushed through.

"You son ... of a bitch," Colleen panted. Her erratic breathing was a sure sign she was in the middle of a panic attack. "Where's my magazine?"

Like he was going to give her ammunition now. "What happened, Coll?" He wasn't sure he wanted to know given she was dressed in a t-shirt and nothing else as far as he could tell.

"I ... want ... my ammo."

"You need to breathe," he said. He turned to Donovan. "What the hell did you do to her?"

"I," he stammered, "I don't know. We were just, she was sleeping and ... shit."

"Colleen, come on, honey, deep breaths," Devon said, hoping to ease her out of the panic.

She shot him a dirty look. It wasn't the first one he'd ever been the recipient of. Knowing Colleen, it wouldn't be the last.

"I'm not giving the ammo back, so you may as well focus on your breathing."

Leah got her a glass of water and Colleen took it. Donovan leaned against the counter on the opposite side of the room, keeping his eye on Colleen, guilt bleeding off him as if he had an open wound. Devon didn't know what had happened, and even though he wanted to kill the guy, he couldn't help but feel bad, having been in the same shoes.

"You alright?" Devon asked after her breathing slowed to normal.

She was on her second glass of water.

"Fine," she barked before turning to Donovan, her expression softening. "Jake, you didn't do anything wrong. I'm sorry."

"I don't want you to be sorry, Coll. I want you to tell me what happened."

"You just surprised me, that's all."

"Oh, for the love of ... she has post-traumatic stress," Leah burst out.

Devon couldn't believe she said it and based on Colleen's expression, she couldn't believe it either — and she wasn't happy about it.

"Post-traumatic stress?" Donovan asked. "From what?"

"Nothing," Colleen growled, turning that dirty look on Leah.

"She was attacked in college and again about a year ago," Leah finished.

Donovan looked as stunned as Colleen at Leah's revelation. Devon wasn't sure what his partner was playing at. Leah was a methodical detective. She wouldn't just throw this information out there for no reason, but damned if he knew what she was up to.

"What? When? Coll, is that true?"

Colleen walked right up to Leah. Standing nose to nose, she looked like she was going to burst with anger. "Get. Out," Colleen snarled.

"You can thank me later," Leah said before she walked out of the house.

~ ♪ ~

Colleen ran upstairs to the room Jake had given her when they first arrived. She had yet to sleep in it but now she was grateful she hadn't moved her suitcase over to his room. She pulled on underwear and the shorts she wore to bed, trying to ignore the humiliation of standing in Jake's kitchen with nothing but a t-shirt. It was long enough that it didn't give away her secrets, but that didn't seem to ease the embarrassment.

Maybe the humiliation had nothing to do with underwear and everything to do with the panic attack. Again.

Right, because it had nothing to do with Detective Paige's news flash.

In a single day, all of her secrets had been broadcast. It was bad enough Jake knew she'd slept with Paul to get him to play Jake's demo on air. Paul's remark only poured salt on the wound. Having Detective Paige lay it all out, Colleen may as well have had her heart cut out.

The door handle rattled, but she had locked it because she couldn't face Jake right now. "Let me in, Coll," he pleaded.

She stood at the foot of the queen size bed that divided the room in half, looking at the door, praying he didn't have a key or if he did, he wouldn't use it. She never wanted him to know she was broken. Now that he knew, he would want details and with details, he would blame himself. Colleen had to live with the shame of what had happened. She didn't want Jake to live with it since he had done nothing wrong.

She looked at the clock. It was after midnight. "Let's just get some sleep," she said.

"I'm not going to be able to sleep and my best guess is you won't either."

The sting of tears caused her to close her eyes in an effort to fight them off, but the wet drops streamed down her cheeks. She focused on breathing again. If she could just breathe, she wouldn't cry and if she didn't cry, maybe all of this would go away.

But it wouldn't go away. It had been eight years and she still struggled with the aftermath. Post-traumatic stress, Detective Paige had called it. Colleen never thought of it that way. She had lost a piece of herself that night when Spencer Mardin attacked her. For all her trying, she'd never gotten it back.

Colleen padded across the room, the plush carpet soft under her feet. Resting her head against the door, she wished it hadn't come to this. All these years, she had kept the secrets from Jake. It had been easier with him not knowing. Now that he knew, she somehow didn't feel worthy of his friendship or his love. She certainly didn't want to be his charity case.

After turning the lock, Colleen moved to the other side of the bed. She couldn't hide from him forever, but maybe he had given up.

She knew that wasn't the case when she heard the swoosh of the carpet as the door slid against it.

"Coll, look at me," he said from right behind her.

She brushed the tears away and took a deep breath as she faced Jake. The sadness in his eyes had her choking back a sob.

"Come here, baby," he said, pulling her into his arms. He stroked her hair with one hand, the other splayed with a firm hold at the center of her back. "Let it go," he whispered.

With the side of her face planted against his chest, she cried and sobbed until her chest ached and her eyes felt like they'd been washed out with a scouring pad.

Colleen backed away, embarrassed but feeling as though some burden had been lifted. "I need to wash my face," she said, "and I've made a mess of your shirt."

Jake tugged the shirt over his head and stuffed his hand inside before wiping Colleen's face. She laughed at the gesture.

"I don't care about the shirt," he said. "I do care about you."

Falling onto the bed, Colleen shook her head. "I didn't want you to know, not about any of it."

Jake sat next to her, the mattress sinking under his weight, gravity making her lean against him. "Why?" The simple question overflowed with confusion, his brow furrowed in surprise and his voice just a whisper.

"You knowing doesn't change anything."

"This is why you carry a gun, isn't it?"

She nodded. It was a year and a half ago, after a woman in Granite Beach was attacked, when Colleen bought the gun. Still new to town, she didn't know a lot of people and lived alone except for Nola who wasn't much of a watchdog. It seemed a smart move and Colleen felt safer for having it and knowing how to use it.

"I'd like you to tell me what happened," he said, "but I understand if you don't want to talk about it."

He was sweet and while it was tempting not to tell him anything, it would eat at him. Jake was detail oriented. He liked to know everything. When he was left in the dark, it made him broody.

Jake rested his hand on her knee. She wove her fingers through his for a little extra courage.

"The night we kissed in the campus center ..." she started.

His fingers gave hers a quick squeeze. "That was the best night of my life ... well, until last night."

"Me too, at least until I walked back to my dorm," she admitted.

His entire body stiffened next to hers. "Shit, Coll. You didn't."

She squeezed his fingers this time, her other hand caressing the top of his hand. "I know it was stupid, but the path was well lit and I didn't want to wait for the shuttle. I wanted to get to the club as soon as I could and see you again."

She'd been naive to think she was safe, but after that kiss, she hadn't been thinking straight.

"Tell me," he encouraged when she couldn't seem to find the words to continue.

"I never saw him, he was hiding in the shadows. No one else was around. He grabbed me from behind and dragged me behind a building. He had me pinned face down. That's why I freaked when you woke me up. I've never gotten over that."

"I never should have left you. Dammit. I should have made sure you got back to your dorm before I headed to the club."

"Stop it," she said, releasing his hand and pushing off the bed to face him. "This is why I didn't want you to know. It's not your fault, not your responsibility. I made a stupid decision. I'm the one to blame."

"No," Jake growled, standing and gripping her arms. "The son of a bitch who attacked you is to blame. Dammit, Coll, I'm sorry. That never should have happened to you, or anyone."

Broken Strings

Colleen cupped his cheek, brushing her thumb over the light stubble. "I got away. He didn't rape me."

"Thank God," he whispered, pulling her against his chest. "Was it the same son of a bitch who attacked Rebekah and those other girls?"

She nodded against his chest. "I was the first," she admitted.

"That's why you didn't want to be with me," he sighed.

She nodded again. "It messed me up and I didn't want you to know because I knew you'd blame yourself."

"I loved you, Coll. I was supposed to keep you safe. I'm not doing a very good job of that now, either."

"I'm fine. I panic sometimes, but …" she trailed off, not sure what else she could say that wouldn't be a total lie.

"What about the other attack?" he asked. "Detective Paige said you were attacked a year ago."

"I was doing a remote broadcast, a grand opening of a new music store in the mall. When it was done, I spent some time in the station editing clips. It was late, dark when I left to go home."

She stopped the attacker from getting the upper hand. "He caught me by surprise in the parking lot, but I fought him off long enough to pull my gun and call 911. He must have seen me shaking because he ran off." Colleen couldn't shoot him, but after that, she bought a second gun for easy access at home.

"Jesus, Coll," he muttered, pulling her into his arms. She indulged in his warmth and strength long enough to push the panic away.

Colleen stepped back and looked at him, devastated by the sadness on his face. "Nothing changes," she demanded. "No sadness, no guilt."

Jake nodded but that wasn't enough.

"No looking back," she reminded him. "Say it, Jake."

He cupped her face and kissed her before the sadness disappeared from his face. With a firm nod, he said, "No looking back."

♪ Chapter 24 ♪

From Viper:

Eyes r open. Check ur app.

To Viper:

Can see everything.

♪ Chapter 25 ♪

AFTER COLLEEN left for work early Wednesday morning, Jake sat on the couch in her living room, missing her as much as he missed the farm. It was good to be away from all the destruction, but Jake was ready to settle down and the farm was home.

Maybe Rebekah was right. Maybe he was hiding out at Colleen's. It was a good place to hide and there was no one else he'd want to be hiding with.

The thing was, Colleen wasn't so good at hiding. She was good at keeping secrets, damn good, and that pissed Jake off. He was trying to be understanding, to not look back as he'd promised, but her secrets weighed on him.

As soon as they'd arrived in Granite Beach Sunday night, it was business as usual and had been for the last two days. Jake had been giving her space, sleeping in the guest room because he didn't want to spook her again. She hadn't invited him back to her bed.

Every morning she went to work with Nola, leaving him to hide out and replay their conversation over and over in his mind. The attack in college, how she'd come to sleep with Paul, the attack a year ago.

It was all too much.

He should have been there. Jake had always put his music first and he thought it was okay because Colleen let him. Now he knew it wasn't okay. He should have been there, walking her home, not letting her know how desperate he was for a record deal, just being with her. She had always been there for him but he'd never been there for her.

That was over.

Jake had never been good at relationships because he didn't want to be good at them. Colleen was the one exception. He'd never felt for anyone what he felt for her. She'd always been the one for him. *Always*. He may not know what he was doing, but he was determined to prove to her he was a man worth sticking with.

How to prove it was the challenge. He'd failed her so far.

His first instinct was to write her a song, but he'd been doing that for a decade and it hadn't gotten him anywhere. He needed a new approach.

~ ♪ ~

The look on Seager's face warned Colleen of doom. She noticed the newspaper rolled in his fist, the tense line of his jaw, the sadness in his eyes. It made Colleen sick to her stomach with dread.

"I'm sorry, but I thought you should see this sooner rather than later. Everyone's been advised not to broadcast anything about it and all inquiries are being diverted to Val's office."

Val was the station manager and their boss. She was a force to be reckoned with, a woman you wanted on your side. Colleen just hoped she wouldn't let her boss down.

Colleen took the paper. It was a tabloid — joy of all joys — and there was a grainy picture of her and Jake on the front page. The headline read "Playboy Pimps Out Girlfriend for Record Deal."

"Shit," Colleen grumbled.

"Val's calling the station's lawyer to see if we can take any legal action."

Oh, God, this was like an avalanche picking up speed and destroying everything in its path.

"When you're done reading, Val wants to see you," Kyle said.

"Is she pissed?" Colleen asked.

"Concerned. Chin up, CC," he encouraged, giving her shoulder a pat. "Let me know if you need anything."

Kyle left her in peace to read the article in all its graphic and frighteningly accurate detail.

How, no, *who* the hell had sold the story?

Rebekah was the obvious choice, maybe too obvious. She'd have no problem making Colleen look bad and it would give her an opportunity to clean up what she would refer to as Jake's mess.

But there were too many details. Unless Rebekah had an in depth conversation with Paul or Jake, there's no way she could have known all this.

That left Paul. He had nothing to lose. Everyone already knew he was a sleaze bag and he didn't seem to care. With Jake not signing a new contract, Paul would want to take Jake down any way he could.

Would Jake's fans care? Probably not. He already had the playboy reputation. It would be no surprise that he and Colleen were sleeping together.

So, the only one who was going to suffer in this was Colleen. Was Val going to fire her, or ask her to resign to save the radio station from having to deal with the aftermath?

She guessed that's why Val wanted to see her. No one wanted a sell out on the air during the most listened to airtime of the day.

Colleen folded the paper and headed down the hall. Val's office was at the end and it felt like walking a long, lonely mall. Colleen imagined a green line and everyone whispering "dead woman walking" as she passed by offices.

Val's door was open and she glanced over the dark rim glasses as Colleen stopped at the door.

"Close the door," she commanded and Colleen did, not saying a word. "I think that shirt's perfect given today's doings."

Colleen got dressed in the dark and grabbed the t-shirt that was on top. She looked down to find *Hi, don't care. Thanks.* in white block letters on black cotton. She supposed it was perfect.

She sat in the chair opposite Val and Nola sat next to her, the perfect, always loyal companion. Colleen knew for sure she would lose her mind if she didn't have such a loyal friend. Actually, she had two, because Jake was just as loyal and protective as Nola. "I'm sorry about this," she offered because she truly was. Colleen loved her job and the radio station and didn't want to see it suffer because of the bad decisions she had made in the past.

"No need to apologize. If this is true, it happened long before you came to work here and your work here is excellent, so these allegations about sleeping your way to the morning show are unwarranted."

"Thanks," Colleen said, unsure what else to add.

"I talked to our lawyer and since the article doesn't defame the station, there's no legal action we can take from that angle, but if this is slander, the station will support you if you want to pursue a lawsuit."

Colleen appreciated that Val didn't come right out and ask if the story was true. It meant Colleen didn't have to admit to anything. Unfortunately, the article didn't say anything that wasn't true, so she had no grounds for a lawsuit.

"I'd just prefer to ride it out and let it fade when the next celebrity scandal hits the front page. I understand if you need me to resign."

"At this point, no, but I'm not going to lie and say it's not something we would consider in the future. I think if you resigned now, it would only fuel the scandal. With any luck, it'll be history pretty quick. What concerns me is the timing. JD Donovan postpones five shows on his tour, shows up at your house, your tires were slashed, and now this. Is it all a coincidence?"

Colleen sighed. "No. Margot Potter was stabbed after the show at Red Rocks. She was receiving threatening text messages leading up to that. That's why they rescheduled the five shows. I started receiving messages after Jake arrived at my place. We went to his farm last weekend and someone burned down the red barn he'd converted into a recording studio. Everything is under investigation."

"Are you in danger?" Val asked.

"I don't know. I'm not sure if I'm being targeted because Jake is here or because we're friends."

"Do the police have any leads?"

Colleen shook her head. "Not that I know of, but I haven't talked to Devon in a few days."

"Devon?"

"Detective Taggart. He and Detective Leah Paige are investigating things from here. I think they are also working with the investigators in Colorado and Vermont."

Val shook her head and tapped her pen on the desk as she stared at a copy of the tabloid. "You're not fired, let me be clear on that, but I think it would be best for you and the station if you took some time off until this is all sorted."

"I don't want to hide," Colleen objected. Wasn't that empowering whomever was doing this? She didn't want to give him that kind of power.

"I'm not asking you to, but all of this is going to generate a lot of inquiries to the station and there's too big of a risk that a hostile listener will call in or Tweet or post on Facebook while you're on the air."

Colleen shook her head. "They'll do that whether I'm here or not. I think we should just operate as usual, like none of this matters. If I suddenly disappear off the air, that's going to generate even more inquiries."

"How long is JD visiting you?"

"Through the weekend. He'll head to Detroit on Monday for his Wednesday show."

"Take the week. Spend time with your friend. Lay low for safety's sake. I'll write it off as comp time so you don't have to use vacation."

"Val—" she pleaded, but she could tell there was no negotiating. Her boss had made a command decision and Colleen had no choice but to take the rest of the week off.

"We'll see you Tuesday," Val said, dismissing Colleen.

~ ♪ ~

There were days when Colleen wished Nola was a runner so the two of them could take off down the boardwalk together. Instead, she had to go home and face Jake who would probably insist on joining her.

He had backed off since the incident three nights ago and she wasn't sure if she was grateful or horrified.

This was exactly why she didn't want him to know. Things were different now, he was different. No, Jake backing off wasn't good. She wanted things to be the way they were before she freaked out on him.

She plastered on a smile and headed up the porch steps. The door was locked. Good. He was taking personal security seriously for a change. She was disappointed not to hear him playing his guitar, though. It was comforting to know he could turn to his music no matter what. He hadn't picked up the guitar since they'd been back. She knew this because it was still in its case instead of the stand he stood it in when he was writing.

She had done this to him, taken away his muse.

He was in the kitchen peeling an orange when she walked in. His smile was encouraging, lightening her heart.

"Hi," she said, smiling back at him.

"Hi." He dropped the orange on the island and came toward her as though he was a man on a mission. Then he kissed her, not a chaste kiss like the ones he'd planted on her cheek the last couple days, but a *tongue in her mouth make the butterflies in her stomach dance* kind of kiss. She dropped her bag and wrapped her arms around him and he held her tighter.

She felt like warm, gooey butter when he let her go.

"I missed you," he said, that smile making his eyes sparkle. There was mischief there, mixed with a healthy dose of desire.

"I see that. I missed you, too." And not just today. She had missed this Jake, the man she loved, for the past couple days.

"How was your day?" he asked.

"Better now," she said, hoping to forget about the tabloid and just move forward.

He kissed her again, a long, slow dance of their mouths. One hand cupped her face, but he didn't touch her anywhere else. It made her insane with want.

"Can I talk you out of your run today?"

Tempting, but Colleen knew if they ended up in bed right now, she'd be a puddle of satisfied goo the rest of the day.

"I have the rest of the week off, so no, you can't talk me out of it, but you can join me."

"You going to let me set the pace?" he asked.

Colleen laughed. "I'm going to whoop your ass into shape."

Jake groaned as he turned and headed down the hall. "I'm in fine shape," he countered.

"You look fine." Colleen smacked his very fine butt and followed. "But you need to trade in that treadmill for some real cardio. There's nothing like an actual run."

They parted ways at the end of the hall, Jake going into the guest room, Colleen going into her room.

It was a few minutes later when they met in the kitchen. Colleen attached Tania to her waistband and secured her running pack around her waist.

"You don't really think you need your gun, do you?" Just like Devon, Jake didn't like that she carried but she'd been doing it for so long now, she couldn't imagine not having the pistol within reach.

"Luck favors the prepared," she shrugged and headed to the front door.

She jogged to the end of her street before stopping to stretch her warmed up muscles. Jake mimicked whatever she did. When she felt good and loose, she asked if he was ready. He nodded and they took off toward the boardwalk. She didn't leave him in the dust this time, partly because the memory of the last time they'd run down here was inching its way forward in her mind. She also liked running beside him. She'd never had a running partner and there was something comforting about having a strong body next to hers. Maybe she didn't need the gun after all.

"So," she started because it was safer to have this conversation while they were moving and Jake was out of breath. "Do you still want me to manage the radio station?"

Jake shot her a look. "Are you kidding? Of course I do. Why would you think otherwise?"

Colleen shrugged. "Things have just been weird the last few days."

"I know. I'm sorry. I wanted to give you some space. I thought you needed it after everything that happened this weekend."

"I get that," she said, and she supposed she did need it. "I can't promise I won't ever freak out like that again. It's not something I have any control over."

"That's okay. Now that I know what happened, I can try not to molest you while you're sleeping." His tone was light and Colleen laughed.

"It's being pinned down," she admitted. The same thing had happened when Devon tried to rouse her awake. She'd been lying on her stomach and when she woke up with him on top of her, her brain switched into survival mode. "When Spencer Mardin pinned me to the ground, I head-butted him and gave myself a concussion. It stunned him enough that I was able to get away."

"I'm sorry I wasn't there," he said, too much sympathy in his voice.

Colleen stopped and crossed her arms as he stopped and faced her. "I don't want you to be sorry, Jake. You didn't do anything wrong. I made the decision to walk back to the dorm that night. It was stupid and I accept full responsibility for it. If we are going to move forward, you have to accept that this isn't about you. You're not at fault."

"I know, but I just wish I'd been there. I'm never going to let anything like that happen to you again. You have my word."

She touched his face and smiled. "You're sweet and noble, but I can take care of myself."

"And you're stubborn as a mule."

She dropped her hand and stepped off, "I guess that beats being called a jackass," she quipped, picking up her pace. It was time to make him sweat.

~ ♪ ~

Jake was grateful for the cool-down walk up her street because if he had to run another ten yards, he was going to collapse. He didn't realize how much more endurance was required to run on actual streets than on the treadmill. Colleen had barely broken a sweat.

Nola greeted them as they entered the house, doing a vertical hop before spinning in circles of excitement. Colleen crouched to give the dog a kiss and a hug before heading to the kitchen.

She offered him the first glass of ice water and he shamelessly took it. He downed all the water and refilled as she sipped hers.

"If we shower together, we can save water," he suggested, waggling his eyebrows.

"Us showering together means a whole lot of water is going to get wasted," she said, stepping up to him. "I'm okay with that."

He put his water on the island and slid his hand behind her neck, pulling her to him. Every lust-filled instinct had him screaming to take her right there, but he knew he had to ease back into it. He'd scared the hell out of her the last time he'd tried to make love to her. No way did he want to do that again, so he kept the kiss slow and sensual instead of manic and needy.

But damn, he was needy. He was already painfully rock hard.

"Let's get in the shower," she said, pulling away. "You stink."

At least she was laughing. He stripped on his way to the shower and turned on the water before she was undressed. He enjoyed the show of her peeling her fitted t-shirt over her head to reveal a form-fitting sports bra. She was fit, not too muscular with curves in all the right places. The bra compressed her breasts, but when she peeled it off, he was rewarded with the sight of her soft breasts tipped with very erect nipples.

"Good lord, you're a sight," he said.

She put her gun on the sink counter and shed her spandex shorts and panties in one firm push over her hips.

Jake soaped up, wanting to get rid of his after-run odor as quickly as possible. He had plans for her, plans he hoped would get her past the trauma of those attacks. Colleen released her hair from the band and joined him in the shower.

"You going to share the soap?" she asked.

"I like you dirty," he said.

"You ain't seen nothing yet, country boy," she said pushing him against the shower wall and pressing her body to his.

The soap slid from his hands as Colleen's mouth landed on his. Her breasts pressed against his ribs, her stomach against his erection and Jake was in heaven. His slippery hands slid around her back and down the curve of her butt. She moaned against his mouth, so he kept his hands there, pulling her more firmly against him.

She felt so good, so right, just as she had that first night at the farm and the second night when he'd taken her in the shower. He wanted that again, but he realized he hadn't grabbed a condom.

"We need to slow down," he said after pulling away from her perfect mouth.

"No," she said, kissing his jaw, his neck, nipping his ear. He was losing his mind.

She lowered off her tiptoes, kissing a seductive trail down his body, her thumbs brushing across his nipples as she kissed his chest. As she moved lower, her lips and tongue leaving him delirious as she zig-zagged across his abs, he realized where she was going.

Dirty, he thought.

"Coll," he sighed, looking down to find her crouched in front of him. The warm water of the shower rained over them.

She smiled up at him as her hand circled around his length, making his hips jerk forward. "You'll like this, I promise."

When her mouth closed around him, Jake saw stars. His last coherent thought was that it was like being in the cockpit of the

Millennium Falcon when they hit light speed.

♪ Chapter 26 ♪

To Viper:

Time to up the stakes. Same as before.

From Viper:

Stab u lata.

♪ Chapter 27 ♪

"I HAVE an idea," Jake said after they dried off and fell onto her bed in a tangle of arms and legs.

"This should be interesting," she quipped, loving that she'd reduced him to a grunting, incoherent mass of sexy and satisfied man in the shower.

He caressed her cheek. "Memories of your trauma are triggered when you're pinned down," he said. She didn't like where this conversation was going. "What if we start with a massage? You face down, it's daylight, you're wide awake. I'll talk to you the whole time and we can position the mirror so you can see me without putting a kink in your neck."

"A mirror?" She raised her brow. Sounded like some erotic fantasy.

He shrugged but the smirk on his face gave him away. "I'll admit the mirror is for me too. I like the idea of you watching what I do to you."

"I don't know about this," she said, remembering how she'd lost it Saturday night and the time she'd lost it with Devon. Could she get through this? Jake was sweet for wanting to try, but she wasn't convinced it would work.

"If it goes well, we can try again in the dark."

"You don't have to coax me into making love with you, Jake. I'm game."

"I want you in every possible way and I don't ever want to scare you again." She could see the sincerity in his eyes and hear it in his voice. What happened Saturday night scared him. She wanted him to get over it, so if it was that important to him, she was willing to give it a try. Besides, it was a massage. With all the tension her body had stored up in the past week, she could use a release.

"Okay, if you want to get kinky with me, I'll let you try the massage."

"Call it kinky if you want, but I look at it as being thorough."

He was thorough, she'd learned that much about him already.

Jake pressed a quick kiss to her cheek. "I'll be right back. I bought some massage oil today."

Colleen laughed as he ran out of the room. She pictured him in the sex shop down by the boardwalk and that made her laugh even harder. He could have gotten massage oil just as easily at one of the chain drug stores in town, but the vision of him in the sex shop was too amusing to let go.

"What are you smirking at?" he asked when he came back in with the small bottle.

"Just imagining you shopping in a sex shop."

He laughed. "You are dirty. I think I'll keep you." The playfulness left his expression, his eyes speaking of one thing. "Lose the towel."

"I don't know," she said, clinging to the spot where she had it secured. "I'm shy."

"Hmmm, shy, hard to get. You're turning me on." His voice was husky and his towel now looked like a pitched tent. "I'll show you mine if you show me yours," he said.

She released the towel and even though he'd seen her naked, he sucked in a breath and licked his lips, making her feel all warm and gooey again.

"Now you," she said, wiggling her finger at the pitched tent.

He pulled a pair of shorts from behind his back and released the towel.

"Shorts?" she asked. "Going somewhere?"

"I'm going to want to violate you six ways to Saturday, so it's best if I keep this guy under wraps for a while."

She laughed and rolled onto her stomach, grateful for daylight streaming in through the sheer curtains.

"You wreck me, you know that," he said from the side of the bed. With her head turned toward him, she looked up, appreciating the fine male specimen in front of her.

Jake squatted down, stroking her still wet hair. "I love you. We can stop anytime if it gets to be too much, okay?"

"Thank you," she said.

He kissed her, a soft caress of their lips. "Turn around, I'll bring the mirror over."

Colleen swung around so her head was at the foot of the bed as Jake moved the pedestal mirror from next to her closet.

He climbed onto the bed and knelt beside her. "I'll start like this and when you're relaxed, I'll straddle your legs for a better angle."

"Okay," she said. Panic threatened, but the fact he was beside her and not pinning her down eased her worries. He poured the cold oil over her back, making her suck in a breath at the shock.

"Let me warm that up," he said, leaning across her to put the bottle on the nightstand before spreading the oil over her back.

His hands felt good, the skin not too smooth, yet not too rough. He applied the right amount of pressure as he started working her muscles. Watching him in the mirror was erotic, but as Colleen found herself drifting off, she closed her eyes.

"Don't fall asleep on me," he said in a voice that was as lulling as his gentle touch.

"I'm so relaxed," she sighed.

"Yeah? You ready for me to change positions?"

She wasn't but the whole point of this was to work through her issues. "Yeah," she said.

"So brave," he whispered, leaning down to kiss her cheek. "Do you want to open your eyes?"

She did, angling her head to face the mirror, her chin resting on her hands. His hands never stopped their firm caress as his weight shifted and he moved over her. His eyes met hers in the mirror.

"I'm okay," she said. "Keep working your magic."

He straddled her thighs, not putting any weight on her so even though his body was over hers, she didn't feel pinned. Even if she did, seeing him in the mirror, his eyes now focused on where his hands worked over her, was comforting. This was Jake. He loved her. He would never hurt her.

He continued the massage, his movements becoming more and more sensual. The neck to the small of her back path he followed soon expanded to her sides where his gentle caress teased her breasts before moving south and over her butt.

"What are you doing?" she whispered, smiling at him in the mirror.

"I told you I'm thorough. I don't want to miss a spot."

"You're driving me insane," she admitted, wishing he would touch her more.

"Yeah?" he asked, a cocky smile curving one side of his mouth. He leaned forward, bracing his hands on either side of her. Their eyes were locked in the mirror and his breath was warm on her cheek. "I want to make love to you like this."

"Yes," she whispered.

"I'm not going to hurt you, Coll. I promise."

"I know," she said. "I want you like this too." The thought was intriguing. Because of her issues, she'd only had sex in limited positions, those she considered safe. That had changed some with Devon but even with him she had never made it this far.

"I need to get a condom," he said, kissing her cheek.

"Top drawer," she said, glancing at the nightstand in the mirror.

Jake leaned back to reach inside the drawer. "What the hell?" he asked and she chuckled, knowing what he found in there.

"Are you kidding, Coll? You keep one in your nightstand, too?"

"That's Vasily," she told him, having named the Glock 9mm after the sniper in *Enemy at the Gates*. "He likes to sleep next to me."

"Tania and Vasily. That movie left a hell of an impression on you, didn't it?"

"It was the first time you kissed me. Of course it left an impression." And if only she had waited for the campus shuttle, she wouldn't have pushed him away and missed out on having him like this for the last eight years.

The memories threatened to knock down the barriers Jake had put in place with his gentle massage. She fought them back, focusing on his weight, the warmth of his body, the press of his erection. "Can you ignore the gun and get back to making love to me?"

He withdrew his hand from the drawer, a condom pinched between his fingers and slammed the drawer shut. Colleen startled at the sound, her heart starting to race.

"I'm sorry," Jake whispered. He pushed her hair aside and kissed her neck, her shoulder, her jaw. "I need you," he said, his hip lifting from her. A few seconds and several wriggles later, she felt the heat of his erection pressing against her.

"I have to put the condom on," he said, meeting her eyes again in the mirror.

She nodded and he lifted his weight. She watched in the mirror, amazed at how beautiful he was, all strength and chiseled perfection. "I'm going to touch you," he said and the rough timber of his voice made her anxious for his touch. His hand moved between her legs, his gaze focused on where he touched her and Colleen felt herself writhe against his hand.

"So perfect," he said, lowering himself. She felt a push and wasn't sure what she should do. Her legs weren't spread at all and she couldn't move them because his were planted on the outside of hers. She lifted her hips and he slid all the way in. Colleen nearly came.

Jake lowered his body again, sliding one hand under her to cup her breast, the other hand moving across her hip and under to stroke her clit.

"Oh my God, Jake," she cried out.

"I love having you like this, being inside you, my hands on you, seeing the ecstasy on your face," he said. "You're the sexiest woman I've ever known."

She turned enough to kiss him, her body falling into a frenzy of lust and desperation. She wanted — no, needed — more.

"Baby, you keep moving your hips like that and I'm going to come too soon," Jake growled.

She pressed against his hand, the glorious sensation of what he was doing there coiling like a storm cloud getting ready to unleash its power.

"I can't stop," she said, her hips pushing back as he pushed inside her, then pushing against his hand as he strummed her in a perfect rhythm.

"Come for me, Coll," he said and when she met his heated gaze in the mirror, the coil of pleasure released like a tight spring being freed.

He continued to pump into her as she cried out over and over. His own grunts turned to groans of pleasure as he leaped into the frenzy with her.

~ ♪ ~

Jake's face was buried in a mass of curly hair that smelled like the ocean. He was right where he wanted to be for the rest of his life, on her, in her, clutching her because he never wanted to let her go.

"You okay?" he asked against her neck.

"Better than okay. That was amazing. You should write a song about it."

"Words wouldn't do it justice. You're amazing, by the way."

"We're amazing," she said.

"I don't ever want to move from here," he confessed.

She laughed, and other than the sounds she made during orgasm, it was the sweetest sound in the world.

He rolled off her because he had to take care of the condom. "Stay right there," he instructed and she gave him a sassy salute.

Broken Strings

As he crossed the hall to the bathroom, he heard Nola's quiet whimper and noticed her doing circles in front of the door. When he finished in the bathroom, he found Colleen in the exact same position he had left her in.

"Either someone's here or Nola has to go out," Jake informed her.

Colleen rolled over and sat up, glancing at the clock. "You can set your clock to her, so I'm guessing someone is here."

As if to confirm that theory, three loud thumps sounded from the front of the house.

She sighed as if she knew who it was.

"Who?" he asked.

"Devon," she said.

"We could just ignore him."

"He doesn't just go away."

Jake sauntered across the hall to put on the clothes he'd worn earlier even though it was tempting to answer the door naked. That would get rid of the detective in a hurry.

Colleen had slipped on jeans and a giant t-shirt and was opening the door when Jake came out of his room.

"You need to answer your damn phone," Devon snarled as he pushed by her, Detective Paige on his heels.

"Come right in, Devon. Make yourself at home."

Jake loved her sarcasm, except when it was directed at him. He joined her in the kitchen, putting his arm around her and pulling her tight against him.

The detective picked up her bag and pulled a folded newspaper out of it before dropping the bag on the floor. "So you have seen this."

"Yeah. So what?" Colleen barked.

"We've been trying to call you and your little boyfriend here for over an hour. Rebekah Charles is in the hospital. She was stabbed this morning."

"What?" Jake demanded, crossing the room to turn on his phone. He'd turned it off when Colleen got home because he'd had an agenda and didn't want to be disturbed.

"She checked out of her hotel on D Street. After passing the alley at the back, she was grabbed and stabbed, just like Margot Potter."

"Shit," Jake groaned. He hadn't spoken to Rebekah since Sunday when she'd pissed him off. She'd texted him that she was back in Granite Beach and again yesterday stating she was heading to Detroit. He was relieved to have her out of his hair, but this, he hadn't wished this on her.

"Where were you at nine this morning?" Detective Paige asked.

"What?" Jake asked, turning to the detective. "Am I a suspect? Rebekah is my assistant. I'd never hurt her."

"Just trying to rule you out," Detective Paige said, no sympathy in her voice.

"I was here," he said.

"Alone, I'm assuming, since Colleen had just wrapped up the morning show."

"Yeah," he sighed, not missing the irony of another stabbing of another woman he was responsible for, and he had no alibi.

"Perfect," Detective Paige said as if she was amused by the situation.

"What about you, Coll?" Detective Taggart asked. "Can anyone at the station verify you were there after the show finished?"

"Of course, but, really, you think I could stab someone?" She sounded as perplexed as Jake felt.

"We witnessed what unfolded between you and Ms. Charles this weekend," Detective Paige said, playing bad cop today. "After what she said about you when I interviewed her, I'd said you have motive."

"You interviewed her?" Jake and Colleen asked in perfect harmony.

Detective Paige rolled her eyes instead of answering.

"Is Rebekah alright?" Jake asked.

"She's recovering. As with Ms. Potter, the knife didn't hit any vital organs but the cut is deep and required stitches. She's at Saint Raphael's Hospital."

This was a nightmare. "And you have no leads?" Jake demanded. Two women stabbed, Colleen's tires, the threats, the barn. It was out of control.

"We're not at liberty to discuss the case," Taggart said.

"Not at liberty? This is my life. These are my people. I am your damn case."

"Calm down," Detective Paige said, taking her turn as good cop. "What Detective Taggart means is we can't discuss any leads."

"Do you know who is responsible for this?" Taggart asked, tossing the newspaper he'd pulled from Colleen's bag on the bar next to Jake.

He picked it up to find a picture of him and Colleen on the front page. It looked like the picture was taken right in front of her house. "What the hell?" he spat, reading the headline. He looked at Colleen. "When the hell were you going to tell me about this?"

"Later," she said, then sighed. "Never."

The fury took him and he tossed the paper across the kitchen. Secrets. She was still keeping secrets. Hadn't they had a break-through? Was this how it was always going to be with them?

"I'm going to see Rebekah," he said, knocking his shoulder against Taggart's as he passed. Jake took his keys out of the red bowl on the table next to the door.

"Don't leave town," Taggart said. "We have questions for you."

"Great. You can question me after I call my lawyer." He was done playing the nice guy. Cooperating wasn't getting him anywhere and if he was going to continue to be the first guy they looked at every time something went wrong, he was going to be sure his ass was covered.

When he stepped off the porch, Colleen's voice called to him, his name a desperate plea. "Jake, don't go."

"I can't keep doing this with you," he said. "I can't handle all the secrets. Why didn't you tell me about the paper?"

"The tabloid?" she said. "That paper is a rag. Everyone knows what it prints is complete fiction."

"Not everyone, Coll. I've lived in the tabloids for the last eight years. Not all of it is fiction. Why didn't you tell me?"

"I love you and I don't want to see you hurt by something this stupid."

Jake shook his head. "You throw around phrases like I love you and best friend, but you don't show me the respect that those words deserve. I can't keep singing this song with you."

Colleen stepped back, her arms folded across her chest as she pinned him with a harsh glare. "What does that mean?"

"It means you need to stop keeping things from me." Jake shook his head, frustrated with this whole situation, with his life. It wasn't supposed to be like this. "I need to check on Rebekah," he murmured and headed for his car.

~ ♪ ~

Colleen's heart shattered as Jake walked then drove away. It wasn't supposed to be this hard. They were best friends, shouldn't that make for an easy transition to something more?

Then again, nothing was easy for her. She made bad decisions about men — always. Her track record was complete and total crap, so why should Jake be any different?

Jake always tried to take responsibility for everything even when it wasn't up to him to do so. He blamed himself for his parents dying, even though he'd only been ten at the time. They'd been hit by a drunk driver after a night out and killed instantly. Jake hadn't wanted to spend the night at his grandparents farm that night. He claimed if he hadn't been such a brat, they wouldn't have been driving out to the farm to get him and they wouldn't have been hit.

What Colleen had learned from Gramps was that they weren't even heading to the farm when they were hit. He didn't know where they were going, but they were heading south not north. Jake had conceded it wasn't his fault, but she was sure he conceded just so they wouldn't talk about it anymore and not because he accepted he wasn't responsible.

When Colleen had gotten a C on a test, Jake took responsibility for that, too, because instead of studying, she had helped him write a song. The C put her scholarship in jeopardy, but she had made the decision not to study. It wasn't Jake's fault nor was it his responsibility.

And that's why she had chosen not to tell him about being attacked in college. Not only would he blame himself, he would live with the guilt for something he wasn't responsible for.

That's also why she wasn't going to tell him about the tabloid. Yes, he might find out at some point, but she hoped it wouldn't be until after this whole situation had blown over.

She shuddered, thinking about his anger, thinking about another person being stabbed. Walking back into her house, she found Devon and Detective Paige whispering. They stopped when the door closed behind her.

"Do I need a lawyer?" Colleen asked.

"No, but we would like you to come down to the station to answer some questions," Devon said, his voice stern.

"Station? Why can't we do it here?"

"Procedure," he barked. "You know we prefer to handle formal questioning in house."

"So you can lock me in that little mirrored room and record everything I say. No thanks." She hated that room, hated knowing someone was on the other side of the glass watching her.

Devon's brow furrowed, his face twisting into an angered snarl. "Do you even get how serious this is? The best lead we have is your boyfriend. He has no alibi for any of these crimes and he has motive and opportunity." The frustration in Devon's voice was as clear as the summer sky, something she could relate to.

"Motive? What motive does Jake have for stabbing Margot and Rebekah and for burning down his own barn?"

"You left out your tires and this nifty little tell-all article," Detective Paige pointed out.

"For all I know, you're the one who blabbed that story to the tabloid since you seem to like to reveal information you have no business revealing."

Colleen wished her gun wasn't in the bathroom. What would the charge be for pulling it on two detectives who had barged uninvited into her house? She had a right to protect herself and they had no cause to be there.

"Anger. That's a new emotion I haven't seen you wear yet," the detective said.

"Enough, Leah," Devon cut in. "Come down to the station, Colleen."

"No. If you want to verify my whereabouts at ten this morning, then do your job and investigate. Maybe along the way you'll find the person who is actually committing these crimes and leave the victims alone. Now get out before I call the police."

"We are the police," Detective Paige said.

"And you barged into my home without a warrant or just cause. I know my rights." She was talking out her ass, but it had to hold some weight. She'd gotten an A in government in high school and college. Maybe she didn't have a working knowledge of the law, but she was pretty sure any cop couldn't just come into her house.

"Don't make me get a subpoena," Devon warned, but she'd heard him complain enough times about how slow that process was to recognize the empty threat.

"Go ahead, Devon. I double dog dare you." Okay, yeah, it was an adolescent comment, but that didn't make it any less satisfying.

Detective Paige laughed. Whether it was at Colleen or at Devon, she didn't know and didn't much care.

Devon stepped up to her. He had nearly a foot on her in the height department and she knew from experience how strong his body was. Alpha male oozed from his pores, but she also knew from very intimate experience what a gentle man he was. There was a time when being this close to him would set her body on fire. There had been many moments when the lusty heat between them was scorching enough to burn a city covered in the frigid air of a nor'easter blizzard. That was before his lie — well, at least before she found out about his lie. It had taken her months to get over him.

Now the only thing between them was that cold air.

"Watch your boyfriend, Colleen. He's involved in this. You can mark my words you are going to get hurt."

That cold air turned hot, her anger now raging and demanding he get out of her house and out of her life.

She had to look up to meet his indignant gaze. His anger only served to fuel hers. "You would know all about hurting me, wouldn't you?"

♪ Chapter 28 ♪

From Viper:

Pigs have no leads.

To Viper:

Time to feed them.

♪ Chapter 29 ♪

"I'M LIKING Donovan for this," Devon admitted as they headed back to the station.

"Biased much," Leah drawled. She didn't always resort to sarcasm, but she was beginning to sound a lot like Colleen and that was enough to drive him over the edge.

"He has no alibi, has motive, and had opportunity for all the crimes. I bet if we search his car we find a stash of no-contract cell phones."

"I'm liking your girl for this," Leah said, her tone so matter of fact Devon thought she was serious.

"She's a victim," he pointed out.

"They're in it together. I just haven't figured out who the mastermind is yet."

"Donovan is the mastermind and if there's a co-conspirator, it's his executive director."

Leah laughed, the same sarcastic laugh she'd let slip at Colleen's house. "The woman who was stabbed and is recovering in the hospital? Seems a little extreme to me. All Ms. Cooper has had are some nasty text messages and her tires slashed. I think she's faking the post-traumatic stress to create sympathy and keep a certain detective at her beck and call."

"I've witnessed her PTSD firsthand and I can assure you, she's not faking it." As far as being at her beck and call, Devon wished that was the case. The anger had been rolling off her in waves when they were at her house. He had to fight off the urge to shake some sense into her.

"She's sleeping with him," Leah said in that same annoying *I know everything* tone.

"We have no proof of that," he said.

"Come on, Dev. Wake up and smell the coffee. Neither of them answered their phones for two hours and they both had flushed cheeks and mussed hair when you stormed in there. Great move, by the way. Very professional."

"Right, professional, just like your outburst at the farm about Colleen having PTSD."

"She needed the nudge," Leah insisted with a shrug.

"What exactly is your problem?" he asked, wondering what he'd done to become the target of her angst.

"Your feelings for her are affecting this case. You can't think objectively and when I try to do that for you, you fight me tooth and nail. This case is challenging enough without having to fight with you, too."

He didn't hear an ounce of frustration in her voice, but Leah was good at keeping her emotions in check. He could stand to take a lesson from her.

"Let's hit the war room and check all the evidence again. Maybe the cell phone records are back," she suggested.

His phone rang and he spied the caller ID to find his brother's name. "Hey, Campbell," he said casually. "What's up bro?"

"Okay, so I get you're not alone, but that's not going to stop me from interrogating you."

"Good to hear," Devon said, glad his brother understood his code. He only ever called him 'bro' when he couldn't talk.

"I was blind copied on an email from you to you."

"That's right," Devon confirmed.

"I figured it wasn't a mistake, so I worked my magic and got you the records you want. Your email is too traceable, by the way, and if someone digs hard enough, they'll find my email was BCC'd on that message."

"Glad the dog isn't digging for that bone anymore," he said.

"You remember how to access the secure site?" Campbell asked. He was so cloak and dagger, but it helped make him a successful private investigator.

"Of course. You planning on coming home for Thanksgiving?" Devon asked, realizing how ridiculous this conversation might sound to Leah. Since she wasn't dumb, he figured he better throw something personal in there to make it less suspicious.

"Access the secure site from an Internet cafe. Don't do it from the police station or from any of your devices."

"Sorry to hear that," he said, knowing the protocols. Campbell always reminded him because Devon often took shortcuts for the sake of time.

"I'm not kidding, Devon. It's not easily traced back to me. Make sure the same is true for you since you can't use this in court."

He smiled at Leah who was studying him a little too closely. "You know, if you moved back here I could fix you up with my partner and fix that problem for you and her. I think you both could stand to get laid."

"Fuck you," they both said and Devon laughed. Campbell didn't bother to say good-bye. Devon pocketed his phone and worked up a plan to ditch Leah so he could retrieve the cell phone records his brother had hacked for him.

Her phone rang and after a brief conversation that consisted of one-syllable words, she turned to him. "Rebekah Charles is out of surgery. Let's head over there."

~ ♪ ~

Jake watched Rebekah sleep. If she had just listened to him and gone to Tennessee, this wouldn't have happened. She was so damn stubborn. He'd been here for a couple hours, first in the waiting room because she was recovering from surgery. Once she was moved to an in-patient room, they let him in, but she'd been sleeping the whole time. At least if she slept she wasn't in pain.

She made a noise and stirred. She'd done this a couple times and didn't wake up so he didn't bother to get his hopes up this time either. He wanted to talk to her, make sure she was all right, find out what she knew about who stabbed her.

He read the article in the tabloid again after finding a copy in the waiting room. Why hadn't Colleen told him about it?

More secrets. Her specialty.

"What are you doing here?" Rebekah asked, her voice scratchy and tired.

"I'm watching you sleep. Does that freak you out?" He kept the humor in his voice.

"Go away," she said.

"How are you doing, Chuck?" He hated seeing her like this. It was just like looking at Margot, but instead of dark hair, there was blonde. What was the same was the oxygen tube in her nose, the IV protruding from her hand and the constant beeps from the machines connected to her.

"I hate it when you call me that," she said.

"I know."

"I quit, by the way. You're paying all my hospital bills." He was going to anyway, just like he planned to for Margot.

"You can't hand in your resignation under the influence of anesthesia and pain meds," he joked.

"What does it matter? I'm fired anyway."

"What makes you say that?" he asked.

"I know, JD. I know everything. Colleen managing the station, you owning Old Red Barn Records. My pink slip."

How the hell could she know? He'd been careful about when and to whom he discussed his business. While he talked openly about the radio station, he had never mentioned to Rebekah that he wanted Colleen to manage it.

"Who have you told?" he growled, not at all happy with her

knowledge of his very personal business.

She smiled, but it wasn't friendly and he hoped it was the medication making her look like that.

"Dammit, Rebekah, who did you tell?"

♪ Chapter 30 ♪

From Viper:

Cold steel is under the wheel. Going to let the dog out.

To Viper:

Woof.

♪ Chapter 31 ♪

IT HAD been hours since Jake took off and Colleen was going out of her mind. She hated to leave Nola, who had been sulking all afternoon, but Jake wasn't responding to text messages or calls and she needed to find him, to talk to him. So here she was, standing at the registration desk of the hospital, trying to convince the woman on the other side that she was a close personal friend of Rebekah Charles.

"We're like sisters. That's why she's in here in Granite Beach. She came to visit." Colleen tried to sound convincing but the truth was she didn't like to lie. She was good at lies of omission, but not so good at blatant lies.

"She's in room B17," the woman instructed. "If the detectives are still there, you'll have to wait to go in."

Great. Just who she wanted to see. With any luck, Devon and Detective Paige would be gone.

The long hall was quiet, not a lot of people milling about. Colleen had to turn left to head away from the main hall and toward the patient rooms. When she arrived at B17, there was a uniformed police officer sitting outside the room and sure enough, the two detectives were inside.

She ignored the officer and what the desk attendant had said and walked in.

"Tell us again who did this to you," Devon said when he spotted Colleen.

Rebekah looked at her, something flashing in her eyes for just a moment before she plastered on her distraught facade again. "It was JD."

"She's lying," Colleen objected.

"You weren't there, CC. I was. It was JD."

"You saw him?" Colleen asked, wanting to know every detail to see just how far Rebekah was going to take the lie.

"No, he came up behind me. I recognized his voice and his cologne and he was the right height."

Colleen laughed. "Why would Jake stab you?"

"Why does he do anything? He's the most selfish, self-serving, egotistical person I've ever met," Rebekah huffed.

"Project much?" Colleen snapped.

"Go to hell, CC. Why are *you* here anyway?"

"I wanted to make sure you were all right," she said.

"Liar," Rebekah drawled.

"Well, that seems to be the theme. I'm just trying to fit in," Colleen snarled.

"Ladies," Devon cut in. "While this exchange is charming, it's not getting us anywhere. Ms. Charles, do you know where Donovan went when he left here?"

"I figured he went back to his little slut, but since she's here, I have no idea."

Colleen opened her mouth, but Devon tugged her from the room before she could retaliate. "What the hell are you doing here, Coll?" he asked after they passed all the patient rooms.

"Like I told the ice queen, I came to make sure she's all right."

"You don't even like her," he pointed out.

"That doesn't mean I wish her any harm."

"Where's Donovan?" he asked.

Colleen shrugged but didn't offer any information.

"Don't be stupid. He's been identified as the perpetrator of a crime. I have to arrest him and if you obstruct this investigation, I'll have to arrest you, too."

"Jake didn't do this. I'm sure she figured out she's out of a job when his contract is done, so she's trying to punish him."

"Coll—"

"No, Devon, that's what she does. She manipulates people."

"Coll, she identified Donovan as the man who raped her in college. She said that's why she didn't testify against Spencer Mardin."

"What? No, she's lying. Jake would never—"

"He's going to jail. The statute of limitations for rape in Massachusetts is 15 years. Add to that all the felonies he has committed in the last couple weeks and his music career is over." Devon sounded smug and that pissed Colleen off.

"Whatever happened to innocent until proven guilty?" Colleen demanded.

"We have a witness. He's guilty."

"No, you have Rebekah. You're going to end up looking like a fool, Devon."

Colleen spun around and stormed off, taking her phone out to call Jake once again. Once again, he didn't answer.

"Dammit, Jake," she murmured as she walked out of the hospital.

When she got home twenty minutes later, Colleen knew something was wrong. Nothing seemed out of order as she looked around the open space of her kitchen and living room, but something was definitely wrong.

Where was Nola?

The dog was a faithful greeter. On the rare occasions when Colleen left her at home, she sat on the back of the chair in front of the window and waited for Colleen's return. Then she'd spin in circles and whine, her very own happy dance and song, to let Colleen know how much she was loved.

Jake's car wasn't in the driveway but his guitar wasn't gone. She checked the back yard and the guest room and even her bedroom.

No Nola.

No Jake.

Had he taken her dog? Where?

She called him again, the call going to voice mail. "Please tell me you have Nola," was the message she left.

She sent a text asking the same thing.

~ ♪ ~

Now that Jake had calmed down, he figured he should replace the cell phone he'd chucked against the brick wall when he walked out of the hospital yesterday. Walking the beach in York, Maine for hours had been soothing enough, as had the sunrise, but none of it helped him figure out the mess he was in.

He hit a coffee shop first. Coffee was priority number one after being up all night. He'd been lucky enough to find a place that had a whole pile of tabloids. In addition to the one he'd seen yesterday, there was another with his picture on it.

Playboy Country Star Burns Down Barn the headline read, a picture of the fire blazing out of control taking up most of the front page with an inset picture of Jake standing in front of the rubble.

It wasn't supposed to be like this.

He wondered if Colleen had seen this one too and if she planned to tell him about it.

Probably not. She preferred to keep secrets. It was going to cause problems between them.

It was time to up the stakes.

He ordered his coffee, the barista giving him a second glance. He didn't think the baseball hat was the best disguise, which was why he wore sunglasses, but it was a little too obvious to wear those inside.

Jake didn't mind being recognized in public, but he was trying to lay low, so he didn't even offer a smile.

After his coffee was served, Jake hit the street and returned to his car. He searched for cell phone stores on his GPS app and found one not too far away. It took over two hours to get the phone set up with his old number and all the data. He sat in his car, going through the voice mails and text messages.

All from Colleen and Detective Paige.

Colleen wanted to talk and, well, shit, Nola was missing?

Jake didn't call back. He didn't pass go. He didn't collect $250. He drove straight to her house.

And lucky for him, when he pulled up, Detective Taggart's black SUV was parked out front.

Jake was walking up the steps when Colleen busted through the front door. "What the hell, Jake? Where's Nola?"

Jake raised his hands in surrender. "I don't have her."

"Did you come back yesterday? Did you leave a door open?"

Jake shook his head. "No, Coll. I went to see Rebekah and then I drove around until I hit York. I spent the night walking the beach."

"You shouldn't have come back," she whispered, tears streaming down her cheeks as Taggart and Detective Paige came up behind her.

"Jacob Donovan," Taggart said, moving around Colleen. "You are under arrest for assault and attempted murder."

"What?" Jake said, backing down the steps. "Assaulting who?"

"Rebekah Charles, for starters," Taggart said and proceeded to read Jake his rights.

"I didn't assault Rebekah," he said as Detective Paige came around with handcuffs in hand. Jake jerked his hands away.

"Ms. Charles identified you," Detective Paige said when Taggart finished his spiel.

"What?" Jake demanded. "Rebekah said I stabbed her? Why? I mean ... shit."

Dammit. Was she just messing with him or did she plan to see this through?

"Jake, she also said you were the one who raped her in college," Colleen added.

"You don't believe her, do you? She's just pissed that I was going to let her go when my contract is up. She's messing with me, Coll, you know she is."

"I know," she whispered and the tears started again.

Jake wanted to wipe them away, to take her into his arms and assure her this was all a big misunderstanding. With his hands cuffed behind his back and Detective Paige tugging his elbow, he had no choice but to go.

"I'll call my lawyer and make bail and we'll look for Nola together," he said as Taggart took his other elbow and turned him around.

Colleen gave him a subtle nod, but she looked hopeless and that made Jake's heart drop like a brick into his stomach.

~ ♪ ~

Her run had done nothing to ease the tension or calm her down. She needed to help Jake but she was feeling helpless. She'd called Gramps who had already been contacted by Jake's lawyer.

Jake's lawyer was on his way from Vermont. Gramps offered to come, but Colleen asked him to wait. It was a long drive and there was nothing he could do here. She was grateful he agreed. The man was such a gentle soul, reassuring Colleen that everything would be fine.

She wished she believed him.

God, she wanted to help, but how could she? She wished she could lie, say they were together when Rebekah was stabbed, but there were too many people who could place her at the radio station when Rebekah was attacked.

Why was Rebekah doing this? What did she have to gain?

Maybe Colleen couldn't lie about yesterday, but she could certainly be Jake's alibi in college.

She sat on the couch, her hand moving to pet Nola, only to realize the dog wasn't there. Another call to animal control had resulted in nothing. She had also knocked on every door in the neighborhood, but no one had seen the dog.

Colleen clutched a pillow to try and distract herself from the absence of her loyal companion. She thought back to that night when her RA had come by to let her know Rebekah was at the emergency room, that she had been raped while walking across campus.

She remembered the moment vividly, the horror replaced by panic. She had felt helpless then, too, but once she got the panic under control, she had called Jake and asked for a ride to the hospital. She and Rebekah might not have been that close, but they were roommates and Rebekah didn't have any close friends.

No one else was with Rebekah when they arrived at the hospital. Jake had stayed in the waiting room while Colleen sat by her roommate's side. She'd already been examined and questioned by the police and they were keeping her there until the resident psychiatrist could stop by and talk to her.

Rebekah had claimed she didn't know who attacked her, never saw his face and only heard his voice.

Colleen remembered it so clearly because she was sure whoever had attacked her was the same man who had attacked Rebekah and if only Rebekah could identify him, maybe the police would catch him.

The disappointment was more than she could handle.

Thinking back, she tried to remember what Jake had been doing when she called. He wasn't in his room, because she remembered it took him a long time before he met her in the lobby of the dorm.

A date. That's right, he'd been on a date. Colleen remembered how regret and jealousy surged through her when he apologized for taking so long, but he had to bring his date back to her dorm on the other side of campus. She'd let him go, so she had no right to feel the emotions storming through her, but she was already awash in panic, so it's not like she'd had any control.

She wondered if Jake would remember who he'd been out with, and if they found her, if she'd remember. It was a hell of a long shot.

Colleen dialed Devon and was surprised when he didn't answer. He always answered when she called, but maybe he was too busy harassing Jake. When his voice mail beeped, she left a detailed message about Jake being on a date in college and they should find out who to follow-up with because there was no way Jake had done this to Rebekah.

Her stomach rumbled like a bear. Not only had she not slept, she hadn't eaten since Jake left yesterday. She opened the pantry and stared at the contents for an eternity. Nothing jumped out at her but the shadow that appeared under the cabinet startled her. She reached for her gun, but had stowed it in the monkey upon returning from her run.

She stepped back and searched her mind for the self-defense tactics she had learned in that class she'd taken so many years ago. She held her breath as the cupboard door closed, her chest seizing when she saw a man she wished she didn't recognize standing on the other side.

"Hello, CC," he said, his head cocked and a smug grin marring his face. "It's been a long time."

"Not long enough," she managed to say before the adrenaline defeated the panic. She put her hands behind her and backed up to the counter, hoping she could get a knife out of the drawer without her biggest adversary realizing what she was doing.

Spencer Mardin chuckled. "Don't even think about it. I've also rounded up both your guns. It's just you and me."

His voice made her nauseous and his smirk made her skin crawl. He'd gained some tattoos since she'd last seen him in the courtroom. No, that wasn't the last time. She knew without a doubt she had seen him last week on the boardwalk. He wore the same hooded sweatshirt.

"What do you want?" she asked.

"I think you know."

Revenge? Sex? All of the above?

"You don't want to do this," she insisted, but her voice was so unsteady, she didn't sound convincing.

"You have no idea how much I want to do this." Colleen backed around the island, but he continued to stalk her. She debated between the front door and the cell phone. If she made a run for it, he would no doubt catch her since her front door was locked.

Locked. How the hell had he gotten in?

If she got to the phone, she'd be caught too, but if she managed to dial 911 before he got her, maybe she stood a chance.

When Colleen thought she could make it, she made a run for the living room and snatched the phone. She continued the game of cat and mouse around the table.

"No one can help you," he snarled, that smirk sending a shiver of fear up her spine. She heard the call connect, but Spencer lifted the table and sent it flying in her direction. She was able to dodge it as she yelled his name into the phone, but he took a couple fast strides over the love seat and tackled her. As she hit the floor, the phone slid across the floor and under the entertainment center against the wall.

Then he slammed her head against the floor and as the pain shot through her, a darkness she couldn't escape claimed her.

♪ Chapter 32 ♪

From Viper:

Scored the big prize.

To Viper:

Explain.

From Viper:

UR BFF

To Viper:

That wasn't part of the plan.

From Viper:

Was always MY plan.

♪ Chapter 33 ♪

DEVON JUMPED the curb when he arrived at Colleen's house. His heart had been beating triple time ever since someone came into the war room to inform him there had been an emergency call from the department cell phone he had signed out to Colleen.

Three patrol cars were already parked in her driveway and he ignored Leah's curses and reprimands for reckless driving as he bolted out of the SUV and up the steps of Colleen's house.

He was familiar enough with the house that a quick scan of the front rooms revealed what was out of place. A chair in the dining area of her kitchen was on its side. The love seat in the living room was on its back, one of the plants by the window knocked over.

"The door was closed and locked when we arrived," Officer Scott said when Devon stormed through the room. "We found her phone under the entertainment center."

Nothing else looked out of place. Devon saw the monkey on the back of the couch and knew as soon as he lifted it that her gun wasn't in place. God, he hoped she had it on her and the perp didn't know about it.

"What did we get from the call?" Devon asked Scott.

"Dispatch said she yelled the name Spencer Mardin before they heard the crash, which is when we assume she lost the phone. They heard more bangs, but nothing from her. They think they heard the door close and then it was silent. They helped us locate the phone once we were in."

Devon raked his hand through his hair.

"We're running a search on Spencer Mardin now."

"He's been in the wind for a couple years," Devon informed the uniformed officer. "He attacked Ms. Cooper in college and served some jail time." He turned to Leah. "Maybe that *was* him she saw on the boardwalk last week."

Dammit. He should have had Colleen work with a sketch artist to render a picture, but no crime had been committed and Devon was convinced she imagined it.

"Or maybe her post-traumatic stress kicked in again," Leah suggested.

Devon didn't believe it and he didn't think it was just his feelings for Colleen clouding the issue. He also didn't believe Jake Donovan was the mastermind behind all this. After interrogating him, Devon was filled with a hell of a lot of doubt.

Leah's phone rang, interrupting the emerging debate. "Follow her. I want to know where she goes," she said before hanging up. "Rebekah Charles is being discharged."

"What? She was stabbed yesterday," he pointed out, as if Leah didn't already know that.

"It appears she's well enough to not be taking up the bed anymore. From what Officer Cole overheard, she insisted on leaving."

"What's she up to?" he asked. She didn't have a car at the hospital. As far as he knew, her rental was still sitting in the parking lot near the bed and breakfast where she'd been staying. "I want to know who picks her up."

Devon looked at his watch. He doubted they could make it to the hospital before she left and his SUV wasn't discreet. "We need to switch cars so we can pick up the tail," he suggested.

"Let's swing by the station and grab my car," Leah said, agreeing with him for the first time all week.

"Yeah, but I'm driving," he insisted as they headed for the door.

"Not in a million years," she said without humor as she led him out of the house.

Fifteen minutes later, they were in Leah's car and Devon was on the phone with the officer who had been assigned to Rebekah's room. She was in a cab heading north on route 1A.

"If she goes into Maine, my money is back on Donovan," Leah said as she sped toward 1A. Five minutes later, they spotted the cruiser in Rye Harbor.

Devon instructed the cruiser to break off discreetly and they picked up the tail. Leah's car was a silver Honda Accord and looked like a thousand other cars in the area. It was one of the most discreet cars you could ask for and Devon was once again grateful Leah owned it.

A few minutes later, the cab turned onto a side street. Leah slowed down to give them some space. They turned in time to see the cab turning left again. Leah sped to the cross street and they saw the cab turn left again.

"You think she's heading back to Granite Beach?" Leah asked.

"That'd make things easier for us," he said. Devon didn't want to deal with jurisdictional restrictions and egos. As far as he was concerned, this was his case and he was going to see it through to the end.

The cab did head south on 1A back to Granite Beach. It was only a few miles to the town line and soon after they crossed it, the car turned onto a side street. Leah kept her distance but they never lost site of the car.

"Whispering Meadow," she suggested and Devon agreed. Whispering Meadow was a campground with cabins as well as campsites. Some of the cabins were nestled deep in the woods.

"We're not going to be able to follow her in there with the car."

Devon's phone rang. "Taggart," he answered.

"This is Scott. We searched the car on Cooper's property and found a bloody knife under the spare tire in the trunk."

"We have Rebekah Charles' blood type on file," Devon snarled. "Have the lab type it and see if there's a match."

"Will do."

"Where are you at with processing the scene?" Devon asked. "We might need some back-up at Whispering Meadow."

"I can send a few guys out," the sergeant said.

When he ended the call, Leah brought the car to a stop. "Let's wait for the cab to come out and ask where he dropped her."

"Good plan. That was Sergeant Scott. They found a bloody knife in Donovan's car."

"No way he left that in his car," Leah suggested. "He's not dumb. He would have disposed of it when he disappeared to Maine."

Devon had to agree. Donovan wouldn't have a reason to hang on to a bloody knife and it would be too easy to trace blood evidence back to him after he returned the rental. If he was the perpetrator, he'd been careful to this point. Devon didn't believe he'd make such a mistake now.

Security cameras at the toll plaza had verified Donovan's story. The department's researchers were still going through the data to ensure he hadn't crossed again at a time other than the ones he specified, but so far, it looked like his story was holding up. Plus, he had produced a receipt for a new cell phone from a store in Maine with a date and time stamp of yesterday morning, shortly before he showed up at Colleen's.

Devon and Leah sat outside the campground for about ten minutes before the cab appeared. Leah stepped out, her badge in hand and stopped the car. Devon joined her as the driver lowered his window.

"The woman you just drove in there, where'd you take her?" Leah asked.

"Shit," the guy grumbled.

"Where?" Devon demanded, not at all as patient as Leah.

"To one of the cabins. Eighteen or twenty-eight. I'm not sure, the number was worn."

"Can you give us directions or take us there?" Leah asked.

"Are you kidding me?" the driver scoffed. "That place is a maze. I couldn't find it again if my life depended on it. The lady had a map. She was directing me."

"Where'd she get the map?" Leah asked.

"I don't know. Pulled it from her bag, I guess."

"Why'd you take her to Rye Harbor?" Devon cut in.

"She told me to drive north, so I did. Then she told me to turn around, so I did."

"Did she say anything else?" Leah asked.

"Nope. She seemed pretty pissed off and was typing away on her phone the whole time."

"Did the cabin look occupied?" she asked.

"There was a car there. It was blue."

"Ford Fusion?" Devon asked, hopeful. Colleen's car was MIA and maybe if they found her car, they would find her, unharmed.

"I don't know. Could have been. I'm not all that great with cars and I wasn't really paying attention."

Devon hated cab drivers. They never seemed to pay attention. He wished it were a requirement for them to detail all of their surroundings whenever they picked up and dropped off a fare, but it was a tedious job that generated little income, so most of them didn't care. It was only on rare occasions questioning a driver got the details they needed.

Leah took down his information in case they needed to contact him later and Devon accessed the Whispering Meadow site map through their web site. Cabins one through fifteen were scattered throughout the campground while sixteen through thirty were on the perimeter. Unfortunately, there wasn't a perimeter road and cabins eighteen and twenty-eight were nowhere near each other.

"You wait for back-up. I don't want to risk her coming out. I'll check the registration to see who is in cabins eighteen and twenty-eight and we'll come up with a plan from there."

Leah agreed and Devon got in the cab. "Take me to campground registration."

~ ♪ ~

Muffled voices roused Colleen out of sleep. She tried to reach across the bed for the gun in her nightstand, but couldn't move. A sharp pain cut into her wrist as she tugged. The same sharp pain in her ankles made her cry out as she jerked her legs.

She was tied up.

Shit. Where the hell was she?

Memories of those last moments in her house played in her mind, Spencer Mardin stalking her in the kitchen and then into her living room where he tackled her. She had dialed 911. Did the call go through?

The back of her head throbbed. He must have slammed it against the hardwood floor. God, what had he done to her once she was knocked out?

Her clothes were all on, thank God and she didn't feel as though she had been physically violated. That didn't mean he didn't plan to rape her, to finish what he'd started that night he'd attacked her on campus.

"Are you out of your fucking mind?" a voice growled from the other room. It was a woman, but the voice wasn't clear enough, or maybe Colleen's mind was just too fuzzy to recognize the voice. She wanted to say it was Rebekah, but she was still in the hospital recovering from a stab wound.

"This is better. This gives us more leverage," Spencer said.

"This gets us caught," the woman said. Could it be Rebekah?

"Relax, doll, no one saw me. I'll get everything set up for the ransom and then we'll have enough to live high and dry for the rest of our lives."

"Can she identify you?" the woman asked.

"It doesn't matter. I'm not letting her walk out of here."

"This is not what we agreed to, Viper," the woman said.

Viper? Was that his nickname? Colleen remembered the tattoo on his arm. It was how he'd been tied to all the attacks in college. She'd thought it was a dragon, but now that she thought about it, it could be a snake.

"Becks, you need to relax. My plan is better."

Becks? So it was Rebekah.

There was silence then, accept for a whimper that sounded like it came from inside Colleen's room.

"Nola?" she whispered. She wished she could sit up and look around, but the wire that had her wrists and ankles bound was tight and restricting. She was able to lift her head, but the room was dark and she couldn't see much. "Nola, baby, is that you?" she asked a little more loudly, hoping they didn't hear her in the other room.

Another whimper and the rhythmic sound of a tail thumping against the floor was Colleen's answer. "It's okay, Nola, we're going to be all right."

She wasn't sure if she was reassuring her dog or herself, but Colleen repeated the words in her head as she tried to figure a way out of this mess.

A door slammed shut and the nightmare she was trapped in continued as the very distinct sounds of sex echoed in the next room.

Being restrained, she couldn't cover her ears, so she kept talking to Nola, only mildly drowning out the sound.

They were loud, absurdly loud, and Colleen wondered how Rebekah was able to take a ride like that after being stabbed.

Colleen set her mind to figuring a way out of the bindings so she and Nola could make a run for it. The wires were tight, offering no slack or resistance. Escape seemed hopeless.

She wasn't sure how much time passed when the ruckus in the next room stopped, but she'd made no headway in loosening the bindings.

Voices broke the silence again. They talked more calmly this time, but the walls in this cabin were paper thin.

"You willing to be reasonable now?" Rebekah asked.

"I want her to suffer for what she did to me," Spencer whined.

"She will. JD is in jail, her reputation is ruined, and so is his music career. I make the call to Paul, get the money transferred into my account, and we are on our way to Belize."

"Come on, doll, I already have her tied up with her boyfriend's guitar strings. Let me have a little fun first."

Panic seized Colleen's breath, bile racing up her throat. The memories of the night he attacked her fogged her senses. She tried not to sob, not wanting to alert them she was awake.

"The longer we linger, the bigger the risk. Her car sitting out there is an invitation to disaster."

"I swapped out the plates," Spencer said.

"That'll only stall the police. That sexy detective is hot for CC. He's not going to rest until she's found, which is why we need to get dressed and get out of here now."

Colleen listened to mumblings around the house, doors slamming inside and out. She guessed they were packing up, loading everything into her car. Panic bubbled up as she tried not to think about her fate. Would they just leave her or would Mardin have his *fun* first?

"Where's the guitar?" Rebekah asked.

Colleen spotted Jake's guitar in the corner near Nola. The strings were all cut, a few of the bridge pins missing, and most of the machine heads broken off. A sob threatened as she took in the destruction of Jake's beautiful guitar, the one his grandfather made and his mother named Rêver. He treasured the old instrument, holding it like a lover as he composed new songs. Colleen couldn't even fathom the devastation he would feel when he saw it like this.

"I'll get it," Mardin snickered.

"I'm calling a cab. You need to get rid of that car," Rebekah insisted. "I'll get the money transferred and text you once I have the tickets."

There was a long pause filled with a few moans before heavy footsteps grew louder. Colleen pinched her eyes closed and turned away from the door as it flew open.

His footsteps slowed and stopped. The floor next to the bed creaked under his weight. The right side of the mattress sank just before his breath prickled her cheek. "I'm not done with you," he whispered.

Colleen swallowed the terror as he licked her face. Then his weight was gone as he banged the guitar against the floor with each step.

The door slammed before two sets of footsteps stomped through the cabin. Another door slammed before a car engine buzzed to life. Then there was silence and that was as terrifying as hearing the sounds of Mardin banging around the house.

~ ♪ ~

"We've got a cab coming in," Leah said when he answered her call.

"Did you stop it?" Devon asked.

"No. I didn't want to make the driver nervous. I sent one patrol car in and one back out so they wouldn't draw attention sitting here. I've got the hood up so I don't draw suspicion."

"All right. Registration was no help. I'm at cabin twenty-eight now, but there are six kids playing outside and a couple moms sitting in lawn chairs. I'm heading to cabin eighteen, but based on this map, it's going to take a few."

"When you get there, you wait for the patrolman, Devon. Do not in there with guns blazing."

"Colleen is in there, I can feel it and who knows what Mardin has done to her."

"Wait. For. Back-up." Leah's voice was stern and commanding and Devon knew he should listen, but he couldn't leave Colleen up there.

"I'm going in, Leah, whether the patrolman is there or not."

He disconnected the call, muted the ringer, and directed the cab driver to cabin eighteen.

Devon kept track of where they were. He didn't want to drive all the way in and give away his position. When they were close, he instructed the driver to stop and wait.

"I don't want to get involved in whatever is going on," the driver said, his voice shaky.

"There's a woman out there who may need medical attention. We may not be able to wait for an ambulance. You could be her only hope,"

Devon informed him.

"Aw, hell," the guy moaned and cut the engine.

Devon knew he looked out of place trolling the campground in a suit. He just hoped no one was looking out the window of the cabin as he approached.

There was no car outside, but if Mardin and Rebekah left, Leah would stop them at the entrance.

He circled the cabin to find all the curtains closed, so he climbed the steps of the small porch and standing to the side of the door, gave a few solid knocks.

Devon heard no movement inside.

Trying the door, he noticed it wasn't locked. When he stepped in, he found he was in the kitchen. It was a mess, as though it had been used but not cleaned up, maybe because they left in a hurry. He eased his way into the living area, finding it also empty. He checked the room with the open door before going to the room with the closed door. He heard a quiet whimper, one he recognized immediately and hope bloomed. He eased the door open, first seeing feet bound to the end of the bed. Even though he wanted to barge in, he continued to call on his training and opened the door slowly.

"Devon," Colleen sighed. "Oh, thank God."

"Is anyone else here?" he asked, scanning the room and checking the closet.

"They left. It hasn't been very long, about three songs."

"Three songs?" he asked.

"I was playing songs in my head to keep from panicking."

Devon holstered his gun and pulled out the Leatherman he carried in his pocket. "Hold still, Coll. I'm going to cut these wires off you."

Her ankles and wrists were raw and probably numb but he knew as soon as she was released the blood would start rushing and the pain would kick in. "Who did this to you?" he asked, already knowing the answer based on her phone call.

"Spencer Mardin and Rebekah," she snarled. What had been relief was now replaced with anger. "And Paul. He wasn't here, but I heard Rebekah say he was paying them."

By the time he got her free, she was crying and Devon pulled her into his arms. She went willingly and for a moment Devon allowed himself to believe it was because she wanted him, wanted his comfort and strength. In the back of his mind, he knew he was convenient, that he was the only one there and given a choice, she would go to someone else, namely Jake Donovan.

"Oh, God, he was in my house. How did he get in?" she sobbed against his chest.

Devon didn't have an answer, so he just held her tighter, determined to find all the answers.

About ten minutes later, he heard noises on the porch. Devon released her. "Stay here," he instructed, gripping his gun and heading out of the room. When he was clear of the door, he saw Leah in the kitchen.

"Call an ambulance," he said, "and get CST out here."

"Who is the ambulance for?" Leah asked.

"I don't need an ambulance," Colleen said from over his shoulder. Her confident, stubborn voice was back and he assumed the adrenaline had kicked in. "Where's Jake?" she asked, not hiding the angst.

Devon sighed. "I'll call the station and have him released but the hospital isn't negotiable," he insisted.

"Fine," she conceded, her hand moving back and forth on Nola's head. "But not by ambulance. I need to call Seager to see if he'll take Nola."

Devon tossed her his phone before turning back to Leah. "Tell me you stopped them," he demanded.

Leah shook her head. "Neither the cab nor Colleen's car ever left the campground. Either they're still in here or there's an exit we don't know about."

Devon uttered a string curses that would give his mother a coronary.

"We've got a couple patrols combing the campground," Leah assured him. "Your cab is still outside. Take care of her. We'll handle

Susan Ann Wall
everything here."

♪ Chapter 34 ♪

WITH HER wrists and ankles bandaged, Colleen felt like she should be on suicide watch.

"What do you need?" Devon asked, putting his arm around her.

She shrugged it off. "I need to see Jake. I need my dog. I need to go home."

Devon walked beside her, keeping his hands to himself. "We released Donovan," he informed her, his empathetic voice gone, "and your house has been cleared."

"You should have released him after you got my message," she asserted. When she had asked why he didn't answer when she called, he said was questioning Jake and had turned his phone off. She wasn't sure she believed him, but none of that mattered now.

What mattered was going home. It was a scary prospect, but if she didn't, it was like letting Spencer and Rebekah win.

The ride in the cab had been long. Devon held her the whole time while barking orders into his phone. Rebekah was in custody, picked up after she tried to leave town in her rental car. There was no sign of Spencer Mardin, and Colleen's car was still MIA. Despite his threat, she figured he was long gone by now, on a plane heading to Belize.

Good riddance.

She'd rather see him in jail, but Belize was far away and somehow that was more comforting than having him in a jail only an hour away.

As they turned the corner to walk down the main hallway, Colleen saw Jake at the check in desk. Her heart kicked into high gear at the sight of him. She picked up her pace. Jake lifted his head and spotted her, breaking into a jog. He swept her into his arms, holding her tight as his mouth covered hers.

"God, Coll, are you all right?" he asked, letting her go and checking her over.

"I'm fine. No damage that won't heal," she assured him.

"I'm so sorry. This is all because of me."

"It's not, Jake. It's Rebekah spinning her evil web."

"But you warned me, all those years ago. You told me not to hire her but I didn't listen." There was regret in his voice, but there was no changing anything that had happened.

She cupped his face, stroking his stubble-roughened cheek with her thumb. "No looking back," she whispered, swallowing the threatening sob.

"No looking back," he agreed with a nod. "Let me take you home."

"Wait," Devon said. He reached behind his back and produced a small handgun. "They took your guns."

"You're giving me a gun?" she asked.

"Mardin is still on the loose," he reminded her.

"I'm sure he's halfway to Belize by now," she said.

Devon shook his head. "I wouldn't be so sure. With Rebekah in custody, she's not controlling him anymore and based on what you overheard, when left to his own devices, he can be a dangerous man."

Colleen took the gun and pulled it from the holster, surprised to see it was the same kind of gun as Tania, except it was all black instead of black and pink. She checked the clip and returned it to the holster, which she clipped to her waist.

"Your phone has been inactive so we're giving it back, but if you get any messages or calls, anything at all out of the ordinary, you call me. Got it?"

"Are you going to answer this time?" she snarled.

Devon pinned her with that alpha-cop expression she was sure made criminals shake in their shoes. It only served to annoy Colleen.

"I got it, Devon," she said, not showing any sarcasm even though she really, really wanted to. Colleen understood how serious the situation was even if she believed Spencer was long gone. She also understood Devon's concern. He cared about her, more than he should, and he was the one who had found her tied to the bed.

"I'd feel a lot better if you stayed in a hotel tonight."

"I'm not going to let him uproot my life. Plus, Nola has been through as much as I have. She needs to go home."

"We'll be fine," Jake said, his voice hard and cold. She couldn't say she blamed him, after all, Devon was the cop who had arrested him.

~ ♪ ~

Jake didn't want to agree with the jackass cop who had arrested him, but he would also feel better if they didn't go back to Colleen's house.

The cop had offered them a ride, but Colleen refused and for that, Jake was grateful. Instead, Colleen called her morning show partner. Seager seemed more than happy to give them a ride and Nola was thrilled to be back with Coll.

"Maybe we should head back to the farm," Jake suggested.

"The farm isn't any safer than my house," she said. "I need to go home. I need to face what happened there."

"Okay, we'll face it together. No looking back."

He wanted them to get through this, to have that ass-hole Spencer Mardin caught and put behind bars. Then they could start this new life together.

The ride was quick and Jake did a walk-through of the house before he let Colleen come in. He noticed a dark SUV parked just up the street and figured it was Taggart. Even though Jake didn't like the guy, and yeah, that had a little bit to do with jealousy, he knew Taggart wouldn't let anything bad happen to Colleen.

Colleen entered the house with slow steps and pursed lips,

apprehension pulsing like the treble in a guitar solo. Nola, ever the loyal companion, stuck close to her.

"They cleaned up," she said, scanning the living room. "He tipped over the love seat and I knocked over a plant when he tackled me."

She pointed to the area, but nothing looked out of place.

"I need a shower," she said. "Will you keep an eye on Nola? I don't want to leave her alone?"

Jake was sure that was just an excuse, that she wanted him to stand guard. He was fine with that. Whatever helped her get past this horror. Though he'd rather be in the shower with her.

"Come here, girl," he said, and Nola joined him on the couch. She had been through a hell of an ordeal too.

After checking the locks on all the windows and doors, Colleen took a long shower. When she joined him on the couch, she was dressed in yoga pants and his old high school football jersey — something she'd borrowed in college and never returned. Jake didn't mind, she looked sexy as hell in it.

"Rêver is gone" he sighed.

"Mardin and Rebekah took it," she told him.

He figured as much. "That guitar is my legacy," he said.

"I'm sorry, Jake. I know how much you love that guitar. It's a part of you."

He couldn't imagine writing a song without it, but as she leaned into him and his arm went around her, the guitar somehow didn't seem so important. Colleen mattered. She couldn't be replaced. Now that she was safe in his arms again, it felt good, so right to hold her. Jake relished the feeling, knowing he had to let her go.

"You seem distant," she said, picking up on his emotions.

"I've put you in danger. I never should have come here. I didn't know it was Rebekah. I swear, if I had, I never would have come."

Colleen turned to him, her hand cupping his jaw and her thumb caressing his cheek. "I'm glad you came."

"Are you? You're hurt. You could have been killed. You're in the tabloids."

"But I wasn't and as far as the tabloids go, what does it matter? I didn't want *you* to know. You're the only one I care about."

Jake kissed her, regret stinging his eyes. How could he have been so blind to all Rebekah had planned? He'd been stupid, naive even, letting her do whatever she wanted, bossing him around, running his life. All he wanted was to make her feel valued, build up the self-esteem she lacked when she first came to him for a job. She'd been so desperate back then, but now he thought it was just another manipulation, like Colleen had said all along.

"I'm going to postpone the tour until this guy is caught," he told her.

"Jake, no. You've postponed long enough. Your fans want you and you need to finish this tour so you can record that last album for Southern Rebel and get things moving with your new label."

It was going to take months to rebuild anyway, so there was no rush, but the bigger issue was Colleen's safety. "I'm not leaving you," he said.

"You know I can take care of myself. I'm not some helpless damsel in distress."

"I know that but I don't like the idea of you going to Taggart for help if I'm not here," he admitted.

"Jacob Donovan, are you jealous?" she laughed.

"Yes, as a matter of fact," there was no point lying about it. He saw the way the detective looked at her and the two of them had history. Jake didn't like it.

She snuggled up closer to him, warming his body and triggering his arousal. All he wanted to do was lay her down and make love to her, but it would be inconsiderate to let his baser urges take over. She'd been through hell and Jake knew she needed a friend.

"I love *you*," she reminded him, "not Devon."

"Then let me take care of you. Let me protect you."

She kissed him, her mouth tentatively touching his but soon her tongue was brushing across his lips and pushing into his mouth. She shifted and moved until she was straddling his legs.

"Coll, baby, are you sure you're up for this?" he asked, desperate for her to say yes.

"Yes. I want to move forward, Jake. The doors are locked and the police are watching the house. We are safe, at least for tonight and I've missed you."

~ ♪ ~

Devon was all done playing nice guy. He was tired of Rebekah's damsel in distress act.

"Spencer has been after me for a long time," Rebekah insisted. "He called and told me he had CC and that if I didn't have sex with him, he would kill her. So I made the sacrifice to keep her alive. I was on my way to the police station when you stopped me."

"According to Colleen, you were rather enjoying yourself," Leah pointed out.

"CC has never liked me so she wants to believe I'm the bad guy here, but I haven't done anything wrong."

The phone in the interview room rang and Devon picked it up. "Taggart," he said.

"Come up to Tech. We found something on Rebekah's phone."

Devon hung up and looked at Rebekah but he gave nothing away. If she continued to play the innocent card, she was just going to dig herself into a grave. "I'll be back," Devon said to Leah who looked at him in question. "Erik's got something for us."

Leah nodded her understanding and Devon headed out, opting for the stairs to expedite getting there.

Erik was smiling when Devon walked in.

"This is sweet stuff. There are three cameras as far as I can tell, one in the living room, one in the bedroom, and one that looks down the hall to what I'm guessing is the front door. I don't know the layout of the house, but this provides a lot of coverage."

Erik had Rebekah's phone hooked up to the computer so it was displaying on the large screen Erik used. "See, you click on the number 1 and it shows the bedroom. Number 2 is the hall," he said, clicking on the two and displaying that camera.

"That is the front door," Devon pointed at the screen where the picture was displayed. "So the camera must be mounted near the back door."

"I'll take your word for it," Erik said. "This is the living room, oh, uh, they were just talking."

In living color was Colleen straddling Donovan on her couch, the two of them lip locked and their hands all over each other. Devon grabbed his phone and hit Colleen's number. "No audio?" he asked Erik.

"Nope, just the low resolution video feed. It's live, by the way."

"Yeah, I get that," Devon groaned.

The phone rang and he watched the camera as the two of them ignored the call. They didn't even acknowledge the phone was ringing.

Devon wrote down Colleen's number. "You dial Colleen," he directed Erik. "I'll call Donovan."

Maybe if both phones rang, they would stop.

Only Donovan tugged Colleen's shirt over her head and there she was in her bra with his hands on her breasts.

And still the phone went unanswered.

"Look at this," Erik pointed to the feed from the camera near her back door. It looked like the door was opening.

"What the hell?" Devon muttered.

He dialed Colleen's number again, praying the third time was in fact a charm.

"Call dispatch and have them send the patrolman in," he told Erik.

He watched as Colleen pushed Donovan back. Devon waited, watching as they exchanged words before she finally picked up the phone.

"This better be important, Devon," Colleen snarled.

"Someone is in your house."

♪ Chapter 35 ♪

"WHAT?" COLLEEN muttered. "No. We checked the house and locked everything."

"There are cameras," Devon said, his voice so filled with anger it scared Colleen. "They feed into Rebekah's phone. You need to put your shirt on and get the hell out of the house now. He's moving down the hall toward you."

"Shit," Colleen cursed, putting an arm across her chest and searching the room for a camera, but not finding anything.

"Get out now, Colleen," Devon commanded.

"What's going on?" Jake asked, his hands firm around her waist.

"We have to leave," she said.

Colleen put the phone down long enough to put her shirt on. She snatched the phone and the gun Devon had given her off the table. "Devon?" she asked quietly.

"I'm still here, Coll. You need to get out of there." The anger was gone, but the concern in his voice wasn't any less terrifying.

She walked to the front door, Jake in tow. "Don't even think about turning that deadbolt," a voice warned from behind them.

A whimper followed the command and Colleen turned to find Spencer Mardin standing in the hall with Nola next to him, hooked to a short chain.

"Let her go," Colleen pleaded, pointing the gun at him.

Mardin snickered and it was only then that she realized he held each of her guns in his hands, the Ruger pointed at Nola and the Glock pointed at Jake.

"Drop the phone and the gun," he warned.

"You're not a killer," she said.

"You have no idea what I'm capable of. You learn a lot of things in prison."

Colleen hit the speaker button before putting the phone on the table by the door. She hoped Devon kept his mouth shut and didn't give away that the call was still connected.

"Now the gun," Mardin said.

At the shooting range, Colleen had perfect aim, but as her hands shook, she wasn't confident she'd be able to hit him. If she missed, she'd be sealing her fate, as well as Jake and Nola's. She prayed Devon had police on the way.

"How did you get in here?" Colleen asked. She had checked every door and window. Unless Jake had unlocked something while she was in the shower, Spencer shouldn't be standing in her house.

"Becks gave me a key," he chuckled, his head cocking to one side as he glanced at Jake.

"Son of a bitch," Jake muttered.

"How do you know Rebekah?" Colleen asked.

"College. She liked sucking dick. She was a keeper from day one."

After what she'd heard in the cabin, Colleen should have known better than to ask.

"The gun," Mardin demanded, nodding at Colleen's hand.

She placed the gun next to the phone. "Let her go," she demanded.

"I'm not interested in your dog or your boyfriend. You're the one I have a score to settle with."

With that, Jake moved in front of her. "I'm not going to let you hurt her again."

"It's because of you this all started," Mardin snickered.

"How so?" Jake asked. Colleen was grateful for the stall-tactic, even if it wasn't deliberate. If they kept Mardin talking long enough, the police would show up.

"Rebekah was going to offer to help you, with her marketing background. She said you were going to make the big time and she needed to get on board before you did so she'd be guaranteed a job and money." Mardin snickered and turned to Colleen. "She knew you wouldn't allow that, so she asked me to take you out of the picture."

"You son of a bitch," Jake growled.

Mardin snickered again. "Then the little cunt got away," he snarled. "Rebekah thought if she was attacked too, she'd be a shoe-in for a job with the pretty boy here."

The plan made sense to Colleen, given Rebekah's devious personality. "What about the other girls?" Colleen demanded.

Mardin laughed now. "That was my idea. I convinced Rebekah it would look suspicious if both of you were the only ones, so I got to have a little fun."

Those words sent a shiver of disgust up Colleen's spine. He's said the same words at the cabin while she was tied up. Now, with a gun pointed at her, the potency of his intent had her stomach roiling with fear.

"Enough talk. Come with me, Colleen," her name a sneer across his lips, "or you'll find out just how accurate my aim is."

"No," Jake said, stepping forward and keeping Colleen behind him.

The Glock went off, plaster shattering on the wall beside the door. "Consider that a warning shot," Mardin said.

"Jake, please, don't. I don't want you getting hurt."

"Take me," Jake insisted, his focus on Mardin. "If it's all because of me, then leave Colleen out of this and take me."

Mardin moved back a couple steps, unhooking Nola's chain from his belt and tugging Nola into the bathroom before slamming the door closed. He only shifted his focus for a second, but with Jake standing in front of her, it was enough for her to grab the gun off the table.

With his glowering gaze back on them, Mardin stepped forward and used the gun to point at the barstool. With his other hand, he retrieved something out of his pocket and tossed it at Jake. "Tie her to the bar stool."

Colleen slipped the gun into Jake's waistband at the center of his back. He stiffened for a moment, but didn't give them away. She prayed he knew how to use the gun.

"I said leave her out of this," Jake growled.

Mardin seemed to ponder Jake's demand before his lip curled in a snarl and he nodded. "Becks has always wanted a little taste of you. Tie her up. Then you and I leave out the back door," Mardin said.

Jake shook his head, but Colleen needed him to do this, just to delay Mardin longer. "Just do it," Colleen whispered. She was confident Devon would show up soon, or at least dispatch someone.

"Coll," Jake said, turning his head to look at her over his shoulder.

"It's fine," she promised, pressing her hand against the gun at his back. It was loaded but the first round wasn't chambered. She had no idea if Jake knew to do that, and there was no way for her to tell him.

Colleen moved over to the barstool. "Sit down. Tie her ankles first, then her hands to the back. Tie them tight."

Jake's eyes pleaded with her, but she gave him a nod. She still had the bandages on, so hopefully that would keep the guitar strings from cutting her again.

"Where's my guitar?" Jake demanded as he crouched and wrapped a string around Colleen's ankle.

"Halfway to Belize, I'm guessing," Mardin chuckled.

Hope ignited as Colleen realized Mardin didn't know Rebekah was in police custody. She had no idea how many cameras were in her house, but she hoped they were giving the police a birds-eye view of what was happening, allowing them an easy way to capture Mardin.

"I thought you were going to Belize with her?" Colleen asked.

"I had some unfinished business to wrap up." His sneer sent a shiver down Colleen's spine.

Jake finished binding Colleen to the chair, the apology in his eyes heart-wrenching. She wondered what was taking the police so long and tried to figure out how they could delay Mardin longer.

As Jake turned, Mardin swung his arm around, hitting Jake aside the temple with the Glock. Colleen screamed as Jake fell to the floor.

The back door crashed open. Colleen jumped on the bar chair, toppling it over. Pain shot through her left side, from her thigh all the way to her head as she crashed to the floor next to Jake.

A shot fired, but she didn't know from where as voices yelled from the back of the house. "The house is surrounded, Mardin," Devon yelled. "Drop the gun and put your hands in the air." Her vision was blurry, but she could make out Mardin's profile as he stood against the refrigerator, out of sight from the back of the house.

She blinked her eyes into focus to find Jake looking at her. "I love you," he mouthed before she recognized the distinct sound of a round being chambered. He rolled onto his back, Ruger in hand and unloaded the six rounds.

Mardin fell to the floor. A frenzy of dark uniforms converged in the kitchen before Colleen's blurred vision went black.

~ ♪ ~

Jake dropped the gun as the police stormed the house. "Coll, baby, wake up, please," he pleaded, his hand brushing the wild curls from her face. She landed hard, her head knocking against the tile floor. God, he prayed she wasn't hurt.

"Is she all right?" Taggart asked as he crouched between Jake and Colleen.

"I don't know. We need to get her to the hospital."

"Ambulance is on the way," Taggart said.

"What about that guy?" Jake asked.

"You hit him twice. Once in the gut, once in the arm. I'd like to let him bleed out, but it's not my call. He'll probably live."

"Shit," Jake muttered, wishing the bastard was dead.

"You did well for a guitar player. You ever fire a gun before?"

"Just a rifle. My dad took me hunting, then my grandfather did. I've never used a handgun."

Jake moved around Colleen, his shaking hands desperate to free her from the guitar strings that had her bound to the chair.

"Here," Taggart offered, a Leatherman in his hand.

Jake took the tool and cut through the strings.

"You're bleeding," Taggart drawled as Jake moved the bar chair away and hauled Colleen into his arms.

"It's nothing," Jake said, ignoring his throbbing head. All that mattered was that Colleen was okay. "Where's the damn ambulance?"

Detective Paige released the dead bolt on the front door. "First ambulance arrived. We called for a second."

"She goes first," Jake said.

"Not our call," Detective Paige responded as the EMTs entered the house. Two headed to the kitchen, two stopped and crouched in front of Jake and Colleen.

They insisted Jake let her go, and reluctantly he did, only because he knew they'd take care of her.

"We need help over here," one of the medics called from the kitchen.

"It's good, I've got this," the woman taking Colleen's pulse said to the man working with her. The man strode off as the woman offered Jake a reassuring smile. "Her pulse is strong, her pupils are fine, and her breathing is steady. Those are all good signs."

Jake swore as the medics took Mardin out on the stretcher, but it was only minutes later when another team invaded the house and got Colleen strapped to a board. In the ambulance, they bandaged Jake's head and monitored Colleen.

The ambulance was in motion when Colleen gasped awake. "Easy," Jake said, caressing his hand over her hair. "We're in the ambulance, on the way to the hospital. You're going to be okay."

When she turned to Jake and spotted the bandage on his head, her eyes widened. "I'm okay too. This is just a fashion statement. All the hot new country artists are wearing them."

She chuckled and shook her head before the smile faded. "Mardin?" she asked.

"He's probably going to live."

"Oh, Jake," she sighed.

"It's okay. Taggart says there's enough evidence to send him to prison for a long time. Rebekah and Paul too. I'm so sorry, Coll."

"Sshhh," she said, pressing her finger to his lips. "No looking back."

"No looking back," he agreed, taking her hand in his before leaning over to kiss her mouth. Her other hand moved around his nape, holding him there as their lips danced.

"I love you, Jake," she whispered against his lips, the sweetest music he'd ever heard.

"I love you, Coll, more than anything."

~ ♪ ~

All Devon wanted to do was follow the ambulance to the hospital to make sure Colleen was okay, but he had a job to finish and duty called.

Four uniformed officers were assigned to the hospital to make sure Mardin wasn't going anywhere. The EMTs said he'd go straight into surgery and could be there for hours, something Devon already knew based on his experience with gunshot wounds.

It wasn't in his nature to wish a perp dead, but this guy had hurt Colleen and Devon couldn't keep himself from wishing he'd been the one to pull the trigger instead of Donovan. Not only would he have hit the bastard more than twice and made it count, but he'd have the satisfaction of taking Mardin down.

"You alright?" Leah asked as they entered the war room.

"Not by a long shot," he admitted, "but at least we have Mardin in custody and Colleen's safe."

"You ready to question Rebekah?" Leah asked.

Devon was more than ready. He guessed the woman was going to be

Broken Strings

livid when she found out her boyfriend had gone after Colleen and got himself shot in the process.

"Any status on Curran?" Devon asked as they made their way down to the holding cells where Rebekah was locked behind bars until …

"Captain is working on the warrant," Leah said.

Devon hoped the process was expedited. He didn't want to give Curran a chance to run and hide, and once Rebekah secured herself an attorney, she'd be able to get word to him that their plan had unraveled. With Mardin in custody, he hoped Rebekah was ready to offer up the full scale of that plan instead of more lies.

"I've got her phone. Erik loaded it with the video of Colleen and Jake. You going to be able to handle that?"

The image was going to bring Devon nightmares, if not sleepless nights, but he'd endure it again to get Rebekah to confess … for Colleen's sake. "I'm good."

Rebekah was sitting in the interrogation room when they got there. "What now?" she snarled.

"Your boyfriend's in custody," Devon said as he sat across the table from Rebekah.

"I don't have a boyfriend," she said.

"That's not what Spencer Mardin claims. He's ready to sell you out for his freedom," Leah added.

"You're lying," Rebekah insisted, turning to Leah.

Leah shrugged. "Got some great live porn off your phone," she said, playing the video and turning it toward Rebekah.

After watching for a few seconds, Rebekah slapped the phone from Leah's hand. "I've done everything for him. Everything. He's so blinded by that little cunt he can't see any of it."

Devon noted how Rebekah used the same vile term to describe Colleen as Mardin had. It was also used in one of the text messages.

He appreciated Leah's level, calm demeanor. She didn't even flinch when the phone flew across the room or by the fact a perp had made physical contact. She simply folded her hands and dropped her chin, giving Rebekah her undivided attention. "How so?" Leah asked, a touch of sympathy in her voice.

"She bats a friggin' eyelash and JD jumps through hoops. What has she done for him? Nothing except spread her legs whenever it's convenient."

The knowledge that Colleen has slept with that record label douche bag rankled Devon's temper. It was the second time in a week he'd heard this news about Colleen. The first time he'd doubted it was true, but as soon as he'd seen the look on her face, he knew otherwise. He hated the thought of it, but it was years before he'd met her and he chalked it up to naiveté.

"CC's not as innocent as everyone thinks she is. I was her roommate in college. Her bed was seldom empty. Then she set her sights on JD. He was sweet. I didn't want to see him hurt."

"So you had Spencer Mardin attack Colleen," Leah suggested. He was grateful she took the lead because if Devon opened his mouth, only poison would come out.

"Oh, no. You're not pinning that on me. Spencer likes it rough, likes to get women to submit to him. He knew I didn't like Colleen and took it upon himself to attack her. I had *nothing* to do with that."

Devon's instincts pegged everything Rebekah said as a lie, but his feelings for Colleen sparked doubt. He *wanted* to believe it was all a lie.

"What about the other girls?" Leah asked.

"Spencer liked it. I tried to get him to stop, but he threatened me, too. When I told him enough was enough, he raped me too."

"But you said Donovan raped you," Devon reminded her.

Rebekah sighed and rolled her eyes. "When Spencer got out of jail, he started stalking me. I was scared, but he wouldn't leave me alone. I didn't know he stabbed Margot. Then he showed up here, told me he was going to take care of Colleen once and for all and we could be together. I didn't want that. I thought if you focused your investigation on Jake that this would all go away and I could get Spencer to stop before he hurt someone else."

It all seemed too convenient.

"We know you were planning to go to Belize," Leah said.

"Right, to get away from all this," Rebekah said, her arms flailing about.

"With Mardin," Devon added.

Rebekah's snarl turned into fake disbelief. "He was following me to Belize?" she asked.

Devon slammed his fists on the table, making Rebekah jump. "Don't play with me. When Mardin gets out of surgery, he's going to talk. I've been doing this a long time and I know a rat when I see one. He's already been in jail. He's not going to want to go back. He'll throw you and Curran under the bridge to stay free."

"Surgery? What do you mean?"

"Jake Donovan shot him when Mardin went back to Colleen's house," Leah said, much more calmly than Donovan could.

"Shot him? Oh my God, is Spencer …" her words were swallowed by a sob, the truth making a welcome appearance.

"He's fine," Devon drawled. "Fine enough to confess."

"No! It was all Paul," Rebekah insisted. "He knew JD wasn't going to sign a new contract. He found out about him starting his own label."

"And enlisted your help," Leah added.

"He said my job was history once JD broke out on his own. I didn't believe that until JD started talking about the radio station. That's when I knew CC would be a part of it and I'd be out of a job."

At last, something Devon could believe. It seemed Spencer Mardin was Rebekah's weakness, not the other way around. It was a risk admitting he was shot, but Leah's approach wasn't getting them anywhere.

"So Paul was the mastermind?" Leah asked.

Rebekah nodded. "He threatened to have me fired if I didn't help, promised me a marketing position at Southern Rebel when JD signed a new contract."

Once again, she was making herself the victim.

Leah opened the folder she'd placed on the end of the table and pulled out pictures of the five girls Spencer attacked in college. "Once we got the school records, it didn't take long to identify you as the common link between all these girls. You had a class with each one of them. I'm guessing you talked your boyfriend Spencer into attacking each one to take the focus off Colleen."

"But that didn't work, did it?" Devon added. "It only turned up the heat. That's why you claimed you were raped. By not identifying Mardin, you were hoping to throw a wrench in the investigation. Little did you know the DA had enough evidence and testimony to convict."

Rebekah stared at the pictures, anger marring her face. "Stupid," she whispered before repeating it more emphatically.

"Mardin's vendetta with Colleen, is that because she got away?" Leah asked.

Rebekah shook her head. "It's because she fought back. He likes his prey scared and submissive. He swore he'd make Colleen beg for mercy once he got out of jail. I thought it was just words," and then she added on a whisper, "not that I cared."

They wrapped up the questioning and headed upstairs. Devon felt like they'd made progress, that they had enough evidence to convict all three perps on multiple charges, but only the jury would prove that.

"Heading home?" Leah asked as they made it to the main floor.

"I thought I'd head over to the hospital, check on Mardin."

Leah's smile told him she wasn't buying it. "Check on Mardin or check on your girl?"

"She's not my girl," Devon corrected.

"No, I suppose not," Leah said with a sympathetic smile, patting his shoulder. "You okay with that?"

"I will be. Donovan cares about her, makes her happy." That's all he wanted, for Colleen to be happy. While he wanted to be the man to bring that happiness to her, he knew he'd blown his shot.

"You going to let Mr. Donovan know we have his guitar?" Leah asked.

The guitar was in Rebekah's possession when they apprehended her. It was in rough shape, the strings and other pieces broken off. "He's better off getting a new one," Devon muttered.

"I dated a guy in high school who played guitar," Leah said, her voice reverent and her smile warm, as if the memory was one she endeared. "He had one similar to Mr. Donovan's, loved it more than he loved me."

"That was his mistake," Devon insisted.

"No, it wasn't," she said, the smile lighting her face. "I suspect our country superstar would want his guitar back regardless of the condition."

"I'll return it after it's processed," Devon said, hoping Donovan didn't hold a piece of wood in higher esteem than Colleen.

He smiled at Leah. "Case is over. You going to find a date now?"

Leah laughed. "Yeah, maybe. Right after I clean up the war room."

"Maybe you should look up your old musician boyfriend," he said.

She shook her head. "We're still friends. That's all we'll ever be."

♪ Epilogue ♪

COLLEEN SASHAYED across the white sand to where Jake sat on a blanket with his guitar, the crashing Caribbean waves creating a calming harmony with the guitar chords.

Nola slept in a curled-up ball at his side, content under the mid-day island sun. She'd been stressed during the flight on the private jet Jake hired, but had settled in on the big yacht to Jake's private island.

Colleen paused before she reached the blanket, admiring Jake's concentration as he strummed the chords on his beloved Rêver. When Devon returned the guitar, it was a massacred mess. Jake and Gramps spent countless hours refurbishing the sentimental instrument until it sounded as beautiful as it had before all the tragedy.

When Jake set the guitar aside and jotted a few notes, Colleen seized the opportunity to break the news to him. "Margot got bumped from the Number 1 spot," she announced as she straddled his thighs.

"Shit," he muttered. Margot's album *Humble Tides* had been sitting at the top of the charts for almost three months.

Colleen pressed a sympathetic kiss to Jake's lips before turning her phone to show him this week's chart-toppers.

His eyes widened, "No shit."

"It's not Photoshop, baby. *Broken Strings* is Number 1."

He set his guitar aside and wrapped his arms around her, rolling her onto the blanket. "That's cause for celebration." *Broken Strings* was the final album he recorded with Southern Rebel. Given the charges against

Paul Curran, the execs cut Jake some slack and let him record some of his own songs. The album was edgy with a heavy southern rock influence, true to who Jake was as a musician.

It had released six weeks ago, debuting at Number 20 and holding steady in the Top 10.

"Did you read them all?" she asked.

Jake grabbed her hand and looked at the phone again. "Holy shit. This is real?"

She laughed, "I promise. I just pulled it up."

"JD Donovan has the Number 1 spot and Old Red Barn has four artists in the Top 10?" The surprise in his voice added to his boyish charm.

"That's what I read too. Must be true," Colleen mused.

Jake had bumped Margot to Number 2, while Owen Foster had risen to Number 5, Lacey Graham was sitting tight at Number 7, and Greg Felton claimed the Number 8 spot.

"I can't believe this," he said, shaking his head at the phone.

Colleen put the phone down on the blanket and cupped his face. "Believe it. You made it, Jake, on your terms."

"With you," he added, pulling her against him.

"We're better together," she agreed.

It had been fourteen months since Jake shot Spencer Mardin in Colleen's house in Granite Beach. Jake finished the tour and recorded his last album with Southern Rebel while Colleen oversaw the rebuilding of the barn in Vermont with Gramps. Old Red Barn Records had continued to operate out of the small studio in Nashville until three weeks ago when the transition was completed. JD Donovan's Heart and Soul Internet radio station had been up and running for the last eight months after Colleen convinced Jake she could launch the station before the barn was finished. So far, things were running smoothly and the station was receiving accolades.

A week ago, right after Spencer Mardin, Rebekah Charles, and Paul Curran had all received their sentences for kidnapping, arson, attempted murder, and all kinds of conspiracy charges, Jake completed production of his first album with his own label. *No Looking Back* was due to launch in three months. They were both exhausted from the events of the past year, so Jake thought it was the perfect time to sweep Colleen off to a private beach in the Caribbean.

"You promised to teach me to paddleboard today," she reminded him.

"I did. Let's go," he said, pushing off the blanket with her wrapped around him. She loved his strength, not just the physical strength, but the strength of his character.

They'd agreed not to hide away as their lives were broadcast in the media with every new development in the case. Now that it was over, the burden of her long-held secrets and bad decisions had been washed away with the changing tides.

As they headed to the shack near the shore where the paddleboards were propped up, the warm air refreshing as the sun kissed her now-tanned skin, Colleen was happier than she'd been her whole life. She had the job of her dreams and the man of her dreams to not just thank for it, but share with.

Before they reached the shack, Jake stopped, tugging Colleen back to him. "I love you, Coll," he said.

"I love you, Jake." It had taken almost a decade for them to come together, not just as best friends or even lovers, but as partners, in love and in life.

"I've been meaning to ask you something," he said.

"Yeah, what's that?"

"I tried to write a song, you know, something just for you, so you'd know how much you mean to me, but there's no words, no chords that could ever ..." he shook his head as his words trailed off.

"What is it?" she asked.

He cupped her cheek, kissing her with such tenderness that it almost felt like good-bye. "Jake," she whispered, "you're scaring me."

He shook his head, a smile pushing aside the serious expression.

"No. There's nothing to be scared of. I love you. Forever, Coll. Always. It's always been you."

When he dropped to his knee, Colleen's heart plummeted to her stomach, her breath caught on the rescinding wave. "Marry me, Coll. You're my best friend, my partner, my everything. Say you'll be my wife."

Colleen dropped onto the sand with him, kissing him as tears of joy streamed down her cheeks. "How could I not?" she said against his mouth. "Yes, Jake, yes, I will marry you and be your wife."

He kissed her again, so fiercely it stole her breath. "Here, I have this," he said, showing her the modest and beautiful diamond ring pinched between his fingers.

"It's beautiful," she said.

"Like you. I wanted to buy you something flashy, but I know that's not your style and I don't want you to have an excuse to ever take this off."

Colleen sucked back a sob, loving that he'd put her tastes above his own.

"Come on, give me your hand before my shaking hands drop this in the sand and lose it."

Colleen's hand shook too, but Jake managed to slip the ring on. "It fits perfect," she said, astonished. She didn't wear jewelry, so he would have had to guess at the size.

"*We* fit perfect," he added. "Oh, I have something else for you."

He reached behind him, tugging something from his back pocket. A t-shirt hung from his hand when his arm swung back around.

"You got me a shirt?" she asked, amused by the gift.

"I know how much you like those snarky t-shirts," he laughed. "Read it."

She took the hot pink shirt from his hand, hanging it in front of her to find fluorescent green letters with a black border. "*He asked. I said, "Hell Yes!"* she read aloud.

Jake's proud smile amped up her heart. Since all Colleen wore was cut-offs over a bikini, she started to put the shirt on, but he stopped her, his smile turning into something a little more mischievous.

He pulled her to him before easing her onto the sand.

"Jake," she whispered, as his body pressed against hers.

"I know," he whispered back.

♪ ♪ ♪

A Note from Susan

I am so thrilled to bring this new romantic suspense series to you. When I first started writing Broken Strings, it was going to be a stand-alone novel, but I fell in love with Devon and knew he needed more stories. He will eventually find his own happily ever after, but it will be a rocky road getting there. I'm also looking forward to writing Leah's journey into love. I promise it'll be as rocky as Devon's!

All the best,

Susan

Books by Susan Ann Wall

Fighting Back for Love Series

Relay For Love (May 2011)
A Flame Burns Inside (January 2012)
Worth the Fight (Coming Soon)

Puget Sound ~ Alive With Love Series

The Sound of Consequence (April 2013)
The Sound of Betrayal (August 2013)
The Sound of Suspicion (January 2014)
The Sound of Deception (June 2014)
The Sound of Circumstance (December 2015)
The Sound of Reluctance (Coming Soon)

Superstitious Brides Series

Marrying for Love (January 2016)
For the Love of Chocolate (February 2016)
3rd Trip to the Altar (Coming Soon)

Devon Taggart Suspense Series

Broken Strings (April 2016)

Sunset Valley Women's Fiction Series

Whisper to a Scream (May 2016)

Broken Strings

Multi-Author Anthologies (ebook only)

Book Boyfriends Cafe *Summer Lovin'* (May 2015)
14 summer romances from USA Today and National Bestselling authors (includes Relay For Love)

Book Boyfriends Cafe *Tall, Dark, & Loaded* (January 2016)
6 billionaire romances from USA Today and National Bestselling authors (includes Marrying for Love)

Love Notes (April 2016)
8 Country Music themed romance novels from USA Today and National Bestselling authors (includes Broken Strings)

First Glance (April 2016)
13 first in their series romances from USA Today and National Bestselling authors (includes The Sound of Consequence)

Summer Solstice (June 2016)
10 friends to lovers romances from USA Today and National Bestselling authors (includes The Sound of Deception)

About Susan

Big dreamer and certifiable overachiever Susan Ann Wall embraces life at full speed and volume. She's a beer and tea snob, can be bribed with dark chocolate, and the #1 thing on her bucket list is to be the center of a Bon Jovi flash mob.

Susan is a multi-genre author of racy, rule-breaking romance, women's fiction, and erotic fiction (her erotic titles are published as Ann Victor). Her bragging rights include nine books in three different series, three perfect children, adopting two amazing rescue dogs, and a happily ever after that started while serving in the U.S. Army and has spanned two decades (which is crazy since she's not a day over 29).

In her next life, Susan plans to be a 5 foot 10, size 8 rock star married to a chiropractor and will not be terrified of large bridges, spiders, or quiet people (shiver).

You can find Susan online at:
www.susanannwall.com
Facebook: Author Susan Ann Wall
Twitter: @susanannwall

Picture by BLC Photography

Made in the USA
Middletown, DE
16 April 2016